FIVE SISTERS

A Modern Novel of Kurdish Women

KIT ANDERSON

CHARACTERS

Burhan m Aysel

|

Aden Ruya Alev & Hassan Songul Mangat Aliye Ridvan
Kadir & Salih Sakina Osman

Ruya m Anwar,	oldest son is Semih, youngest daughter is Kader
Alev m Mehmet	
Hassan m Hatice	
Aliye m Omer	only son is Zafer
Sakina m Ibrahim	
Kader m Ahmet	
Kerim	admires Aliye, goes to mountains to follow Ensar Biter
Rakim	sons are Yashar m Yagmur, & Elbil m Shariye

Mountain fighters are Miriam, Hakim Bey, Hulya & Esra, Pinar, Ayse, Aynur

Mahmoud m Shahrazade	Oldest son is Rajiv m Nur
	Third son is Omer m Aliye
	Youngest son is Ferhat
	Guards are Baran and Bektas
Magrit m Uur	friends in Istanbul
Elif	
Ison	
Saladin	Kurdish hero of the Middle Ages
Sheikh Said	Kurdish hero of early 20th C.
Ensar Biter	Fictional rebel leader in the novel

INTRODUCTION

Flying east across the length of Turkey, looking down at the crumpled landscape, Ruya marveled at how different the mountains looked from the air. "The mountains are the Kurds' only friend," went the Kurdish saying. During the war, when she had been a guerrilla fighter for her beloved Kurdistan, those mountains had been both her friend and her enemy. She had grown up in the mountains, and it was true they had hidden and protected the fighters, but life in the mountains could be very cruel.

She marveled that in less than two hours the plane had flown 2000 kilometers crossing Turkey over rugged mountain terrain all the way. She remembered the agonizing forced marches, the bitter wind on high passes, the brutal distances they had covered on foot. She shivered, recalling countless nights in icy caves. Then, with a rush of love, she remembered the clean cold air, the high blue sky stretching over vast spaces, the thunder of mountain rivers, the morning light touching the high peaks to rose and gold. Once again she felt the pain of fallen companions and the loneliness of night watches. She remembered the warm comraderie around evening fires., and the joy of finding Anwar's love. For her, looking at mountains would always bring back memories of her years as a guerrilla fighting against the Turkish army.

Those were hard times back then, with much suffering. So many had died. But in recent years only sporadic conflict had gone on in eastern Turkey, in the region its native people thought of as Kurdistan. It was not Kurdistan, nor were they Kurds, the Turkish government insisted, as it banned the very use of the word or their language or their native dress and music. Not Kurds, they said, but Mountain Turks. Well, probably most people only wanted peace and security now. Probably they were willing to be Mountain Turks.

She wondered where her old comrades in arms were now. Many dead, she knew. Many Kurds had scattered all over the world. Some of them, like her, had fought at one time for their national independence. They were a nation which had no land of its own. That was what the fighting had been about, but they were too few, too weak, to stand against the powerful modern nations within whose boundaries their ancestral lands were divided. Too primitive, too tribal, too divided. Fighting had been so hard, the odds overwhelming.

Those memories were much more vivid than the ones of her early life growing up. It was as if her early memories had disappeared with her high mountain village. Long ago Sicaksu had been bombed to rubble by the Turkish army.

Shocked to think she had forgotten, she forced herself to remember Sicaksu. Little brown houses, each surrounded by its mud brick wall and beds of bright flowers. Each with its flat roof, shaded by fruit and nut trees. Much of the household work over the passing seasons took place on the roofs. In the winter the flat surfaces were warmed by bright sunshine, in summer they were cooled by mountain breezes.

There the sheared wool fleeces were spread out to dry after washing. There the women gathered on the roofs to spin and later to weave on the big, wooden looms. There strings of vegetables and bunches of herbs were hung to dry, while fresh onions and tomatoes were chopped into salads or sauce. There grain was ground, chickens were plucked, and meat cut and prepared. Under shady canopies the women rested and chatted while they drank their tea before returning to their familiar tasks.

If only things could have stayed the same as they were while she was growing up, she thought. But she caught herself. Life in the village could be peaceful and sweet, but the rules were very strict. Through no will of her own she had broken those rules. That was why she had gone to the rebels, because if she had stayed, she might well have been killed by her family or forced to kill herself. Life was rigidly controlled in the old villages.

Ruya had grown up in Sicaksu, eldest daughter in a big Kurdish family. With mingled love and pain she remembered them, especially her mother Aysel, Aunt Kader, and sisters Alev, Songul, Aliye and Sakina. Aysel, Songul and Aliye were dead now, as was her father and some of her brothers. From long habit she made herself turn away from the sadness, and think of good things. Soon she would be back "home," or at least back to Van, where she would meet Kader, her long time correspondent, and Sakina, for whose wedding she was returning.

It was because she had joined the rebel army that she had been exiled from her beloved home and family for so many long years. Only now, with her precious American passport, could she return to this land she still loved. She had changed so much from the girl she had been, and she knew everyone else must have changed, too. She was afraid of what she would find coming back. Was anything going to be the same? Would her family, her sisters, be changed? So many had died. Would the warm family life she had so bitterly missed still be there?

Ruya Returns to Her Family for Sakina's Wedding

Ruya craned her neck as they approached the western shore of Lake Van to see the gaping black volcanic crater of Nimrut. She marveled at its size. In the early fall dry season, its five lakes were reduced to only two, but she could see their green pools standing in the dusty plains where nomads tended their flocks. In a moment they were over the turquoise waters of Lake Van, the largest lake in Turkey. Local people called it "The Sea." It had been made sixty million years ago when streams were dammed by the boiling lava from Nimrut

By the north shore, the tall cone of another volcano, Suphan, was already dusted with winter white. Its lower slopes, like the fields along the lake shore, were still brown with autumn's dry colors. Close to the lake stood the massive rock outcrop on which fortresses had stood for thousands of years, guarding the various cities built on the land where Van now stood. She could see the even higher, whiter cone of Mount Ararat shining far away to the north. That was not far from their second farm, up in Cansu. The farm she had never lived on, where her family had resettled

1

after their home village of Sicaksu was bombed, and where her father and brothers had been killed. She, with her sister Songul and two older brothers, had gone to join the guerrilla fighters before that happened.

Ruya was trembling with excitement as her plane crossed the vast lake and swept down to the miniature airport. The whole city seemed such a small fringe of man-designed buildings, dwarfed by the snowy chain of peaks which surrounded it, cupping it against the lake waters. The concrete runway came to the very edge of the water and as they dropped, it felt as if they might actually land in the water. She held her breath, then sighed with relief when they touched down firmly and rolled safely toward the small terminal. Her hands twisted together convulsively in her lap. In a few minutes she would be home, would be back with her family. So many had died. She tried to imagine what they would look like. Had they changed as she had?

She smoothed her knee length navy skirt, crossed her nylon clad legs and surveyed her smart navy pumps with satisfaction. She brushed imaginary crumbs from her flowered silk blouse, and smoothed back her curly, shoulder length black hair. Hastily she opened her purse to smooth on a little more lipstick and dab a bit of powder on her nose. Her large dark brown eyes stared back at her from the little mirror, naturally rimmed by thick black lashes that needed no mascara. The man seated next to her smiled in open admiration, and she blushed, hastily closing her purse again. The plane was almost to the terminal. People were starting to stand up.

She had thought for a long time about whether to dress in Kurdish clothes. Some of her friends in Texas still did so. They still stayed in their homes and spoke no English, too, she thought scornfully. She had become American, and she would show that to everyone. She had looked around the busy terminal in Istanbul as she boarded the plane for Van, she had seen that the women passengers were wearing a wide variety of fashions, from modern to the most traditional Kurdish. Kurdish women wore long, colorful skirts, long tunics or coats, and the tightly wrapped head scarves they felt a modest Muslim woman should wear. A few women were even cloaked and veiled in black. But she was not the only western looking woman on the plane. Were some of them Kurds, she wondered. Were they, like her, coming home from some distant foreign place?

There were going to be big changes awaiting her, that was certain. For one thing, there had been tragic deaths in the years she had been away. Trapped in first Irak and then America, she had been unable to attend the funerals. Only by phone and letter could she join her family in grieving. The pain of that had never gone away. She hoped that returning to eastern Turkey would somehow bring closure to those painful wounds. But life had gone on, and there were other changes as well, good ones to celebrate.

Her youngest sister, Sakina, had finished medical school and was now getting married. Ruya was returning for the wedding. All that was a great deal of change from the family that she had left behind when she had fled. Less than fifteen years ago, she and her sisters had only been allowed to attend their crowded village school for a few short years, barely enough to learn to read and write. Her mother Aysel had never learned to do either, nor had she ever learned to speak Turkish, and it was the same for her many aunts.

In the village, her grandfather had scolded her father for allowing his daughters to go to school. "It was a great shame for girls to get educated," he had declared indignantly. Ruya recalled hearing one Kurdish grandmother in America vehemently argue against the girls in her family going to school. "They'll learn to use telephones, and then they'll talk to boys," she had shrilled.

Only when Ruya and Songul had run away to join the Kurdish patriots fighting for their independence had they received any real schooling. Ruya knew education had changed her life, but now it seemed that so much else had also changed that she hardly knew what to expect.

The tarmac in front of the airport terminal was empty except for a few heavily armed soldiers on guard. Friends and relatives had to wait indoors, back of the security barriers, for those they had come to greet. Ruya deplaned and hurried to the double doors in the midst of an anxious, pushing crowd, all eager to meet their loved ones. Inside, she could see no one she recognized among the noisy crowd. Then a young woman dressed in a skirt as short as her own touched her arm and asked, "Ruya?"

Ruya searched her pretty face, made up as was her own and framed by long, uncovered curls. She could see nothing she recognized, nothing Kurdish except for the telltale dark eyes rimmed in long curling black lashes. Could this be Sakina?

"Yes, I'm Ruya," she replied, hesitating to make a false identification. Her doubts were dispelled as the girl threw her arms around her in an exuberant hug. Behind her, three men wearing big smiles pressed forward to greet her too. All were in western dress and she would not have recognized any of them, although two were her brothers Ridvan and Osman. Sakina introduced the third, older man as their Uncle Ahmet. Ruya knew Ahmet was a policeman in Van. He had married their Aunt Kader in a second marriage for both of them, soon after Ruya had fled from Turkey into Irak, so she had never met him. In fact, her aunt was also nearly a stranger, as she had come to stay with their family in the old village just before Ruya had left home.

It was Kader, however, who had taken Sakina into her home and raised her, insisting on the education that none of the other girls had been allowed. It was Kader who had kept up a steady correspondence with Ruya through all the years, keeping her connected to her family. Ruya was eager to meet her again.

She continued to get reacquainted with Sakina and her brothers as Ahmet went to recover her bags from the carrousel. When he returned, Sakina pulled her sister along to the parking lot and grandly flicked the locking command of a shiny four-wheeled drive vehicle of foreign make. She insisted that Ruya sit in the front passenger seat beside Ahmet, but let it be known that she also drove. She asked if Ruya drove, and Ruya replied that yes, she did. In America you simply had to drive because everyone did, and there were such long distances.

Privately Ruya was breathing thankfulness that she had not chosen to dress in traditional Kurdish dress. She had never imagined that such changes could have happened so fast in her family or in her nation. She had not been surprised to see all the modern changes in Istanbul, which was half a European city anyhow.

4

But that so much could have changed so fast in Van, and among her family, astonished her.

She continued to be surprised almost into speechlessness as they drove through handsome developments of apartment buildings, and into a city of many modern looking storefronts. There were even some colorful glass office towers set among them. She thought of the narrow dirty streets crowded with foot traffic and push carts that was the Van she remembered. Now the broad divided boulevard was crowded with expensive modern vehicles. The crowds that thronged the streets were dressed in the same mix of modern dress and traditional Kurdish clothing as she had seen on the plane.

As they drove out of the city, she saw that tall eight and nine story apartment blocks seemed to stretch endlessly in all directions beyond the central shopping area. Only here and there stood one of the small, square, mud brick houses surrounded by flowers and fruit trees that she thought of as Kurdish. Van had been a small, shabby little town of one story mud huts when she had last seen it. Surprise kept her silent, but it didn't matter at all as Sakina kept up a running flow of chatter about family matters and wedding plans.

Until the wedding, Sakina was staying with Ahmet and Kader. Ruya would stay there too, so that was where they were going now. Ruya knew that Kader had taken Sakina under her wing at the time when multiple tragedies had shattered their family. It had been her faithful support that had enabled Sakina to pursue her education and end up as a doctor. Now Kader, proud of her niece, was determined to give her the finest wedding Van had ever seen.

Once again Ruya was lost in amazment as she was ushered into Kader and Ahmet's comfortable, modern house. They led her to a room that she could see was where Sakina was staying, and left her to wash up before joining them at a midday meal. When she returned, Ruya found a crowd of their relatives seated around a large cloth spread Kurdish fashion on the floor. Everyone had questions about America, and she got such confusing and scattered fragments of their family history that she was not much wiser in the end that she had been before. But the laughter, friendliness, and the delicious food made it a happy time and she realized how she had missed the special warmth and security of a really big Kurdish family.

Her own four children lived an American life style that was quite different. She had thought she was coming back to her own family, but the realization that, although she had come back to eastern Turkey, she was never going to find her own family or her own past struck her like a blow. Everything had changed too much. Tears welled up and her hand flew to cover her mouth. Ahmet looked at her sharply, but no one else noticed.

After lunch Ruya sat in the front room with the men, talking with Ridvan and Osman, while Sakina helped Kader and her daughters clear and do the dishes. They wouldn't hear of her helping them, they said. Osman had taken the day off from his school, and Ridvan from his job at a local carpet store. He didn't like his job very much, he said. It was boring and didn't pay very well. He told her he would like to talk with her about coming to America. There wasn't much work in eastern Turkey, which was still recovering from the war. He limped and suffered from painful arthritis which had resulted from an accident many years earlier, when he had been struck by a car. He couldn't do anything very physically demanding, but his condition had saved him from the obligatory military service that all young men in Turkey owed the government.

Thinking of her years fighting the Turkish army, Ruya thought again how much things had changed In a few months Osman would be serving in that very army, as were two of Kader's sons even now. That they were fighting against other Kurds like themselves was one of the strange twists that life had taken here. Once or twice she had come close to asking about the political situation in Van, but she sensed that no one wanted to talk about such things. She wondered if it was still unsafe to speak of it.

With a vague sense of guilt, she realized that she felt no part of the life her family was now living in Van. She was very glad for their health and happiness, and she wished them well. But there was such an enormous gulf between their present circumstances and her life growing up in their mountain village that it seemed to her another world, as well as another time. Her present life in

America was yet another different world, which she saw the others couldn't relate to very well either.

Throughout the day her mind was busy with what was going on around her, although it kept straying into comparisons. That night, however, lying beside Sakina, her thoughts were filled with old memories. Sakina's excitement about her wedding plans recalled the time when she had been a girl in love, planning to marry. Vivid memories of the happy days in their village before the war flooded her mind. Sakina's eager chatter died away and she fell asleep, leaving Ruya to go over those long ago events in her mind. How could it all have changed so much?

T W O
_____

The   Village
Before   the   War

Ruya straightened her aching back and used the corner of her white headscarf to wipe the perspiration from her face. Her skin was flushed from heat and sun. She sneezed twice from the hot dust that drifted in the air around her. Squinting her eyes against the bright sunlight, she stared across the stretch of wheat rubble to the red walls of stone that rose high above it. Heat shimmers swirled, blurring its polished surfaces. A tiny waterfall fell from a crack far up in the red wall, dispersing to mist before it reached their level. She thought longingly of its coolness on her face, rinsing her dry throat. She reached for their water bottle, and took a sip of the warm fluid.

Beside her, her younger sister Songul also straightened up, placing her hands in the small of her back to ease the strain on tired muscles. She gathered up a fold of her long skirt and bent to wipe her face and neck with the blue cloth. Songul was fair-skinned, with light brown hair and amber eyes, and her face was bright red from the sun.

The steady swish, swish of the scythes cutting through the wheat continued as their father and three brothers Aden, Hassan and Mangat worked on tirelessly. Their bare heads bobbed rhythmically, their arms and chests shone golden brown with

9

sweat, and great wet patches mottled the thin white cotton of their shirts. The layers of cut grain piled steadily behind them in golden waves.

Under the hot mid-summer sun, the ripe wheat reflected shimmering ripples of light and heat. It flashed like metal, gold and bronze. Steadily it fell into neat piles as the men cut through it. Wild flowers lay purple, pink or white among the golden stalks, and Songul had tucked a spray of bright blue flowers under the edge of her scarf. She loved flowers and was always gathering bouquets for the house. Working together, Ruya and Songul bent again to gather the stalks into sheaves, which they piled on a large unbleached cotton cloth. When the cloth was full, they tied its corners together to form a neat bundle, and then spread another cloth. They had worked since early morning with only a short tea break, and nine of the large bundles lay in one corner of the field, ready for threshing and winnowing.

In the rugged mountainous country where they lived, flat land was rare. The precious, narrow strips along the streams were planted with vegetables. On the rocky slopes, every tiny patch of level ground was plowed and planted with grain as soon as the snow melted. For generations this level meadow had belonged to their grandmother's family, and had come with her when she married their grandfather. It had been his sole request in lieu of other goods or money. Over the years the family had benefited from his wisdom, for they always had bread throughout even the longest winters. Ruya thought proudly about her father, Burhan. She thought he was also very wise and managed their lives very well.

Even so, Ruya thought ruefully, she could wish this field was a little smaller. The faint shouts and splashings of the village folk, playing down by the river, sounded from below. She knew most of the people from their village were enjoying the coolness of the water, their tea clothes spread under green branches, the children and boys sporting in the broad shallow stream. The girls would be sitting demurely together, or with their mothers, staying cool in the shade, their bright skirts spread to best advantage. She longed to be there too.

From the river dogs barked, a donkey brayed, shouts of laughter told of some prank. She straightened her back again and looked to see how much of the wheat was left to be cut. Once it was ripe, any delay in harvesting was dangerous. The capricious mountain weather might bring hail or heavy winds and rain that would cost them some of the precious harvest on which they depended for their winter's bread. It had to be finished today.

The family had two other smaller patches which they had already cut and stored. When this one was done, their harvest would be complete. Then, one day when the wind was right, they would go to the cleft in the rock where the threshing was done. The rocks channeled a sharp breeze down over a natural, level rock floor. There the men would thresh the wheat with flails made of two wooden posts hooked together by a short chain. After it was threshed, they swept it up with brooms and winnowed it by tossing it in large, shallow woven reed baskets. The women gathered the straw into bundles for winter fodder and bedding for their animals, and for making the mud bricks of their dwellings and out-buildings.

Thrashing the grain was always a holiday time for the family. Cool breezes chased down over the rocks, and the men laughed and sported as they took turns flailing and resting. The golden mounds of winnowed wheat piled nearby on the ground grew steadily larger as the chaff was tossed up to blow away on the wind. For the women, gathering the straw into bundles wasn't hard, either. Often several branches of the family came together to watch or take their turns flailing their own wheat. Then the young people would eye one another shyly as the matrons gossiped and nursed their babies.

When the wheat was all piled in its golden drifts and the straw bundles stacked, then the tea urns would be fired up. Cloths would be spread and the urns would begin to smoke as everyone settled down by family groups to drink the good strong tea, sipped through lumps of sugar. As the sun went down behind the mountains, the golden grain would be gathered up into large bags and loaded onto donkeys to be carried back for storage.

As she looked around the high mountain meadow, Ruya saw with relief that her father had stopped scything and her brothers were finishing the last of the wheat in the far corner of the field. Their little sister Aliye, and Ruya's favorite sister Alev, who was Hassan's twin, were close behind them, gathering up the stalks almost as they fell. They would be done very soon. They would gather up the big cloth bundles, loading what they could on the two donkeys and together carrying the rest down to their farm shed. Then they could go and join the other villagers at the river for the rest of the afternoon. She smiled in anticipation.

Later, resting in the shady spot where her mother Aysel had spread their tea cloth, Songul watched with amusement as Ruya and a young man from another family eyed one another surreptitiously, unaware they were being noticed. To speak or show any open awareness of one another was forbidden, but people always knew when a boy and a girl liked one another, Songul thought. Still young, and with an independent personality, she thought it was all nonsense, but she could see Ruya's cheeks were flushed with self-consciousness. Songul noticed that she had changed from the dusty clothes of the harvesting into her prettiest skirt and a becoming, sleeveless blue tunic worn over a snowy white blouse.

Ruya had been promised to an older man in the village, but then he had died in an autobus accident on the narrow, dangerous mountain roads near their village. As far as Songul knew, Ruya had felt relief more than sorrow, but they hadn't talked about it. Perhaps, she thought, Ruya was feeling anxious about getting too old to marry. She was nineteen, and all the other girls her own age were long since married. The period of mandatory mourning for her betrothed had kept her single beyond the normal age, but she was pretty and their family was respected. Soon there would be an offer.

Ruya retied her headscarf, revealing a tantalizing glimpse of her long curling dark hair, and Songul smiled, recognizing the gesture as a flirtatious one directed toward the watching young man. He was the son of the local baker. Strongly built, with curling black hair and dark eyes made darker by their thick curling black lashes, he was a handsome young man. Songul knew him to be cheerful and willing, too. He would make a good husband, she thought. His family had a steady income and, she smiled to herself at the thought, at least they would always have bread on the table.

Three of her younger cousins came up leading her smallest sister, Sakina. Sakina was crying. Songul turned to them, forgetting about Ruya and the progress of her flirtation. The little girls had been picking wildflowers and Sakina had gotten a nettle sting. Songul put a wet cloth over the reddened skin and pulled the little girl onto her lap with a kiss. In a moment she wriggled down again and the girls ran off, the hurt forgotten. The baby, Osman, stumbled after them on his stubby legs, and Songul called to the girls to wait for him. They turned back and one of them stooped obligingly so he could scramble up on her back to be carried piggy back.

A water fight broke out where some of the boys were splashing in the shallow ripples, and there was a great shouting and commotion. The village dogs barked madly, but harmlessly, in the excitement. First one donkey and then another threw back his head and brayed rustily. Relaxed and comfortable, Songul watched it all from her shady resting place and felt at peace with the world.

From the center of their group, Aysel also watched it all, ready to intervene if Ruya flirted too boldly, or the boys became too rowdy. She sent her fourth son, eleven year old Ridvan, to the village, and soon he came back with a bulging bag full of hot nan, the flat round loaves of bread baked on the walls of their clay ovens. She put out platters of olives and the tomatoes and cucumbers she had been slicing. Pots of the garlic-spiced white goat cheese they all loved completed the picnic. Burhan and his older sons, cool and refreshed, came from their river play, along with the wet and sandy twins, Salih and Kadir. The family ate hungrily. Along the banks of the river, others also gathered in family groups for their evening meal. Afterwards everyone drank more tea together.

The long slanting rays of the evening sun turned the water to ripples of purple and gold as the western sky filled with color. Alev and Ruya washed the family's dishes in the river, enjoying the cool water on their arms, while their oldest brother Aden emptied the coals and ashes from the tea urn and carefully buried them in the sand. Carrying the urn, the supper cloth, and their dishes with them, the family returned to their house filled with contentment. Ruya carried little Osman and Songul held Sakina's hand as they walked up the hill to the house. The twins Salih and Kadir had left the picnic earlier to get the sheep and goats back to the barn yard, and were waiting for their father to help them shut the animals into the barn for the night. The older girls washed the little ones' faces, and changed their damp, stained clothing, helping them get ready for bed. As matron of the home, Aysel put away the food and dishes in the kitchen, leaving the tired harvesters free to fall onto their beds, where they all fell instantly to sleep.

Their busy lives geared to the rising and setting of the sun, the other villagers too were soon in their homes and settled for the night. In midsummer the hours for rest were short enough that all were glad to sleep during the few hours of darkness. Only Abdullah the village guard, and Mehmet the baker, working at his ovens, were awake.

Abdullah stopped in at the bakery to chat for a moment before going sleepily on his way, patrolling the dark lanes among the houses. In their high village, even the summer nights were chilly and Abdullah wore his big brown and white plaid shepherd's scarf around his shoulders. There was no alarm, nothing to guard against as far as he knew. He rubbed his face to keep awake, and stole a rest sitting on a wall while he smoked a cigarette. The river chuckled quietly on its course, and a small disturbance in a henhouse brought sleepy mumbles from the chickens. Nearby an owl screamed as it struck some luckless mouse, and Abdullah suppressed a superstitious shudder. By and by he resumed his stroll, and under his drowsy eye the village slept.

THREE

Songul Dreams of Joining the Rebellion

The long winter passed peacefully, and welcome spring brought fresh green to the steep slopes above the village. On her hands and knees, Songul worked automatically, her fingers searching the ground cover for the particular feel and shape of the herb she was gathering while her mind went over and over the events of the previous evening. The early spring sunshine lay warm on her shoulders, but the fresh greenery felt cool to her hands, soft under her knees. Deep patches of snow still lay in the gullies, and the peaks above them were streaked with white, but early flowers everywhere proclaimed that winter was almost over.

Scattered over the hillside around her, her aunts and sisters also gathered the wild garlic. Their brightly colored clothing made darker splashes of color among the wildflowers which dappled the landscape. Blue, gold, white, pink and purple, their fragrance and color had wakened bees and other insects which hummed around them. Perfume from wild rose bushes mixed with the scent of crushed green things in a spicy fragrance that drifted on the little breeze. The busy springtime chatter of the birds mingled with the talk and laughter of the women as they worked. Nearby the men were sitting together under a tree and speaking seriously of the previous night's events as they sipped their tea

All the village had gathered in the square to listen to the visitors who had come. These strangers had told them about the history of the Kurdish people, and had urged them to be proud of being Kurds. This was different from the village school, where the teacher had told them they were Turks, mountain Turks. The Turkish government did not even allow them to speak Kurdish, although of course, when the teacher or soldiers weren't around, they did. Many in the village knew no other language.

Everyone knew it was very dangerous to speak and think as these visitors did. One of the speakers stood out in Songul's mind and now filled her thoughts. Dark and bearded, his clear voice and gentle manner set him apart. He had dark, dreaming eyes. He painted pictures with his words, and what he had said about their proud heritage had made her want more than she foresaw for herself living here among her family. Songul was sixteen, promised in marriage to an older man in the village. With only three years of schooling, she was barely able to read or write but she had a lively and hungry mind.

The dark young man, speaking like music, promised that they could be an independent nation. They had been a nation of warriors, and once, while known as the Medes, they had ruled a mighty empire. In the Middle Ages a Kurd named Saladin had led the Muslim armies to great victories over the hated Christian Crusaders. Strong in their own traditions, the Kurds had lived beside or under many conquerors and served them without changing their own ways.

Long ago the Turks had conquered Asia Minor and claimed the property of those who had lived there before them, but they had not tried to change the Kurdish way of life. An ancient and proud people, the Kurds kept to their own ways under their own leaders. After the first great war, called World War One in the West, their traditional homeland had been promised to the Kurds as their own nation. That treaty was never honored, however. In the fluid politics of the Middle East, new powers had risen. Under various strong leaders the modern nations of Turkey, Iran, Irak and Syria had formed and developed politically, and

16

there had been no separate place for the Kurds who lived within their boundaries.

Through the millennia Kurdish armies had served with one conqueror or another. Their preference had been to live in small, clan villages and practice the simple life of nomadic shepherds, but they had always been ready to fight as well, when it was needed. There had been strong Kurdish leaders, but like Saladin they were more often generals than political organizers. Even now Kurds were not given to political unity, but still desired freedom to be who they were. The young speaker called on the villagers to unite to fight for their identity as a separate people and to claim their own land.

Sitting among the women at the back, Songul had thrilled to the images of a strong brave army of Kurds claiming back their land and heritage. She longed to do something brave to help her people, but knew with a stifled sense of inevitability that she would never leave the small brown houses and crooked stone streets of her village.

Only when one of the visitors stood up and began to speak in a high clear voice did she realize that this was a woman. Dressed as the men were in headscarves, boots and trousers, with ammunition belts across their chests, there were several women in the group. Songul's blood raced and made her dizzy as first one and then another spoke of the need for women to join in the struggle for the freedom of their people.

She saw that they were proud but modest, and that they were treated with respect by the men of the group. They had come together as equals, and left in the same way. Songul knew that some of the old men in the village would sniff and call these women immoral camp followers, but it was obvious to her that this was not the truth. These women were freedom fighters serving their nation, and her head felt like it would explode with excitement and joy, seeing this. Songul knew that her brother Aden had been stirred as well. She had seen his shining eyes and flushed cheeks.

As she gathered the spring herbs among the women on the grassy hillside, Songul glanced at the men talking under the tree. She saw that Aden was listening avidly.

Aden was very devout, reading his Koran every night before the fire. He had been good at his studies at the school, and was restless within the rigid order of life in their village. He chafed under the strict authority of their father. He was a thinker too, Songul realized. Would he leave, she wondered? Would he join the young men who were fighting to make their people free and strong again? She would if she were Aden. For the thousandth time she wished that she, too, had been born a boy.

A thought struck her like a blow. One of the speakers last night was a woman. She had said she was proud to be a woman fighting for their land. She had spoken of the importance of women in their nation, not just to bear children and feed the men but also to share in the struggle to be free by fighting and leading. We are comrades, she had said. The men with her had smiled in agreement. She said she had grown up in a village and hoped one day to go back and be a wife and mother. Right now, she said, there was something more important to do. She had left her village to do it.

Songul's breath stopped and the world seemed to go black. She didn't know how long she crouched on the soft grass, her head swirling, as this momentous realization took hold of her mind. She could go with them. She could join this army and fight for her nation too.

For the rest of the day and all the night Songul planned how to leave. In their big, busy family her distraction was not noticed. She went about her tasks mechanically, doing what was normally required of her. There was so much she didn't know. Where had the group of guerrillas gone? Where did they stay? Could just anyone join them? What would she have to bring?

When she saw Aden go outside the next morning, she followed him. They were close to one another in age, the second and fifth born of the children, separated by the twins Alev and Hassan, and they had always been close. Aden was Songul's hero and she had followed him around like a puppy, eager to run his errands or do his bidding whenever he deigned to notice her. He was no bully, and returned her devotion with a kind of casual kindness.

He stopped when she called his name, turning to see what she wanted.

18

"Aden, are you going to follow the men who came to the village? Are you going to join them?" she asked.

Aden looked nervously over his shoulder in the direction of the house. Brown haired and light skinned like Songul, he blushed easily, and now color flooded up his neck and across his face.

"Be quiet," he said irritably. "Are you crazy? Do you want everyone to hear you? Why do you want to know?"

Songul was crushed. She hadn't thought about hiding her feelings. Would their father object to their going? All in a rush she realized that this would make a great difference to their family, might even get them all into trouble with the police and soldiers. It had not occurred to her that Aden might go secretly, without telling the family.

Aden saw his sister recoil as if he had struck her. She went pale and then flushed deeply, looking away and twisting her hands together. He saw her amber eyes flood with tears. He had no idea why this should be so important to her. What difference could it make to her? Would his going away mean that much to her?

"What's the matter?" he asked. "Songul, come over here away from the house." He led her behind the barn. He didn't think anyone had seen them.

"What's the matter with you? How did you know I was thinking about going? Did anyone say anything to you?"

Songul faced him anxiously, still confused. "Aden, I just thought you would want to go. No one has said anything. But I want to go, too. I can fight and live in the mountains too. I don't want to just stay at home and live the kind of life everyone else lives. I am proud of our nation, and we have a right to be the way we want to be. I want to help."

Aden looked disgusted, and then he laughed. "You, Songul? You're a girl, and just a child. You couldn't learn to fight. A guerrilla's life is very difficult and dangerous. I'm not sure I'm brave enough to do it. You mustn't even think about it. And for goodness sake, don't tell Father. He has forbidden us all from going to any meeting like that again. Stay away from the guerrillas, is what he told us. If he knew you were even thinking about something like that he'd lock you up and marry you off next week."

Songul felt miserable. This was so different from what she had imagined. She had seen herself bravely setting off with Aden into the mountains, the family proudly watching them go. The tears brimmed over, and she hid her face behind her sleeve.

That night, however, as she lay on her sleeping mat among her sisters, she found a new resolution in her heart. A stubborn determination was forming. Those other girls had done it. She was strong, and braver than the other girls in her village. Aden could laugh, but she was not a child anymore, and she didn't want to live the life marked out for her future. Bride, slave to her new family until she bore the first of many children, old in another decade or two from hard labor and privation. That would be the best she could hope for. Most girls seemed to want that life, but she realized that she had been looking for a way out of it for a long time. It seemed as if the talk by the girl guerrilla had given her an answer she had been searching for, without even realizing it.

She wished the young people had stayed, but after the meeting they had melted away into the night without waiting for questions from anyone. How could she find them again? She had counted on Aden knowing what to do, but now she realized she was going to have to think things out for herself.

Trying not to disturb her sisters sleeping around her, Songul lay awake until the early light shone in the window and the farm creatures began to stir. Her mind was too full of excitement and confusion. Finally, however, as she at last fell asleep for the last precious moments of the night, she knew her own mind. Somehow, before she was trapped forever, she would find a way to join the fighters in the mountains.

FOUR

R u y a   i s   R a p e d

Ruya waved the long switch over the last of the sheep as they crowded into the low stone barn, trilling the note they recognized as her command to move into their pen. Snow flurries gusted through the door behind them, and wind whined through the cracks under the roof. A sudden spring blizzard had blown up and her father had sent her to bring the flocks into shelter.

She stooped to lift the pole that closed the sheep pen, when strong arms seized her and threw her to the ground. Before she could react, her skirt was thrown up over her face and her shawl was wrapped tightly around her arms and head. There seemed to be two men at least, as one held her arms above her head and pressed his hand over her nose and mouth, smothering her and pressing her head against the earth. She couldn't scream or even breath, nor could she kick or move as another man fell on her and raped her. He was heavy and hard sharp objects that he seemed to be wearing cut and bruised her. There was a moment when the first one rolled off, but the pressure on her face never lifted as another climbed on her. Darkness blurred her mind.

She became aware that she was lying on the dirt floor of the stable, dazed and bruised. The men had left as abruptly as they had appeared. Gradually in the dusty haze the rough stone walls came into focus. The wind howled and whistled outside the barn, and snow still gusted in the door. Overhead, the closely set branches of the low brush roof were barely visible in the gloom. Leaning on the poles of their pen, the black and white goats peered at her curiously, while the sheep crowded nervously in their corner. As she struggled up, straightening her clothing, she felt the stone of despair fill her chest. It left her with no breath. Blackness swirled across her mind again, and she fell against the wooden manger with a sob. Her father would kill her.

She had been sent to gather the animals into shelter because a late spring snowstorm threatened. Before she saw or heard them, the men had seized her. She had no time to scream or fight. Perhaps they had been soldiers, she might have seen a quick flash of a uniform. The hard objects that had hurt her might have been their equipment.

She fought to stay conscious, to think. What could she do? If she told anyone, she would surely be killed. Her brothers, even her father, would think first of the shame to the family, and how to regain their honor. They would try to hunt down and kill the rapists, but they would kill her too.

Her mind filled with memories of her friend Esra, who had died the previous summer. The last time they had been together the two girls had sat milking their goats. The humming of bees was the only sound in the quiet hillside pasture. In the hazy warmth of the summer sun, the goats were quiet and easy too. But Esra had sobbed with fear as she whispered her secret to her friend. Tanrir, the village headman's son, had found her alone by the village well and whispered a dirty thing to her. He had taken her arm, leaning close to her. Pulling away she had spit at him. Some boys nearby had laughed. She had run off without her bucket, but rumors had spread that she had been secretly meeting with Tanrir. Never, never, she swore, sobbing, and Ruya believed her. Esra thought Tanrir might have boasted of things that had never happened, starting the rumors.

She was terrified that her father would believe she had brought shame to the family. Bright and pretty, she had already attracted a proposal from an older man who was willing to pay a good sum of money. Esra knew the man had two other wives, one of them a real termagant who would be sure to make her life a misery. She had frantically begged her father to refuse the man, threatening to kill herself rather than go to him. Her mother had added her own pleas for her daughter. Esra's father was angry with them both, and called her a willful, disobedient girl who was more trouble than she was worth. There were many girls in their family and he felt lucky to get a good offer for one. If he heard the new stories and believed himself shamed by her behavior, he might kill her.

Ruya had comforted her friend as well as she could, and struggled to suppress her fear about her own future. She had been betrothed at sixteen to an older man from another village, but a mere three weeks before the wedding he had been killed in an automobile accident. Released by the tragedy, she had passed into an unspoken but happy understanding with Vulcan the baker's son. She believed their engagement would have been announced as soon as her two year period of mourning was finished. Last fall, however, Vulcan was killed by Turkish soldiers during one of the frequent military skirmishes that went on in the rugged mountains around them. She never knew if he had been actively fighting for the Kurdish rebels, or just unlucky in getting caught somewhere unprotected.

She knew she was thought to be unlucky, and now, at twenty, she would be fortunate if anyone wanted to marry her. She had felt sorry for Esra, but also envious of her younger, prettier friend. That had been the last time she had seen her. Esra had taken poison, and no one outside the family knew whether her fear and shame had driven her to do it, or whether she had been forced by her father to remove the family's shame by killing herself.

Now facing her own crisis, Ruya scrubbed at her tear-streaked face. In the low roofed stable, her breath smoked and she shivered in the cold. She had been out of the house too long. She must go inside, and what would she say? Distractedly she rebound her scarf about her hair and brushed at her skirt. Shaking out her shawl, she rewrapped it. Whatever else she did, she must never, never tell anyone what had just happened to her.

As she entered the warm house, she saw that she had not been missed. Hanging her shawl on its hook, she went into the wash room to wash her hands and face. Carefully she inspected her skirt, smoothing it. Her drawers under it were torn, but she could mend those secretly. There was blood on them, but that too could be explained away if anyone saw it.

As the women and young children gathered for the evening meal in the kitchen, the men having been fed in the front room, Ruya tried to appear as natural as possible. She set out plates and spoons on the cloth laid out on the floor. As her mother dished up the savory lamb stew from the big pot on the clay, dung-burning stove , Ruya carried it to the others. Alev tore the big round circles of flat bread into individual pieces and piled several at each place on the cloth, and Songul ladled the foaming ayran from the big tin milk can in the corner of the room.

When her mother asked, "What took you so long with the goats?" Ruya was prepared. "That old brindle nanny hid out in the bushes, and when I tried to drive her down, I fell and slipped down the hill. She went back twice before I could pen her."

"She may be about ready to drop her kid," Aysel responded. "They get contrary then, and try to get away."

Ruya felt she had covered herself well, but as they got ready for bed her sister Alev asked, "What really happened out with the goats?"

"Why do you ask?" Ruya gasped, feeling as if she had been hit in the pit of the stomach. Alev looked at her curiously.

"What is it, Ruya? You're white as a sheet, and at supper you blushed like a peach when Mother asked where you had been. What were you doing?" She stared sharply at her older sister.

Ruya lay down on the floor mat, pulling the blanket up to her chin. "It's nothing. I don't feel well. I told you, the old nanny made trouble and I fell, and my period is starting." She turned over on her mat with her face to the wall, hoping her sister would take the hint. That would cover the blood on her drawers if Alev noticed.

Alev said no more. Ruya lay awake, trying to plan. When she could hear the even breathing that told her all the rest were asleep, she rose and went into the kitchen. Pouring some cold water into a basin, she soaked and scrubbed her drawers until there was no telltale stain left to betray her. Returning to the sleeping room, she placed them on the floor by her mat, hoping they would be dry by morning.

She dared tell no one, that she knew. Probably the soldiers who had raped her didn't know who she was, so even if they boasted to their comrades about it, no word would reach the villagers. But what if, somehow, someone did find out? Her fear burned like bitter bile in her throat and stomach.

She would not take poison or hang herself, as some women did when their families' shame became known. But what else could she do? Although there were family members who lived in the nearest big town, no one would take her in if they knew of her shame, and no one would take her in without talking with her family in the village. It terrified her to think of going farther away, but even if she went to one of the bigger cities in the west, what could she do? Would anyone let her work as a shop girl or take her as a servant? It was always relatives who employed people who left the villages, and that usually with an eye towards marriage. Now for sure no one was going to marry her if news of her rape leaked out.

All night she lay awake, tossing and turning. In the morning her mother noticed her pale, drawn face, and asked if she were ill. Her sharp eyes examined her daughter. She had not missed her changing color and nervousness the night before.

Ruya pleaded a difficult period again, and went to sit huddled by the clay stove. Alev brought her a glass of tea. When the others gathered around the cloth for breakfast, she stayed in her place by the stove. All day she huddled there, and the others left her alone.

When her father sent Aliye, her younger sister, out to the stable, she had a pang of guilt. What if the men came back? Thinking quickly, she stood before her father in the position of respect, head bowed and hands at her sides, asking permission to speak. Her father was a kindly man with his daughters, although very stern with his sons.

"What is it Ruya?" he asked.

"Father, I saw a wolf up by the trees last night. May I go with Aliye in case it comes closer?"

"You are not well today. I will send Ridvan out with her." It was what she had hoped, that one of the boys would be sent.

"Thank you, Father." She returned to her seat by the stove.

Weeks passed, and spring became summer. Although she often was given the task of caring for the goats, the men didn't return to bother her. She had taken to carrying a small knife in a little case under her skirts, but she questioned her courage to use it. The men had come so quickly, she had been so completely helpless wrapped up in her shawl with one man restraining her while the other raped her. She couldn't use her arms, couldn't kick, couldn't scream. They were gone before she had recovered enough to scream, and screaming would have brought certain punishment to her, anyway, whether the men were caught or not.

As she had thought it through, if she had screamed and if her family had caught or identified the men, then they would surely have killed them. Then their whole village would have suffered, for the men were soldiers of the government. Of that she felt sure.

There was nothing to do but remain silent for the rest of her life. She could count herself lucky that no one knew. When her menses came after the rape, Ruya began to feel safe from discovery. The bleeding was quite heavy with painful cramping, but she felt sick from relief. That first night, curled up holding her aching stomach, she realized that until that moment, she had been prepared to do quite desperate things rather than give up and kill herself.

Ruya turned over again on her mat. They were so crowded that she bumped Songul as she did so, and Songul mumbled and turned over in turn. The familiar feel and smell of her sister comforted her. For the moment her fears diminished, and she pulled the cover over her shoulders and settled to sleep.

When her period lasted a full five days, Ruya felt sure she had escaped pregnancy. The numbness that had gripped her in a vise of fear faded away, and she was able to think of something else. The family members had born her silences and moodiness cheerfully, involved in their own busy routines. Aysel had questioned her, but accepted her answers, thinking Ruya was depressed because of losing two suitors and having no prospect of more. She worried for her daughter as well, for she loved her and felt she deserved better than the fate of the single woman in a Kurdish family.

Aysel began to notice that Songul too had pulled back from the family activities. She did her work as if her mind were a thousand miles away, and sometimes didn't hear when she was spoken to. Aysel asked Ruya about it, knowing the two were close. Thinking about it, Ruya realized that Songul had begun to act this way after the guerrilla fighters had come to their village to teach them about the fight for freedom. She didn't want to tell her mother that.

As she watched her sister, she saw Songul watching Aden. Ruya knew how restless Aden was. He had not confided in her, but as the two first born, they knew each other well. She guessed that he was thinking about joining the guerrillas, and now she realized that Songul had also been touched by the message the young people had brought. Songul didn't want to marry the man she was betrothed to, and Ruya realized that she might be thinking she had found a way to escape. As she lay thinking about this in the night, she caught her breath. Perhaps that could be a way out of her trouble, too.

The next day she followed Songul out to the pump and began to pump the handle as her sister held the plastic container underneath. "Songul," she asked directly. "Are you thinking about what those people said when they came to our village?

Songul went pale, and inadvertently looked over her shoulder at the house. "Why?" she asked fearfully. "What makes you think that?"

"You have been very quiet since they were here, your mind a thousand miles away. And you watch Aden. Songul, maybe I want to do that too.

Songul gasped. "Why!" she cried. Why would you go? You've had some bad luck. You're twenty, but that isn't too old to get married and have your own family.

Ruya laughed. She had forgotten how old twenty seemed when you were only sixteen. "Not too old," she agreed. Even now she didn't dare reveal her secret, but involuntarily she shivered as she thought once more of what would happen if it were discovered. Probably going to join the guerrillas wasn't any more dangerous for her than staying with the chance of her rape being found out. "But why not?" she added recklessly. "If we go together, it will be better for both of us."

"If Aden goes, and then both of us go, Papa will be furious," Songul whispered. "We could never come back. Have you thought, Ruya," she added anxiously.

"Yes," Ruya answered quietly. "I have thought. It is the best thing to do. "

She continued to pump as Songul filled all the containers. The chickens clucked around their feet, pecking at the wet dust where water had spattered. The sisters returned to the house without speaking again. Neither one had any idea how it could be done, but they had made their decision.

FIVE

The Sisters Leave Home

After the last late, wet snow fall, summer came full bloom to the village. Lambs and kids doubled the size of the flocks, and in the family's yard a new calf peeped cautiously from behind his mother's flank at the people who came and went around him.

The guerrilla soldiers came back to speak in the village square again, and although Burhan would not let the women and children attend, the older boys pleaded until they won his permission. They listened eagerly and later told their sisters what they had heard.

Once again Songul asked Aden to take her with him, and once again he refused, this time scolding her angrily. Still, she was not discouraged. She and Ruya decided to watch him closely. They believed that he would disappear one day without telling anyone where he was going, and when he went they were resolved to follow him if they could.

It was generally known which villagers sympathized with the guerrillas. One warm afternoon when she was milking in the pasture, Ruya overheard Aden arguing with Hassan. Hassan was warning him to stay away from Mehmet the Baker. "He'll only get you in trouble," he said.

"Have you listened to him?" Aden replied. "Are we to sit here while our nation is destroyed, and do nothing?"

"Who is being destroyed?" Hassan rejoined. "Only the people who listen to these trouble makers, and then because of them, all their unfortunate friends and neighbors. "

"Aunt Kader's husband, son, and brother weren't trouble-makers, or sympathizers, but they're dead," Aden rejoined. "You can get killed for doing nothing, so you might as well do something for our people." Their father's brother's widow, Kader, had recently come to their father for shelter after their village was bombed and her husband and son shot in their doorway.

Hassan's voice grew louder. "Fighting the Turkish government isn't going to do anything for our people, Aden. It's just going to get you and maybe the rest of us killed."

"We have a right to our own land and our own ways," Aden muttered stubbornly.

"This is father's land," Hassan rejoined furiously. "You'll just ruin everything for all of us. You'll run off to the hills, and the rest of us will be punished by the soldiers for something we couldn't stop."

"Then come with me. Be a man and fight for your land," Aden shouted.

"I don't have to fight for it now, and I won't be able to keep it if you join the resistance." It seemed to Ruya that Hassan sounded like he might cry. But it was simple for them both, she thought angrily, compared to her own choices. They were men and could decide their own fates. She wouldn't run away if she could be safe staying at home, but if her rape were discovered, she would probably die anyhow.

She rose with her full bowl of milk and crossed the pasture to where Aden was leaning against a tree.

"Aden, are you all right?" she asked kindly.

Aden started, and looked at her angrily. Seeing the milk, he realized what had happened.

"Don't tell Father, all right?" he said.

"I won't tell. I want to come with you."

"What, you too? You girls are crazy. You can't come to the hills, it is for men," he said. "What are you thinking? I can't take care of you there. Who knows what would happen to you, and you could never get husbands if you did that. You would probably be killed. Fighting isn't for women. Your safety and our children are what we are fighting for."

"Aden, don't you see? We understand, and we want to help. For the others." Ruya struggled to find a way to persuade him without revealing her particular problem.

" Songul and I have made up our minds. We believe in the struggle. We believe it is necessary, and that this is the time to save our people. We will be as safe as you are when we join the women there. They will protect us and train us. You just have to take us with you and help us get there. Then you won't have to take care of us any more. We'll help each other."

Aden jumped up, his face set and his fists bunched as if he wanted to hit her.

"It's completely out of the question. Never speak to me about it again. I would never help you to leave home, and that's final." He stormed off down the hillside toward the house.

Ruya felt totally defeated. She sat down on the grass, and put her face in her hands. What was she to do? She and Songul had no idea where to go, or how to get in touch with the guerrillas. If they followed Aden when he was leaving, they might lose him on the way, and then what would they do? Lost in the mountains, terrible things might happen to them. Why were men so unapproachable? They never listened.

Later, she took Songul outside beside the stable and told her what had happened.

Songul thought about it. "What did Hassan say?" she asked. "Were they talking about Mehmet the Baker? Maybe we could ask him how to find the freedom fighters," she said.

"What if he laughed at us? What if he told Father?"

Well, I know his daughter, Jansever" Songul said. "I can ask her about it in a roundabout way, so she doesn't suspect what we are thinking. We often talk at the big water pump."

Several days later she asked Ruya to come outside again as the evening grew dark.

"Jansever says her father knows how to get in touch with the guerrillas, and when someone wants to join them he passes the message along. They come to the village in the night and take people back with them to their camp. Otherwise, no one would ever be able to find them."

"What about women? Would they do that for women?"

"Well, they have hundreds of women fighting with them. They must have arrangements for women to join," Songul said reasonably.

"What, hundreds! Where do hundreds of women live, up in the mountains?" Ruya demanded.

"Not right here, I don't think," Songul answered. "But that is what Jansever said, that there are hundreds of women and that they have women leaders and special training for them. They stay completely separate from the men and there isn't anything impure about what they do. They are good girls, and brave fighters."

"She said a lot," Ruya said skeptically. "Did you tell her we wanted to join them?"

"No, but she has thought about it for herself and has talked to her father about it. He doesn't want her to go, but he has told her all about it. He says the training is very hard, and he thinks she is too lazy and soft."

"Maybe I'm too lazy and soft, too," Ruya said despondently. She turned away and went back to the house without saying anything more. In the kitchen, as she strained the milk through a cloth into a large jar, a wave of panic and depression swept over her. Her hands shook and she couldn't control them. As the bowl in her hands blurred, she realized that tears were pouring down her cheeks. Her mother's warm hands covered hers and steadied them to pour the last of the milk into the jar. Only a little had splashed onto the table.

"What is the matter, Ruya?" Aysel asked. Her manner was sympathetic but practical. "Come," she said, and led her daughter to the porch where they could sit and be cool while they talked in privacy.

Ruya had wiped her face on her sleeve, and now blew her nose in the cloth her mother gave her. She felt as if she were tied up in a hard knot of tension; it was unbearable. She dared not tell anyone, yet she had to tell someone. Her head seemed to be splitting. A sob broke from her, almost a wail. She stood up as if to run away, then she was in her mother's arms. Aysel held her as she sobbed out her story of the rape and her fear that her father would kill her. When her story was out, she felt tremendous relief, but also fear.

She sank back down in her chair while Aysel went inside to get a wet towel for her to clean her face, and brought her a drink of water. Ruya looked anxiously at her mother's face as she sipped the water. What would her reaction be? Families generally approved the honor killings, or at least supported them.

Aysel spoke calmly and reassuringly. "We will keep your secret between us. It will be easier for you now that you have shared it with me. We will tell no one else, and no one will ever know. I will show you how to make it seem you are a virgin on your wedding night. Your father loves you and I don't think he would ever harm you, but I'm not sure what he would do. It is best if no one else knows what happened."

After a little while she went inside to start the supper, leaving Ruya to marvel at the weight that had lifted off her shoulders. She felt utterly drained, however, and didn't get up to go inside until the men returned from the village for their dinner.

Late summer came, and word reached them of more nearby villages being bombed by the Turkish soldiers. Refugees would stream through on their way to find some new place to live, and everyone fed and helped them as they could. It was the time of abundance as the wheat was harvested, the fruit picked and dried or preserved, and the vegetables bottled or pickled and put away for winter. The days were hot under dark blue, cloudless skies, and even the nights felt airless as no breeze cooled them. The pastures burned brown, and the rocky slopes of the mountains shimmered in waves of heat.

Arrangements were completed for Songul's coming marriage as a second wife to a much older man. He had lost one wife, but he was hard working and was faithful to the new wife he had married, having several children with her. The family thought he would be a good husband to her, also, but there were nine children in the family, the oldest nearly the same age as Songul.

No one had asked for Ruya, and she came to feel that if she stayed at home she would wither away as an unwanted spinster daughter. Several offers came for Aliye, who grew more beautiful with every passing season, but Burhan refused them all, saying she was too young. The family understood that she was his favorite, and that only a very good offer indeed would persuade him to part with her.

The Sisters Join the Guerrillas

The days grew cool, the nights frosty. The mountain foliage turned red and gold. The same guerrilla group which had come twice before came again to their town. This time they came in the middle of the night. Mehmet the Baker held the meeting in the large back room of his shop where the big ovens warmed the room. Songul and Ruya begged their father to let them attend, but he adamantly refused. When he left the house with the older boys, however, the two girls sneaked out after him carrying their shoes. Hurrying through the shadows to the bakery, they saw many people entering the front door, while some clung to the shadows to slip in the back way. Some of them were women.

Afraid to enter where they might be seen, they crept around to a side window which someone had cracked open for ventilation. They could hear every word spoken, and watching, they saw which faces were open and eager, which ones closed and disapproving. Along with the speaker's voices, the fragrance of baking bread drifted through the window, making their mouths water.

Suddenly someone was beside them, and they turned with a gasp of fear. A young woman signaled for silence, and beckoned them away from the building. They could see she was one of the guerrillas, in fact they recognized the one who had spoken at the first meeting they had attended.

"I saw you through the window," she whispered. "I'm Miriam. Why don't you girls come in?" she invited, smiling. The sisters were startled to see that she had a repeating rifle on a strap over her shoulder and both a pistol and a big knife on her belt. Her pants were tucked into her boots military fashion, and they saw that her vest was stuffed with ammunition. She looked much more like a guerrilla fighter than like a woman to them, but her voice was soft and her smile friendly. She had a pretty face, and tonight her dark hair was uncovered and bound into a long braid that hung down her back.

"Our father has forbidden us. We don't dare let him see us," Songul answered her. Then, greatly daring, she added, "But Ruya and I want to join you."

The woman smiled again. "You would be welcome, but do you know that it would be very hard? You would have to train, and go to school as well. You would find the living hard."

"We know," Songul rejoined ardently, "but we know we can do it and we want to fight for our nation. We believe we can win freedom, and everything will be so much better for all of us."

"Many of us who fight will never live to marry and have children, nor experience that better world," Miriam replied soberly.

Songul was silent, realizing as never before the truth in what she said. Then she rallied. "We may never have our own children, but we will help to give that better world to the children of others, of our sisters and friends," she insisted.

Miriam turned to Ruya. "And you, do you feel as strongly as your sister or are you just going along to keep her company?" she asked.

"I have my own reasons for joining you," Ruya answered. "I have made up my mind and will not be turned away."

"Not everyone goes to fight, you know," Miriam said. "There are many ways to serve the nation. Perhaps you will just want to come to school for a while, or perhaps you can help in one of the cities in a store or office, or perhaps you can become a teacher."

For a moment the girls were silent thinking about this. "I do want to go to school and learn more," Songul said eagerly. "But

I want to fight, too," she added. Ruya was silent. She didn't really know what she wanted, but she knew it was more than she faced if she stayed with her family. When she saw Miriam watching her, she lifted her head and stared back. "I know I want to come," she said stubbornly.

"All right, then. If you come here after the moon has set in three nights' time, someone will meet you and bring you to our camp. Is that all right with you?" Miriam looked hard at their faces, still looking for signs of weakening.

The sisters looked at each other, and Ruya reached for Songul's hand. "We will be here," she said firmly.

"Don't tell anyone in your family. Believe me, that is essential. It will all go wrong, and we may all be caught and punished, even killed, if the wrong person finds out. You can never tell what people may do," she urged. "After you have reached the base, you can find a way to let your family know you are safe."

She led them back to the window and left them there. For the next half hour they listened to the speakers, but they were dizzy with the momentous thing they had agreed to do and could hardly concentrate on what was being said. Ruya found that she was still gripping Songul's hand, long after Miriam had gone.

She had always been the big sister, teaching and encouraging Songul and cleaning up after her impetuous mistakes. She was supposed to be the leader, the strong one. Where had Songul found this courage to do something so daring and different? Who would take care of whom if things went wrong now? She knew she would never have decided to leave the familiar village life if she hadn't been so afraid of someone finding out about her rape. She didn't want to die, either at home or somewhere fighting a war. Maybe she could find something else to do like Miriam said. But Songul, this Songul, was someone she didn't know, or was her little sister just being impetuous again without weighing the cost? They must talk some more, Ruya decided.

They had plenty of warning when the meeting was breaking up, and ran home well ahead of their father. They couldn't talk as they crept into the house and to their beds, where the other women of the household were soundly sleeping.

The following morning, however, Ruya followed Songul to the water pump again. She could tell by the way Songul eyed her and set her jaw that she was not open to any more discussion. Still, she tried.

"Are you sure, Songul?" she asked. "Think, it is the rest of your life, which has hardly started."

Songul looked around the area where the pump stood. She gestured in a half circle at the small mud brick houses, chickens scratching in their yards, and the broken street. "If I stay here, my life will be over before it has started," she replied. "I want more than this. Don't you see, Ruya?"

Ruya tried to see what Songul meant, for the first time recognizing how limited were the options they faced living here. Even without the threat she faced, the hard, narrow life of a village woman was reason enough to take the risk of leaving, if there was anywhere to go. "Yes," she said slowly. "Yes, Songul. Yes, I see."

During the next three days they secretly hid some articles of clothing under their sleeping mats, and also hid away bits of food for their journey. They continued to work hard at their household tasks to counter any suspicions against them.

Songul longed to tell Aden their plans, believing it would cheer him up. He had been despondent since attending the guerrillas' meeting, poking at his food without eating it and snapping at anyone who spoke to him. But Ruya warned her, saying they should especially avoid giving him any hint of their plans. She had seen on the hillside pasture how much he was set against their going. The hours seemed to drag by slowly, and it felt as if every eye was watching what they were doing. It seemed impossible that the others didn't know what was happening, but the family was oblivious.

Then, suddenly, the night was upon them. Neither could sleep, but lay stiff on her mat, waiting for the moon to set. When it rested on the western mountains, they rose and stealthily gathered the things they had prepared. Creeping out of the kitchen, they hurried through the silent streets to the bakery.

In spite of her excitement, Ruya thought with pain of her mother, of how sad she would be. Ruya loved her mother, worshipped her. For so long her dream had been to be just like her someday. She had never told her that. Now it was too late, and would never happen.

The streets were dark and silent, with only the sound of the wind brushing through the pines on the slopes above them. Ruya reached nervously for Songul's hand as they pressed together, huddled out of the wind in the bakery doorway.

Suddenly, with no sound, Miriam and two men were beside them. Songul saw that one of the men was the speaker with dark eyes and musical voice who had so beguiled her at that first meeting. "Come," Miriam breathed. The men took the bundles the girls were carrying, and when Songul made a gesture of protest, Miriam put her hand on her arm and whispered against her ear.

"It will be a hard journey for you, because you aren't trained. Let him carry it for you."

For hours they climbed narrow paths through the mountains. Ruya's legs grew so weak that at last, when they paused on a high pass, she sank to the ground with her head on her knees. One of the men offered her water from a canteen, and Miriam sat down beside her. "It isn't far now," she comforted. "We'll rest a little, and then you can go on."

It was true. After ten minutes, Ruya found she was able to rise and start down the path again. In less than an hour, they came to a sentry guarding a narrow place between tall rock walls. Passing him with a word of recognition, they entered a steeply walled valley.

With smiles and words of parting, the men handed the girls their bundles, and left them. Songul gazed enamored at the one who fascinated her, but his manner was impersonal. She had imagined that he and Miriam seemed very aware of each other, but there had not really been any word or action to make her think they were a couple.

Miriam led them toward a fire which burned under a rock overhang where it could not be seen from above. She said they could sit down. Gratefully, they sank to the ground and accepted glasses of hot tea with sugar. After a few minutes, a woman brought them tin plates of cheese, bread and olives, and they ate hungrily. They were given more tea, then Miriam led them to an earthen cave dug into a hillside. Several dark mounds lay on the ground, the sound of heavy breathing announcing that these were sleeping people. She showed them piles of blankets where they also could sleep. Exhausted, they lay down and without even talking to each other, fell into deep slumber.

When Songul woke, she lay for a few minutes in warm comfort without thinking about where she was. Suddenly she remembered, and sat up looking around. Ruya still slept beside her, and no one else was in the cave. Songul could tell from the light that it was daytime. The sounds of voices and soft clatter came from outside. Although she had made no sound, Ruya's eyes flew open and she turned her head, looking around with alarm.

"It's all right," Songul said. "We're safe. "

Ruya sat up, rubbing her eyes like a child. After a little, she said, "I need to go to the toilet."

Together the girls went outside. They saw a number of women moving purposefully about their duties. Hesitantly they went to a group of three young girls who were preparing vegetables, and asked where they could go to the toilet. Smiling, one of the girls rose and showed them a latrine area. There was a spring of water nearby, welling into a little pool, and they washed their hands and faces before returning to their cave. Songul began to comb her hair and then bind on her scarf again, but Ruya lay back down on her blankets. In a little while she was asleep.

Songul went outside and joined the girls, offering to help them prepare they vegetables. With no embarrassment, they accepted her offer. While they worked, they chattered among themselves, and just by listening Songul began to have a sense of their life in this camp. She learned that they had been brought here much as she and Ruya had been. They had been staying at this place for several days, but wouldn't stay here much longer.

They told her she and her sister would soon be called to speak with the senior officer, who would probably send them to a bigger training camp somewhere in the south. Already the sun was low over the western mountains and a chill shadow was creeping through the valley.

Miriam came over and told Songul to waken Ruya. It was time for them to be interviewed by the camp commander, she said. When Ruya had straightened her clothes and retied her scarf, they went with Miriam some distance down the valley to the men's area, and entered a rocky cave guarded by two soldiers. Inside, three men sat on the floor on a carpet.

They didn't immediately recognize the women as they continued to speak among themselves. Following Miriam's example, the sisters stood quietly near the entrance with their hands at their sides and their eyes cast down.

After a few minutes, one of the men stood up, greeted Miriam, and asked about Ruya and Songul. Then he spoke directly to first Songul and then Ruya. Without preliminary, he asked, "Why did you want to join us? What do you expect to do?"

Although frightened, Songul rose to the occasion. "I believe we are a people with a right to our own customs, language and homeland. I have seen how the Turks abuse us and steal our land, and I want to fight them."

"Don't you want to be married? Has someone offered for you?"

Songul met his eyes bravely, lifting her chin. "Yes, as a second wife. I do not want to marry him, or anyone else. I will stay alone, and fight for our people."

The officer smiled at her. "You will need to be trained before you can do that. We can send you to a place where you will learn a lot if you work hard. Are you willing to give your life, first to learn and then to fight?"

"Oh, yes. That is what I want to do," Songul said ardently.

Turning to Ruya, the officer asked, "Why did you come with your sister? What do you expect to do?"

Ruya felt she must tell the truth. "I was afraid to stay at home. I had no good place there. All our villages are being destroyed and I wanted to do something to help our people to be safe again. Maybe I will die, but if I can help make a better life for our children, then I am willing. That is what I want to work for, if necessary to fight for. I will learn to fight or to do whatever I can."

The man looked hard into her face. He seemed to be thinking. At last he said, "Why were you afraid? Why are you not married yet?"

Ruya flushed heavily, feeling her voice trapped behind a lump in her throat. What if they sent her back? Panic rose, filling her chest. "I was twice engaged, but both times the men died," she whispered, her head hanging.

"Look at me," the officer snapped. "How did they die?"

Ruya forced herself to lift her head, although she could not make her eyes meet his. "The first died in a car accident, the second was killed by soldiers," she said. She spoke more clearly, but her voice was still choked and thin from the fear she was feeling. She wished miserably that she could disappear into the dust, or be a wisp of smoke that could melt away into the wind.

"And why are you afraid? Someone will probably offer for you in time."

Ruya could not answer. Her breath stopped, and blackness filled her mind. She opened her eyes again to find herself lying on the cave floor, with Miriam and Songul kneeling beside her. "Here, drink this," Miriam said, putting an arm under her shoulders to lift her and holding a cup of water to her lips. Ruya sipped it, and then sat up. She remained hunched over miserably, her head hanging, her arms wrapped around herself. She was desperately aware that the men were nearby, sitting on their carpet.

"Ruya, what is it?" Miriam asked quietly. "You must tell us. For your own safety, and ours, we must understand why you have come and what you want to do."

Ruya hung her head lower, and silent tears began to pour down her cheeks. She couldn't stop them, her throat was closed and she couldn't speak. She couldn't breathe. Her body shook with the contained misery and terror.

"You were raped, weren't you?" Miriam's calm voice penetrated the blackness. She heard Songul gasp. Suddenly she could breathe again, and drew in a long rasping gulp of air with a groan.

"Ruya, you will not be punished here. You are safe. We can help you. You can stay here, and no one else will know, and you will not be punished. You are safe here," Miriam repeated in the same calm, soothing voice.

Ruya drew in another gasp of air. She lifted her wet face to Miriam and felt hope come into her heart. "Really, truly?" she begged for reassurance.

"Yes, really truly. You are safe here," Miriam repeated.

Ruya turned to Songul, still mutely seeking reassurance. Songul threw her arms around her sister and kissed her over and over. "I didn't know," she cried. "Oh, Ruya, I didn't know. I'm so sorry. But we will be safe here, don't worry."

Ruya looked at the officer who had been questioning her. As he rose and came to them, the women stood to meet him.

"Ruya, do you want to stay and train with us to fight for our nation?" he asked her.

"Oh, yes," she breathed.

"No one should be afraid, as you were afraid. We must change that," he said. "Help us to change our ways so that no one is killed for something she couldn't help. We must learn to meet our shame with courage and overcome it by kindness and patience, not by bloodshed. Will you help us fight for these changes?"

"Oh, yes," Ruya answered as ardently as Songul had done.

The officer looked satisfied. He spoke to Miriam. "Take them back to eat and rest with the other women. In two days, on the fourteenth, this group will go to the south for training. You are to go with them."

Turning back to the sisters, he said, "We are glad you have joined us. Study hard and train well, so that you will be an asset to our cause. Together, we can win our homeland and bring our people to better ways."

To Miriam, he said, "Dismissed."

Going back to their sleeping cave, both sisters walked as if on air, their heads lifted and their eyes shining. Miriam smiled secretly to herself. She never ceased to marvel how Hakim Bey could inspire new recruits, transforming raw, confused youngsters into dedicated, zealous reformers with a few words. It was his own passion and single mindedness, she thought, which was so infectious. She loved him with all her heart and would have gladly died for him, and she knew that many others in the camp felt the same.

No one knew what the next days would bring, nor the long future either, but she could be sure that these two girls, with the several dozen others who had gathered here in the first stage of their journey, would give everything they had. They would join hundreds of other volunteers, men and women, and be educated and trained in the skills they would need for the long conflict. They would emerge strong and determined to do whatever was required to win their struggle. They had become revolutionary fighters in their hearts already, and would soon be so in reality as well.

SEVEN

The Guerrilla
Training Camp

That evening after their interview with Hakim Bey, Ruya and Songul got better acquainted with the five other new women recruits who were sharing their cave. For two more days they stayed there, preparing their own food and cleaning their own area of the camp. The weather stayed clear, but it was very cold at night. Ice rimmed the spring by the latrines, and in the early mornings their breath made white puffs of vapor.

Two of the other recruits were also sisters, and the four girls were drawn to one another. Hulya and Esra had fled from a remote farm outside of a village. Their mother was dead, and the household of men whom they served, father, uncles and brothers, had abused and overworked them. They, like Ruya, were seeking a more tenable life, but their other three cave mates were more like Songul. Filled with patriotic feeling for their nation, they believed that by fighting, the Kurds could find a place in history for themselves, and a land of their own. Ayse in particular was a fiery girl with striking beauty, while Aynur and Pinar were more serious, quiet, and intense.

Remembering what Hassan had said to Aden, Ruya undertook to challenge Songul and Ayse one morning as they ate their breakfasts together. "Don't you think that if we had not begun to fight the Turkish government, none of us would have suffered the loss of our villages?" she asked. Ayse kindled into defense at once.

"For almost all of this century any Kurdish leader who showed any power and tried to help the nation politically was murdered," she said. "Don't you know the story of Seyh Sait? He was a brave and able leader who was feared by the Turks and hung. We have never been given a voice to work peacefully, and now they don't even want us to exist. They command our young men to fight and die for them, they steal our resources and give us nothing in return. Kurds are despised by the Turks. If we don't fight for the identity of our nation, we will just disappear into nothing and be forgotten."

Ruya was silent. She really didn't know anything about their history. She could not reply. Hakim Bey had said they would study while they were being trained. Perhaps she could learn some of these things for herself. Beside her, Songul was earnestly questioning Ayse.

Ruya had noticed that her sister deeply admired the beautiful, passionate girl, and she felt a stirring of jealousy as she saw Songul hanging eagerly on every word Ayse uttered. She tried to quench it. Songul herself was the passionate one, ready to fight for the cause she believed in. Of course she would be drawn to someone who felt like she did, and who was much better informed about it. She rose and began to clear up the breakfast things. After the dishes were washed and put away, Ruya withdrew unnoticed, as Songul and Ayse continued to talk eagerly about the hopes and dreams they shared.

When Songul came back to the sleeping cave, Ruya was sulking on her bed and wouldn't talk to her. When Songul realized that something was wrong, she knelt down by her sister anxiously. "What's wrong, did something happen?" she asked. Ruya wouldn't answer.

Songul turned to Pinar, who was sitting at the back of the cave. "Did something happen?" she repeated. Pinar shook her head, looking surprised. "Not that I know about," she said. Songul reached out and shook Ruya by her shoulder. "Ruya, stop this. What is wrong?"

"Oh, nothing. Nothing to disturb a great lady who sits with her new friends and lets her unimportant sister wait on her. Why talk to me? Why even notice me? I don't know anything, I don't matter."

Songul's mouth fell open in surprise. After a moment, she reached out and put her arms around her sister. "Ruya, I'm sorry. I didn't notice. I'm sorry. It's just that I'm so interested in what is happening here, and Ayse knows so much more than we do. But I love you, you're the most important thing to me. Don't be angry."

Ruya felt ashamed of herself, but she wasn't ready to give up her hurt quite yet. She didn't return Songul's hug, but turned aside from it. "I don't belong here," she said. "I don't even know why I came. They are never going to want me, because I don't feel like you and Ayse do."

Songul scrambled across the bedding to sit in front of her sister and take her hand up in both of hers. "Ruya, that's silly. We all belong here, and you meant it when you said you wanted to come. We are all different, perhaps we will do different jobs in the end, but you and I will always be together. You're my sister. Now come, stop this. You'll see, it's all going to work out."

Ruya didn't turn away this time, and she allowed Songul to brush her hair for a long time until she felt calm again. They went outside and helped to prepare the midday meal together. Songul was careful not to excite her sister's jealousy again, although she still felt a great admiration for the beautiful Ayse.

Early the next morning, the new recruits were called to prepare for a long journey. They would not be returning to this camp, they were told. All around them, they could see that the whole area was being cleared out. Pains were taken to erase the marks of their stay, so that no one could easily discover where they had been. They were not told where the others were going, but they themselves joined with about twenty young men who were also recruits and began to walk south through the mountains. They were led by Miriam and the two men who had come with her the night Ruya and Songul left their village.

For ten days they marched, and as they did the three leaders taught them guerrilla crafts of concealment, stealth, and intelligence gathering. Snow now lay on the mountain tops, and when they woke in the morning their blankets were white with frost. Once a dense snowfall drove them to shelter for two days in a cave until they could travel again, leaving a highly visible path behind them in the snow. Until they descended below the snowline, they stayed among trees where their passing was less noticeable.

Ruya felt like she was a guerrilla already by the time they emerged from the mountains into the training camp. The area bustled with activity. Concealed within caves or under groves of trees were the signs of many people living, some areas further protected from aerial surveillance by camouflage netting. Everything looked clean and tidy. Across a level plain, a broad, shallow river flowed, and a narrow plank bridge spanned it. They could see cave openings in a cliff wall on the other side.

Men and women were moving about as if on purposeful errands. The recruits passed an open field where several dozen men were going through practice drills in hand combat. A squad of women soldiers jogged past them at a smart clip, obviously very fit young women who were not panting or sweating, Ruya noticed. She doubted she could ever do what they were doing. Her heart sank. Why had she thought she could do this? Her hand stole out to take Songul's for comfort, but Songul's eyes were shining as she looked around, as if she could hardly wait to be a part of all this.

Miriam called the girls to follow her, and the men went with the other two guides away from the stream. Crossing the river, Miriam went behind a low ridge, and led them to a cave where they were quickly settled. Later they learned that they would live in a completely separate section of the camp from the men. The next morning their classes began. Those who had no formal education were taught basic skills like reading, writing, and numbers. Because they had some schooling, Ruya and Songul found themselves in an advanced class that did more difficult mathematics and focused on political history.

From the first day there was physical training. Although it pushed them to their limits, it wasn't impossibly difficult, Ruya found. By the end of the first month, she too could jog several kilometers without distress. She realized that she felt better than she had ever felt before, and she saw that the women surrounding her all shone with health and confidence in a way she thought was beautiful. She began to realize that her previous life, the life of a village woman, made women weak and fearful and old before their time. She discovered inside herself a growing passion to free her sisters, and all women, from the virtual slavery that was the lot of Kurdish village women.

She still did not share the passion for Kurdish independence that most of the others seemed to feel. She knew that many national groups found their home within the boundaries of the Turkish nation and she couldn't really see why her nation couldn't do so as well. She also noticed that to many of her instructors the establishment of a Kurdish nation meant the freedom to maintain their feudal village life style. Their greatest anger was against the practice of bombing the villages.

The loss of homes and lives was terrible, she agreed. But her own new birth within the ranks of the soldiers had awakened her to the destructive nature of village life for women, and a part of her was glad that such a system was being destroyed. Whatever came of it, she didn't think they would go back to the old ways. And to Ruya, that was a good thing.

Songul, on the other hand, had become a passionate separatist. She was eager to fight and prepared to die to establish a separate Kurdish nation. Her friendship with Ayse had strengthened until the two were almost inseparable. In their busy life of training and study, Ruya became accustomed to this. She missed her former closeness with her sister, but she had become close with Pinar. In part this was because the quiet girl reminded her of her old friend Esra, who had died of poison because of a spiteful rumor in their village. Just one of the things that were better done away with, she thought. To eliminate that kind of injustice was worth any price. She believed in the struggle that would modernize her nation, but she sometimes felt secretly that the enemy was as much their own village culture as it was the Turkish State.

After their first four months of training, they were required to choose whether to go on to more difficult courses in a different camp, or to go out to some assignment elsewhere. The trainees were encouraged to use whatever skills and talents they possessed to carry on their struggle on many fronts. Some scattered across the nations, going to Europe and the Americas, their purpose to teach the world about the Kurds and to win them friends.

Ayse had a beautiful singing voice, and to Songul's distress she went to the western part of Turkey for more musical training. She would help in the propaganda struggle by singing the folksongs of the Kurdish nation. Songul and Ruya stayed together and went to a different camp where they could begin military training in armed combat. They would also continue their schooling with more emphasis on mathematics and history, and of course political science.

Ruya loved learning and pursued all her study courses eagerly. It was Songul who turned out to be an excellent marksman with a rifle and loved her artillery classes. The training filled her days and brought her awards and attention. She missed Ayse, but the first pain of parting was soon forgotten. With Ayse gone, the sisters grew very close again.

They learned that Aden was in this new camp training in the men's area. Miriam had told them that he had joined the first guerrilla group a few weeks after they had arrived, but by then their camp had changed locations. So it was several months before he arrived at the training base where they were now staying. The sisters asked permission to go and see him, but when they did so, Aden was distant and unfriendly. It made him angry that they were learning to fight. He seemed to be offended by their having joined before he did, or perhaps by the fact that they were enjoying themselves. He told them not to visit him again.

The sisters talked with each other and with their new close friends about why Aden was acting as he was. Ruya thought he was ashamed of them and what they were doing. But Songul pointed out that he had not seemed happy or enthusiastic about being with the guerrillas himself. It was almost as if he resented them for forcing him into something that he had not quite made up his mind to do. The sisters were sad, and worried for him. There seemed nothing they could do about it, however. Then their minds were taken off family problems as a major alert took them out of the camp to a conflict on the Iranian border.

EIGHT

A l a r m   i n   t h e
N i g h t

Alev sat on her mat, blankets clutched to her chin, stunned into immobility.   The noise assaulted her, a thunderous clacking that she knew was a helicopter, a bellowing voice shouting over an amplifier, people screaming, children crying. As the blaring message came again and again the sense of it reached her; "Leave your homes. Go now. You have thirty minutes to leave your homes. There will be no other warning. Go now."

Thirty minutes. She knew, they all knew, what would happen then. The shells would come, the bombs blow their houses apart. One half hour. Ruya was not on her mat beside her. In a moment she remembered, Ruya and Songul were gone, run away into the mountains. She heard her mother crying, her father waking her brothers. She tried to think, but her mind was numb. Get dressed, she thought.

Alev got up and lighted the lamp. She slept with her aunts and sisters in the kitchen, where it was warmest. Aunt Kader was already dressed and folding bedding into tight neat rolls. Aliye was burrowed under her blanket, surely not still asleep but pretending to be. Her mother was holding the two little ones, trying to soothe them. No time for that, Alev thought.

51

"Get up!" she hissed to the room at large. "Get up all of you. Hurry! Put on all your warmest clothes, all you can. Aliye, you have to come help." She pulled the blanket roughly off her smaller sister. "Roll your blankets, we must try to take them with us, or we'll freeze."

She was dressing as she spoke, saw Auntie helping her mother with the little ones, saw Aliye emerge from hiding and begin to dress, too. She went to find her father.

He and her twin, Hassan were gathering what items of value they had in the house, some military medals, coins, a silver candlestick, the Koran. They were stuffing them in the woven saddlebags they used when taking vegetables to the market. Her mother came to pull clothing out of a chest and pile it on a blanket.

"Bury the silver in the back yard," Aysel advised her husband. "Someone may rob us if we take it with us into the mountains."

"No time," he grunted. "Besides, the soldiers will come back and look for anything we have left. They would find it."

Alev went to her mother and put a sweater into Aysel's hands. "Put it on, Mother," she said gently. "It's cold tonight. Put on all the clothes you can wear."

"Is there any food left?" Aysel asked her daughter. The freedom fighters had come earlier in the night, taking whatever food they could find. It was why the soldiers were here now, to destroy the village.

"I'll see if I can find anything," Alev promised. She went through the kitchen to the back of the house, taking the lamp as she went out. She opened the cover to the root cellar and looked within, but it was empty. It had been nearly empty when the guerrillas had come, winter having come early and gripped the land hard this year. Their hens were gone too, she knew, and the two orphan lambs they had been caring for. The family had not protested the food the men took, although it would make life very hard. They knew they were starving up in the mountains, and that they were up there fighting for their nation. Anyhow, what could they have done?

What had hurt them most was that her younger brother Mangat had gone with the men. A quiet, serious boy, no one really knew what Mangat was thinking much of the time. But when he gathered some clothing in a pack and came to the men, asking to go with them, the family was shocked.

Aysel screamed and threw her arms around him, sobbing and begging him not to go. She had been broken and subdued since her three older children had gone to the hills in the fall. However, when Mangat turned to his father, quietly asking "Baba?", Burhan merely turned his head aside. Mangat kissed his mother, then pushed her away and left with the men.

Back in the kitchen, Alev lifted the loose board in the floor and took up the two sacks of precious seed wheat. Rolled underneath a cupboard she found three onions that had been missed by the guerrillas. There was nothing else in the house that could be eaten. Putting the onions in one of the bags of wheat, she took them to her father. Wordlessly he received them and put them into the saddle bag he was filling. From the shelf he took the clock that was a family treasure. Her grandfather had looted it from an Armenian home when the owners were driven away.

Now it is we who are being driven out, Alev thought. Why is life so hard?

She went to help her mother, who was still gathering winter clothing to bundle in a blanket. In a few moments they gathered all they could carry and hurried out the door. They knew there would not be another warning.

Escape Over the Mountains

Standing at the edge of the village in the icy night, Aliye pressed against Alev. Her mind was swirling. She felt like she might spin away up into the air like the leaves and bits of trash the wind was blowing across the hillside. Dazed, she clutched her mother's sleeve for support. Although the ground where they stood was dry and bare of snow, the hillside not far above them was white with it. Higher up the great peaks shone silver in the moonlight. White puffs of breath came from the mouths of those around them, and frost crystals sparkled in the icy air.

Having led their heavily burdened donkey to the edge of the village, the family paused. They waited with the many others also fleeing the soldiers. Some people had already driven away in cars or trucks stuffed with relatives and hastily assembled household goods.

The wind was sharply cold, and some of the women squatted, sheltering their little ones against their bodies. The sound of the anxious crowd rose and fell. It sounded like the noise of a storm that calms and then roars again against the walls of the house. Only we will have no more house, Aliye thought. Our house is empty now, about to be bombed, gone forever.

She knew it would be destroyed. She would never live in it again. Theirs was not the first village the soldiers had come to, forcing all the people to leave so that they could bomb the houses, cut down the orchards, and fill the streets with rubble. Sometimes they didn't even warn the people to get out before they started shelling.

No more people were coming out of their houses. Among the crowd on the hillside were the refugees from other demolished villages, who were again being dispossessed and cast out into the night. Her mother was sobbing, other women wailing loudly, but Aunt Kader, who had come to them seven months ago, stood straight and silent, her anger surrounding her like a frozen envelope.

Kader's husband had been shot by the soldiers as he stood in his doorway, although he was not armed. When her oldest son had run to him, the soldiers had shot him, too. Their baby had died from the cough he took that night fleeing over the cold mountainside. They had been taken in by her husband's older brother Burhan, Aliye's father. Kader's three remaining children surrounded their mother, pressed against her skirts. Like her, they were silent as if all too familiar with the scene around them.

Aliye couldn't make any sense of it all. In the village school the children had been required to speak Turkish. They were told they were mountain Turks, part of the great nation of Turkey. Her father had allowed her and her sisters to attend the school when they were small, although not all of the families in the village let their girls go to school. It wasn't easy because the teacher spoke only in Turkish, while in the village everyone spoke Kurdish. But Aliye was a bright eager student. She took to reading, and her teacher encouraged her and loaned her books.

From her reading, Aliye had learned that there were other ways to live than the ones in her village. She understood that a smart girl in the western part of the nation might go to secondary school and even to a university. Women became doctors or the managers of banks, and lived free and independent lives. She couldn't quite imagine what that would be like, but she felt trapped and restless in their small village. She knew she wanted more than she could find there.

It seemed to Aliye that Turkey was a great and strong nation, one she had felt proud to be a part of. It seemed to be pushing toward the future with new ideas that were bringing freedom and prosperity to its people. She wanted to get an education and to be a part of that kind of change.

She knew there was fighting in the mountains around them, where guerrillas fought the Turkish soldiers for the independence of the Kurdish people. The year before, a group of young men and women had come to their village and told them about their history. They explained who the Kurds were and why they had a right to be a separate nation from Turkey. Aliye had heard her father and brothers talking about it. Then her older brother Aden, and two sisters had gone away to help the guerrillas fight. Now her brother Mangat had gone with them too. But Aliye wasn't sure.

There was a fixed role for women in her village, and that was to marry and have many children. A woman who dressed or acted differently from the others was considered to be damaging her family's honor. She might even be killed for bringing shame on her family, if she went away to school or work. A few, like her sisters Ruya and Songul, had run away from the village, but most were afraid to. Aliye knew she was also afraid, so she hid herself in dreams most of the time.

She loved her family and their life in the village, the busy days and long, peaceful nights. The beautiful mountains around them were as much her home as was their small cluster of flat, brown houses tucked against tall rocky walls. She loved the orderly flow of life where everything always happened the same way. She loved knowing everyone and being known by them.

Sometimes, though, she wanted to have more, to do more. She knew she didn't want to spend her whole life doing exactly the same things her mother did, and in the same way. She thought that was why her sisters had gone away with the guerrillas.

Standing with her mother and sisters in the back of the room, Aliye had heard what the guerrillas said. Everyone in the village had gone to hear them, the first time they came. Then her father had forbidden his women to go again, and many others as well had been upset by what they said. She had heard people talking about them when they came back twice again, and not everyone had wanted them to come. Then her two older sisters had disappeared. A few days later her brother Aden had gone after them, and her father had given him his old gun and some money. Everyone knew they had all left to join the guerrillas. Once a man came to speak with their father, bringing a message that all three were well and happy. The family was quietly relieved.

When she got older, she might want to go away, too, but not to fight. To fight to keep their lives as they were in the village didn't seem to her to be such a good thing. Perhaps they should try to learn from the Turks and make their lives better.

Lying in her bed at night she thought about these things. But she knew she could never talk about them to anyone, because in the village things never changed. It was especially unsafe for girls to have ideas or want anything to change. Her grandmother had told her girls should not ask for anything, even from Allah in prayer.

If he knew some of the things she thought about, her father would think she was being rebellious and wicked, and that if anyone knew about it he would lose his honor. Her mother and aunt would tell her what the Koran said about how Allah would punish her. She would be in disgrace, and the family would quickly try to marry her to someone, thinking that would stop her having such ideas.

But now everything would be different, and maybe that wasn't all bad. Now they would find a new place to live, maybe in a city. They might even go to America or Germany like some people they had heard of. There would be new things to learn and perhaps the old rules wouldn't be quite so strong. Guiltily she pushed these thoughts out of her mind. What was happening was terrible and if anyone knew what she was thinking they would stone her. Probably she deserved it.

It was not the villager's fault the guerrillas had come, Aliye thought. The bearded men had been quiet and polite, she remembered. They had done no violence, but there had been no resisting them when they took all the food from the houses. Perhaps her father had not wanted to resist. Whether he had wanted to help the guerrillas, Aliye didn't know. He had not prevented Mangat from leaving with the men. Perhaps he knew they were going to lose their home, so that Mangat might be better off with the guerrillas. Her father was very wise. She looked for him, but couldn't find him among the men grouped nearby, silently watching.

She didn't think it was right for the guerrillas to take their food, and she knew not everyone wanted to fight the soldiers. Her father was still at home, and he didn't seem glad that Aden had gone. After her two older sisters had left, no one could talk about them. Her father had said their names were no longer to be spoken in the home. They were now dead to the family. They didn't really talk about Aden either, but the house had felt strangely empty with three of them suddenly gone, and no one talked very much about anything anymore. She knew her mother was very sad. Now Mangat had gone too, and her mother would be even sadder.

How could this be happening, she wondered. If the Turkish government wanted them to be part of this nation of Turkey, why were the soldiers punishing them and destroying their homes and farms? When the guerrillas came for food, the villagers had no choice. The guerrillas were armed fighting men, used to violence. How could shop keepers and shepherds stop them? The soldiers knew that too, but still they bombed houses and shot people. She supposed they were following orders, as soldiers must do. Someone, somewhere, had decided their village must be destroyed as a part of a war that no one living in the village had made, or wanted. Aliye felt helpless, and thought again that she was like the dry rubble blown by the wind.

A sharper gust of wind whipped up the dust and stirred the women's skirts and scarves. Aliye pressed against her mother's back to shield her from its cutting blade. Alev pressed against her, too. They turned their faces away from the blowing dirt.

Aliye looked again for her father, and found him nearby holding the donkey. He appeared small and uncertain, not the strong figure she was accustomed to depending upon. Her mother, crouching beside her, was a dark mound of scarves and shawls from which muffled sobs escaped. The younger children were crying, too. Aliye knelt and clung again to her mother's sleeve, hiding her face behind it. Little Sakina, muffled in sweaters, leaned against her mother's knees, crying hard. Ridvan stood close, and the twins Kadir and Salih were holding hands. She could tell they were close to tears as well, fighting to be brave but overwhelmed by the general tension.

The silhouettes of armed soldiers stood in pairs or triplets around them. The soldiers were tense and alert as if expecting attack from both the group of villagers and the darkness around them. Their hands were ready on their guns to shoot anything that moved in the night. There were so many of them, Aliye thought. Who did they think would be brave enough to attack them? But if we move suddenly or run away, they will shoot us. She reached out to put her hand on the shoulder of her small brother Osman, who could be silly sometimes. "Stay right here and wait with us," she said to him. "Stay very quiet." The little boy turned his face into his mother's skirt, whimpering.

They waited on the mountainside, watching. They could not refuse the guerrillas, and there was no resisting the soldiers, either. A firestorm of noise and bright flashes erupted as rockets streaked through the air and exploded in the village. Explosions shook the ground beneath their feet. A regular heavy booming accompanied the erratic rocket fire as a large artillery piece shelled the houses, smashing walls and setting roofs on fire. Sheep and goats around them blatted in panic and broke free, running off into the night. Dogs barked and a cow bellowed. Children began screaming, and the voices of women rose wailing in the night air, but Aysel merely continued to sob softly. From her surrounding family there was no loud outcry, either.

Aliye reached for her mother's shoulder to steady herself, and stood, crowding against Alev. She stared hard at the top of Aysel's head, at the black shawl embroidered with black and purple that Ruya had made for her. Biting her lip, she willed herself not to cry. After a time, the noise of destruction ended. The air was filled with dust and smoke, but through it, by the light of the fires she could see that the familiar shapes of the ruined village had changed forever. Aysel still sobbed softly from within her mound of shawls and skirts, and little Osman and Sakina were wailing loudly, but Aliye saw that Kader still stood silently erect. Encircling her, her children were silent too.

Above the crowd noises, they heard the soldiers shouting. They were yelling at people to move on. No one could stay in the village. Aliye forced her thoughts to slow down. She took two long breaths to steady herself. She must concentrate on what was happening right now. They must keep the family together and not forget any of their possessions. She looked around for her father or Hassan, for someone to direct them.

"Come," said the voice of her father. Alev and Aliye each took one of their mother's arms and lifted her to her feet. They all gathered up the parcels and bundles surrounding them, and began to move slowly down the road away from the village.

Through the long cold night they trudged across the mountains following the rutted road. At first it went downhill steeply to follow the edge of the river. High rock walls shut away the light of the moon so they stumbled along in shadowy darkness. Then they had to climb again up a steep hill, to come out on top of the cliffs. It was cold up there because the wind cut against them, pouring up the cliff face from the icy river. But Aliye was grateful for the flooding moonlight that seemed to wash away the fear of the dark riverside.

Little Osman rode on top of the donkey's load with Aunt Kader's youngest child. Sometimes Osman was taken onto his father's shoulders. Hassan carried Aunt Kader's little boy. When Sakina sat down suddenly on the road and began to cry, Ridvan lifted her to his back and carried her.

Around them others moved, but no one talked. The soldiers did not follow them or offer any further directions. Aliye wondered where they had gone to. She didn't wonder where they themselves were going – if she thought about it at all it seemed they would just keep walking. After a long time she was so tired, she wondered why they didn't just sit down. Why walk on and on when there was no where to go?

Finally they stopped, the others as well as her family, and everyone sank down wherever they found themselves, numb with fatigue. "Aliye," Aunt Kader spoke her name. Looking up, she saw she was being offered a cup of water. It was cold and sweet, and she could feel its icy path down through her throat into her stomach. It made her feel alive again. She realized they had stopped by a spring that ran from the hillside, and people were splashing their faces and collecting the icy water in jars and cups to drink.

Surprised, she realized that she could see familiar faces around her, other families from the village. Although the moon had set and there was not yet any color in the sky, a grey light revealed the trees, the people, and the road they were on. In spite of her heavy clothing, she shivered in the bitter air. There was snow on the hillside around them. Rims of ice lay on the edges of the little stream that ran down from the spring.

All too soon they were on their feet again, walking downhill. The little ones were sound asleep, Osman on his father's back and Sakina now in Hassan's arms. Aysel and Aunt Kader walked on either side of the donkey steadying Kader's two little ones who slept there. The donkey's breath escaped in white puffs on the winter air, and his little hooves clicked on the stony road. Aliye wanted desperately to sleep too. Why couldn't they have just stayed at the spring and slept? Was it because it was too cold? Sometime they would have to stop walking and rest. Her mind drifted away into a blur of fatigue, but she kept on putting one foot in front of the other, moving among the bodies of her family around her with no more conscious thoughts at all.

TEN

Finding A New Home

As the first shafts of sun gilded the treetops, the stumbling group of foot-weary travelers straggled into the neighboring village of Kiziltas. The low brown houses lay sleeping against the wall of red stone which towered above them. Snow lay in the crevices of the red rock, and far above the rocky cliff great snowy peaks loomed against the sky. Their tops shone rosy pink in the dawn. Coming into narrow streets, Aliye thought the thin lines of smoke rising from the chimneys was the most welcome sight she had ever seen. Her feet and legs felt like wood, stiff and numb, but her body ached with cold. All she wanted was to be warm again, and to lie down, and to close her eyes.

The village dogs came snarling and barking against the strangers, but a door on one of the nearby houses opened, and a man stepped out, yelling to them. He came forward to greet the travelers, and as the men stood talking, other doors opened. Soon boys were sent running to find relatives of the refugees, and a crowd gathered. Not all of their group had relatives living here, but all found shelter and food in some welcoming household. Their plight might well be the fate of these villagers on another night.

Aliye's family were taken in by Burhan's uncle Artos. Given a hearty breakfast in the warm kitchen, Aysel was once again reduced to helpless tears, but the exhausted children were too tired even to cry. They were soon settled in piles of quilts and blankets in a quiet room and left to spend the day sleeping. When they woke in late afternoon, they ate again, and then sat quietly listening as the men discussed the best course to follow for their future.

It seemed this village was already overflowing with refugees from other places that had been destroyed. Moreover, since most of the villages in this area were already gone, the chances of this one being left alone were not good.

Far to the north was the place that Burhan's grandfather had left to settle in these southern mountains. He had left some trouble behind him, so the family could not be sure of their welcome there, but the area had escaped most of the fighting. No villages there had yet been destroyed. It seemed their best chance might be to go there and try to restore old ties. That village was named Cansu.

If the family caught a regional bus in the morning to the nearest large town, named Van, then from there they could take another bus north to Cansu. In Cansu they could seek out relatives and try to find a place to stay. Having reached this decision, they all returned to their beds to get a good night's sleep before starting yet another long journey.

In the morning Burhan sent Hassan and Kadir back to their old village. They would try to find any livestock that had survived. They would drive whatever sheep and goats were left to Uncle Artos's house, where they were leaving the donkey. If the rest of the family were able to find some land to live on, then they could arrange to bring the animals in a truck to their new home. It was the best they could do.

Waiting in the village square for the bus to come, Aliye jumped up and down a little and squeezed her arms inside her many sweaters to keep out the icy morning air. Her mother and sisters chattered with the ladies of the household they were leaving, and the little children ran and screamed with their local cousins as if they had been friends all their lives. Everyone seemed restored to normal by a day and night of warmth, food and sleep.

There were many people waiting for the bus, all like Aliye's family going to Van. From there, they would scatter to various other places in the hopes of finding shelter with relatives. When the dusty vehicle arrived and emptied out some passengers, there was a great rush to pile into its few seats. Burhan's relatives helped push and shove the family into the minibus, and Aliye felt herself lifted and shoved into a seat by a window, with her mother, Sakina, Osman, and Kader's little one crowded into it beside her. Alev and Aunt Kader with her two older children stood beside them in the aisle, which was packed with people. She could see nothing more of her family. Then, looking outside the window, she panicked as she saw Salih and Ridvan's stricken faces in the crowd outside the bus. Where was her father Burhan? As the bus pulled away the boys disappeared in a cloud of dust and other crowding figures.

As she shivered at the bus stop, Aliye had seen a boy she didn't know watching her from a vantage point under a tree. He had looked away, a flush coloring his neck and face, but then he looked back again and smiled at her. Aliye had always been told she was pretty, but somehow the adoration in his eyes made her blush too. She looked away and resolutely kept her eyes fixed on some houses across the road, not looking at him. But when they were on the bus and it started to move, she looked back. The boy was still watching her, and she was sure he had kept his eyes on her the whole time. Too bad, she thought. We will never meet again.

The boy who had been watching Aliye stared after the bus until it disappeared down the mountain. His name was Kerim. He had noticed the girl at the bus stop, clutching herself against the cold. Her family swirled around her in busy agitation, but to him she was like a single rose in the midst of a tossing storm of branches. After a few minutes, the girl saw him looking at her. Embarrassed, he looked away, but then, wanting her to notice him, he smiled at her. She turned her head away, but there had been a jolt like electricity when their eyes met.

He knew where she came from. The whole village knew about the refugees from Sicaksu who had arrived in the early morning on the day before. It was his sister's husband's cousins who had housed this family, so he would have no trouble finding out the girl's name. They might even know where the family was going. Kerim vowed to himself to somehow find her and marry her when better days came.

He knew why her village had been destroyed. He with his younger brother Mohammet had been returning from a scouting trip over the mountain when they had seen the band of men leaving Sicaksu, laden with sacks, chickens and sheep.

None of the guerillas looked familiar, so they had remained hidden and watched the men pass. The information they carried was for their own chief. It was up to him to decide whether to share their plans or to keep it for an attack by his own small troop. The fewer who knew, the fewer who could betray.

After delivering their information and sketches to their own guerrilla band, Kerim and his brother had gone back to their farm and climbed into bed. Not even their own family knew where they had been or what they were doing. Hopefully no one else knew they had been away at all. But for three days they had watched the military patrol outpost at the pass into nearby Iran, recording exactly how many men were there and at what times their shifts changed, who came and went and on what schedule, and where their sentries were posted. If anyone had caught the boys, they would have protested that they were just shepherd lads, searching for a lost sheep.

One night soon, Kerim knew, armed men would visit that outpost to place bombs against the munitions store and the sleeping quarters, or perhaps the kitchen. They would do whatever made life most miserable and difficult for the soldiers there, whatever killed the most men.

Kerim knew the soldiers were only boys like himself, sent by the Turkish government to lonely, dangerous lives in wilderness country that they hated and feared. But as agents of a government which was oppressing and threatening his Kurdish nation, they had become his enemies, and fair prey.

Meanwhile he took good care to stay visible in his village, leading a normal life, so that none could report to any soldier or policeman that he was behaving suspiciously. Most would protect his secrets even if they knew them, but the special political police didn't hesitate to torture information out if they thought someone knew more than he was telling. Kerim didn't know how he himself would react under torture, or what he would reveal. He hoped he never had to find out.

Kerim's thoughts returned to the girl he had been watching at the bus stop in Kiziltas A crowd was waiting for the bus, and there was a rush of pushing and shoving to get on. A man, perhaps her father, picked up the girl and shouldered into the bus, pushing several others in front of him. The others settled into a seat, with the girl by the window. Shouting and pushing, others tried to force their way onto the bus, and in self defense, the driver pulled away from the station. Those who had been left behind yelled angrily but futilely after him. The girl in the window looked back and saw Kerim still watching her. He waved and smiled at her. She turned her head away, and didn't look back. But he had seen the flare of interest in her eyes, and knew she wouldn't forget. Perhaps he could send her a message somehow. He would ask his married sister to help him find her. She was a rose.

Near the middle of the afternoon, the bus ground and coughed its way into Van. It had been a long, weary journey and sharp pains shot through the dull ache in Alev's back and legs. She had stood the whole way. Some of those who had seats slept, as did the little children on the women's laps, and a few stretched on the floor.

When the bus stopped, the rush of passengers to get off pushed her away from her mother and out onto the pavement. Her father thrust some bundles towards her, and turned back toward the luggage storage to claim their other goods. As her mother and sisters stumbled off the bus, Alev pushed the packages towards them in turn, and went to help her father. There was no sign of her brothers, and she wondered unhappily whether they would ever see them again.

Once their bags and parcels were collected, Burhan went off to buy tickets for the rest of their journey to Cansu. The rest of them huddled nervously over their baggage, fearing it would be stolen away right under their noses. The bus terminal was a bewildering crush of strangers, all seeming to be running around in different directions.

When Burhan returned, it was to relay the bad news that no bus left for Cansu until the next morning. To stay overnight in a strange place was an entirely unprecedented experience for the family. Strange men pressed around them urging them to stay in one hotel or another, but they could not imagine doing such a thing. How could they trust strangers to take them someplace safe? What about their possessions?

They stood dazed and confused, unable to decide what to do. Then, to their joy, Salih and Ridvan appeared. They had caught a ride on a truck that another family was driving to Van, perched precariously on top of stacked furniture as they swayed over the narrow mountain roads. The boys were full of stories about their adventure.

With the boys to stay with their household goods, Burhan could take the rest of the family to a hotel for the night. For the women who had never before been away from their home for even one night, the modest hotel was a strange but not altogether unpleasant experience. The indoor bathroom down the hall, and the shower with hot running water, were entirely new luxuries. The warm room was comfortable, although it felt strange and possibly dangerous to be in a place where so many strangers had touched the furnishings. However, they sat down to eat some of the food they had brought and then spread their bedding. To lie down felt unbelievable wonderful, but the noise from the city streets was frightening, as was the thought of all the strangers under the same roof. In spite of their discomfort, the family fell asleep.

Starting a New Life

Alev and Aliye, curled together under one blanket, were awakened in the early morning hours by their parents, who were moving about preparing to leave. With the bedding once again rolled into portable packs, the family ate the remainder of their food. Before the sun was up they were back at the bus station. Salih and Ridvan had slept beside their possessions after eating some food at the small station buffet. Now they went off to eat again, and a vendor gave the family hot tea.

As light flooded the world, their bus arrived and this time, when the family climbed on, there were places for them all. It was another four hours to Cansu, but having slept well, Aliya enjoyed looking out the windows at the scenery passing by. She saw that although there were high snowy mountains rimming the landscape, this land was very different from the rugged, mountainous region of their home. The most amazing thing was the great expanse of Van Lake, stretching to the horizon.

For more than two hours they drove along the large body of water. It was more water than she had ever imagined could exist in the whole world. It flashed in colors of blue, bright turquoise, and dark aquamarine, shading to dark blue-green in the distance. Little ripples of shining white tipped the waves.

It seemed to have no end, but went as far as she could see to lie against the blue sky, a distinct line of different blues marking the horizon. It was a clear sunny day, and the south edge of the sea as they left it behind them lay against tall white mountains. These faded away in the distance into pale blue shadows merging with the sky. Looking back in the direction they had come from yesterday, she saw a distant wall of saw-toothed peaks she knew were the mountains of her home. Her former home, she corrected herself. There was no home there anymore.

Eventually the road turned north and left the sea behind them. The land was still much less mountainous than what she knew. She loved being able to see so far across gently rolling fields, looking at tiny flocks of sheep and tiny houses. She amused herself by imagining they were the homes of relatives who welcomed them in and fed them, then invited them to stay to work in the wide, open lands around their house. Where there was so much land, there must be plenty for everyone, she reasoned. Scattered among the wheat fields were orchards, patches of plowed, unplanted ground that looked dark and rich, and grassy pastures where flocks of sheep grazed. Each small flock was guarded by one or more shepherds and also by the big powerful sheep dogs known as Kangal.

The bus stopped once for rest and refreshments. Everyone climbed off and went to the toilets, and then ate the simple, familiar food provided by the restaurant. They finished with glasses of tea. It was the first time any of the children had ever eaten food in a public place, prepared by someone other than their mother. Aysel was nervous about it at first, but decided it had been a real treat.

In the early afternoon they arrived at Cansu. Once again the family waited in tense uncertainty beside their piled belongings. This time they had crossed out of the bus station to settle across the street in a little park. They could see they were in the center of the small town. Burhan with Ridvan went off to look for anyone who might remember his grandfather, or know the family, leaving Salih as male overseer of the women. Before very long several men hurried into the town center and wrapped Burhan in their arms, kissing his cheeks and pounding his back. They introduced themselves as Burhan's great-uncle's sons, Yashar and Elbil, with their sons. Their welcome was warm, and soon the family was swept up with all their bags and parcels and hurried to a big two storied house on the edge of the town, where the family patriarch awaited them. He was Burhan's eighty-seven year old Great Uncle Rakim.

Burhan's family was ushered inside and greeted by a large crowd. They paid their respects to Burhan's elderly great uncle, amazed to find him red-cheeked and cheerful, although bound to his chair by arthritis. Then the men were served tea, and later hot food. The women and children went into another large, warm room where they also were offered wet towels for washing, and then refreshments. Old Rakim's daughters-in-law were both kindly, lively women, Shariye fat and Yagmur thin. They bustled around tossing commands at the many daughters and daughters-in-law, at once serving the men and making the new women of their family comfortable.

The kindly women made it clear to the weary refugees that they had found, not only shelter, but a new home. They spent the next hours getting acquainted with these new relatives. The older family members sat together and traced the history of the two branches of the family through its many divisions and alliances. Not even Rakim remembered what trouble had caused Burhan's grandfather to leave, but they all agreed that it was a good thing to have the family back together again. Later the women worked together preparing a meal. The men were served first, and when they were finished the women and children ate. There was plenty for all.

Aliye was aware that after they had eaten, the men went out of the house and were gone for some time. Aysel said the men and boys had gone to the hamam, the public baths. She gathered clean clothes for herself, little Osman, and the girls and told them they would also have baths. At this house, as at their own, there was no running water. Instead a big tank in the downstairs bathroom was kept filled and warmed by a fire under the tank. Bathing was accomplished by dipping the hot water from the tank and pouring it over oneself onto the tiled floor, then soaping and shampooing, and then dipping more water for rinsing. With the men out of the house, all the women and children bathed in turn and put on clean clothing.

After bathing, they went back to the warm women's room and drank tea with cakes. Later Aliye and Alev helped Kader and their mother to lay out their family's bedding in an upstairs room. They were all very tired. The younger children drooped, exhausted, and were put to bed first.

They were all safe in their beds, clean and fed, when Alev and Aliye heard their father and brothers come back. Alev listened as the men talked into the night, and felt reassured by the calm murmur of their voices. It seemed there was going to be a place for them, and family to help them. For the first time since the guerrilla fighters had come to their village, she relaxed. Only now did she realize how anxious and afraid she had been. Sighing heavily, she yawned once and fell into a deep sleep.

It wasn't so easy for Aliye. For a long time she lay awake, trying to lie still and not disturb the others. When she closed her eyes, pictures churned behind her lids of the bombing of the village, the crowds in the bus and the hotel, of the road unfolding in front of the bus from Van. Her skin felt prickly and her limbs wanted to jerk and twitch.

She tried hard to put the bad thoughts out of her mind. Trying to think of good things like the smoke from the houses when they had arrived at Great Uncle Artos' village, she suddenly remembered the boy who had smiled at her while they waited for the bus. He had nice eyes and a funny smile, and he had watched her all the time. She sighed, wishing there could have been more time. She didn't even know his name, and besides, she told herself crossly, they would never see each other again.

Carefully, she turned over again on her mat. They were so crowded that she bumped Alev as she did so, and Alev mumbled and turned over in turn. The varied snores of her parents filled the air, her father's an extended trumpet like their neighbors goose honking, her mothers more like a breathy whistle. Aunt Kader made a small, rattling purr with every breath. She could hear the snores of their uncle's family coming from the other rooms. It was rather like a bog full of frogs, she thought with a stifled giggle.

Surprised, she realized that she was experiencing a sense of relief greater than she had felt for months leading up to the attack on her village. She had been trapped with no escape from the village routine, but now that everything had changed, she might well find an answer to her problems in the new situation of their family. She yawned, and realized that she, too, was ready to sleep.

In the morning everyone was up early. The house teemed with people in every room. Outside the sky was heavy and overcast, and sharp little squalls of sleety rain lashed down from time to time, but inside it was warm. After serving the men, the women ate breakfast together in pleasant fellowship. The children played around them on the floor, and it was as if they had known each other all their lives.

Burhan had learned from his relatives that there was an empty farm outside this village that belonged to their family. An old house was in need of repair, but would be livable. There was no spring for water on the farm, but it was not far to a village standpipe. The women could carry water. There would be hire work for Burhan and the boys when the spring planting began. The women could plant their own fields and vegetable garden.

For three more nights Burhan's family stayed in Rakim's town house with their relatives, while their days were spent cleaning and repairing their new quarters. When the old house was once more clean and tight, they moved their meager possessions and spent their first night there. The kindly family of Rakim gave them enough extra bedding that they could all sleep warmly. They bought some new pots and dishes in the town.

They had come far north from their old village, and the weather was colder than they were used to. Until the ground thawed, there wasn't much they could do about planting a garden, so they lived very carefully, conserving the little money they had. The girls with Kader and Aysel busied themselves knitting and weaving new rag rugs for the floors, the older boys with their father spent their time away from the house in the town.

Hassan and Kadir arrived with half a dozen sheep and a dozen goats, as well as the donkey. The cow with her calf was lost to them, probably to the soldiers, they thought. All their chickens had been taken the night the guerrillas came, but they were able to buy some newly fledged poults from a neighbor. In time, they had eggs again.

When warmer weather came, they were pleased to find several fruit trees coming into bloom around their house. Wild flowers were everywhere, and suddenly the yard around their house was bright with many colors. The fields were large in this open land, and the boys hired on to neighboring farmers for lambing and then planting time, bringing home precious cash for household needs. Behind their house they dug a large vegetable garden and started tomatoes, beans, peppers, and onions. There was no water nearby, however, and the girls trundled back and forth to the neighborhood pump endlessly, carrying the big plastic bottles to fill them with water. A field next to the house turned green with wheat sprung from fallen grains left from former years, and the family planned together to harvest this to supplement the precious grain they had saved, and to bring the field back into production. As the days grew longer and warmer, the family began to gain hope and confidence from the new life springing up around them. The days were long and hard, but it seemed they had survived and would prosper.

Back in the village of Kiziltas where Burhan's family had found their first temporary refuge, the boy Kerim of whom Aliye still dreamed was leaving his home and security to embark on a much riskier adventure. With his brother Mohammet, in the middle of the night he stealthily gathered together some extra clothing. From the kitchen they took some cheese, olives and a few pieces of nan, wrapping them in a twist of cloth which Kerim added to his pack.

He hated leaving his family, but he knew the police were too close. They would be suspicious of his absence and question his family, but if he were picked up and tortured into confessing, the family would also suffer. The men would surely be tortured. Four of his friends had already disappeared, and they might have been forced into incriminating him, although he didn't think anyone but his brothers and father really knew what he had been doing. Mohammet, younger and more optimistic, objected to leaving at all, but Kerim had used his authority as an older brother to make him go. He hoped it was the right thing to do.

Slipping out the door, they moved as quietly as possible through the streets, staying in the shadows, watching for patrols. The bright moon overhead made it more dangerous, but they knew the town like their own house, and also the routine of the patrols. Kerim hated to leave it all, but now he would join the group in the hills for whom they had been spying. The leader, Mahmoud Biter, was famous in their area, and Kerim would gladly die for him. In a way, he thought, it would be a relief to no longer have to lead a double life, to hide and pretend all the time.

In the streets of the town, the snow was gone, but the night air was still chilly. As he neared the forest, it had a clean tangy smell of pine needles that stung his nose. He sniffed appreciatively. Suddenly aware that Mohammet was no longer close behind him, he turned. His brother's figure was a darker shadow hurrying back the opposite direction. Kerim realized that Mohammet was running back home. He was not going to go to the hills with his brother. Checking an urge to run after him, Kerim turned away. He couldn't force Mohammet to leave, and he had already used all the arguments he could think of to persuade him to come.

Checking that the way was still clear, he left the village. Dropping to his hands and knees, he worked his way around the guarded check point at the edge of town, flattening to the earth when a soldier leaned over the guard post's wall to look his way. Apparently satisfied, the guard turned back and Kerim crawled beyond the walled enclosure and the rolls of razor wire until a rocky outcropping hid them from view. Then he started up the mountainside, climbing through the rocks with a hillman's strong legs.

Several hours later, he came out into the open on a mountain meadow. In all directions around him the snow-topped peaks towered, shining and saw –toothed against the sky. A clean, cold wind blew into his face. The moonlight slanted weakly now, casting long shadows as it set in the west behind him. He walked slowly with his open hands before him, waiting to be recognized. A man appeared on an outcrop of rock ahead of him and signaled him, and he turned in that direction. Although there was no longer anyone in sight, he walked into the rocks below the place where the man had stood, and after a few minutes his cousin Anwar joined him.

"What's up?"

"I had to leave. They picked up people who knew me, and it was too risky to stay anymore."

"OK. Come see the chief." Anwar didn't waste time with useless questions. They all knew the costs of the struggle. Their families paid the price of their actions, but a lot of innocent people who had done nothing against the State had been punished just as severely. As the saying had it, a Kurd either died for his nation or his woman, and these young men believed they were fighting for the survival of their nation. Not everyone in their families agreed with armed rebellion, but many were proud of them. Most were willing to support their struggle however they could. The history of the Kurds, their identity, was one of warriors. The police and soldiers made little distinction between those who were rebellious and those who were not.

Anwar led Kerim to a cave mouth, where he spoke with a man guarding the entrance. The grizzled leader of this band, Ensar Biter, appeared in the smoky interior of the cave, rubbing his stubbled cheeks with his knuckles.

"Good morning, Kerim. Have you come to stay? Come have some tea." He led the way to the fire at the back of the cave.

Ensar was a charismatic leader who was famous throughout the region. He had trained at the guerrilla camps in Irak, then returned to his home area. Close to the Iranian border, there was always military action going on. He had gathered a band of resistance fighters around himself, many of them related to one another. Most of the men in the band were local lads who had come to him directly. He sent them to be trained in the south, and they returned to fight with him in the area where they had grown up.

After an hour when Ensar had pried every possible bit of information out of his tired brain, Kerim was allowed to follow Anwar to another cave where he could stretch out and sleep. He had joined the men in the hills, and his life would never be the same again. Everyone knew the men who went to the hills would probably die there. To their families they were already dead. But as he fell asleep, Kerim remembered the flower face of a girl boarding a bus, and his memory became a dream in which they stood together laughing in a sunny meadow, among their sheep.

A l e v ' s
E n g a g e m e n t

In the early months of their first summer in Cansu, Burhan's family was thrown into crisis by a kindly meant offer from a wealthy neighbor to marry Aliye. Just turned 15, Aliye was already beautiful. The neighbor, Mehmet, was a distant relative, an elderly man who had buried two wives and had two still living. He offered the family a very princely sum for Aliye, and assured them he was willing to wait a year until the following summer to hold the wedding ceremonies.

The money would be enough to replace their flock of sheep and assure the family's well-being through the following winter. Burhan and Aysel talked about it for hours, Aysel crying softly from time to time. In the end, Burhan told Mehmet that his honor required that he find a husband for his older girl Alev before he could contract for Aliye. For a lesser sum Alev would make a better, harder working wife than the young Aliye, and Alev was of child-bearing age.

When the agreement had been made informally, Mehmet arrived one day with several respected members of his family to formalize the arrangements. Normally the bridegroom would not have appeared at this meeting, but because he was a man so senior and respected in his family hierarchy, he came to make his own contract. An honorable and wealthy farmer, his terms were generous and Burhan felt no need to bargain. Mehmet would pay 1500 lire and provide festive clothing and shoes for the women of the family including the bridal dress. He would give watches and guns to Burhan and the two older boys, winter school uniforms for the younger boys, and shoes for all the males as well. They agreed that the engagement would take place at the end of July, and the wedding a month later.

A few days before the engagement party, Mehmet again proved his generosity by arriving with two sheep and a dozen chickens as his contribution to the larder. It put the women on their mettle to honor his gift with the best feast they could prepare from it. On the day before the party, the men slaughtered the animals. Then the women washed and seasoned the meat, and also cleaned every inch of the house inside and out.

Early the next morning the first friends and relatives began arriving, only to find the whole family already up and hard at work on preparations. The women guests gladly joined in to help with food preparation, and in the garden the men talked and drank endless cups of tea. Toward late afternoon Alev's brothers and several of the younger boy cousins came to the kitchen and set to work preparing large basins of salad. They chopped and diced small mountains of cucumbers, onions and tomatoes, laughing and joking with one another the whole time, and the women were glad to surrender the field to them.

As the sun sank low in the sky, delicious odors of roasting meat set mouths watering. Soon, large clothes were spread on the floor in every room and even out on both porches. Set with dishes, cutlery and glasses borrowed from several households, the center places were soon filled with large basins of salad, heaped platters of rice, large baskets of bread and trays of roasted lamb and chicken. Small dishes of pickled vegetables and summer greens were scattered to be available to every hand. The men gathered separately from the women, sitting down around the cloths on the porches and in the large front room, while the women and children sat in the back rooms and kitchen.

Boys served the men, running back and forth to replenish the rapidly emptying baskets and trays, while girls kept the women's tables supplied. When all had eaten their fill, the plates and serving dishes were removed, and then the delicious full-bodied tea of the region was served in glasses. Everyone drank it in small sips, daintily sucked through a lump of sugar held in the teeth.

Outside by a level field, a band of musicians began to tune up. They were a group of Mehmet's friends, whom he paid according to custom. To Kadir's delight, these musicians had agreed to let him play with them. He had a musical gift for the saz, the short clarinet-like instrument so essential to their traditional music. Since his arrival in Cansu, Kadir had used every spare moment he could squeeze out of his busy days to hang around the musicians in the town, listening and begging to learn. A kindly farmer had loaned him a saz to practice with and he had become a good player. These men had heard him play before, and knew he would not shame them.

When the band started to play, young men were quick to go out onto the field. Linking little fingers, they formed a line and began to dance. More slowly, giggling nervously, some of the young women went out and formed their own semi-circle. The music, full of emotion and with a strong steady beat, carried them in the familiar steps of their traditional folk dances. As dark fell, two large fires lighted the area and soon a full moon added its ruddy light. More and more of the company joined the dancing circles, stout matrons with sturdy farmers and shepherds of all ages merged into the rings which were no longer separated into one line for men and another for women. Around and around they danced, everyone following the intricate steps easily from long familiarity with the old patterns.

At the front of the line, a leader swung a white scarf. He set the patterns of the dance, with one set of steps or another, but whatever he led, the company joyously followed. It was a matter of pride for the best dancers to take their turn as leader, but also at times an old grandfather would be honored with the place and would delight in showing that he still had the vigor for it.

The circle widened as more and more joined the dance. Sometimes they broke into two lines that circled one behind the other. In their own language, they called this dearly loved activity playing, and there was a spirit of fun in the dancing that grew more hilarious as the evening progressed. Children danced beside parents or uncles, or made their own circles in the center of the larger one. Small contests of vigor and athletic ability would start up, and now and again a group of young men would break from the larger circle and energetically vie with one another with higher jumps and faster steps, the company stepping back to enjoy their performance. Sometimes a group of girls would encourage each other to swing their hips and move their shoulders more provocatively. Broad hipped grandmothers and white-bearded old men pranced and smiled at one another in high spirits, and children fell down in the center of the circle convulsed with giggles over their own silliness.

Sweat shone on the men's faces in the firelight, and as the evening wore on, the parents and grandparents stepped outside the circle to rest on quilts spread on the ground or on chairs provided. Babies slept against older shoulders as their young mothers joined the circles, reliving their courting days. A few of the younger men passed among the crowd with trays of water or tea glasses. Some of the groom's granddaughters passed out small packets of nuts and sweets, tied with pretty colored ribbons.

Twice the band rested and took their tea standing and joking with the guests. Then the men drifted into the shadows where they talked and smoked, and women took the opportunity to settle their younger children indoors on quilts and mattresses.

During the evening two of the most senior and honored members of Mehmet's family, an imam and the local muhktar, went indoors with Burhan, who was attended by old Rakim and his sons. In the sitting room, the money agreed by Mehmet was formally presented to Burhan. In the accustomed manner, Burhan begged them to honor him by taking back a portion, 300 lire. Mehmet's representatives then presented Burhan with the gifts agreed upon, the shoes, clothing, watches and guns that he had promised to the men of the family.

Alev had stayed carefully out of sight throughout the day. In one of the back rooms, she had visited with some of her women relatives, but it was important that she not be seen by the men, especially the prospective bridegroom. In the late afternoon, Mehmet's two wives with their children came with Alev's mother and aunt to the room where Alev was sequestered. The young women with Alev rose and respectfully greeted the newcomers, and then stepped back to allow her to get acquainted with her new family.

The second wife Anise was sharp tongued, thin and dark. She made critical remarks about their poverty, the food their guests were served, and the village they had come from. Alev felt she would not be easy to live with. The older wife, Sumera, was round and jolly. She laughed a lot. She had seven children of her own, the youngest of whom was only two and still nursing. She smiled and spoke kindly to Alev, and this gave Alev some badly needed encouragement.

The visitors wore very nice clothing, with beautiful handwork. Anise did fine embroidery, they said. Alev raised her eyes and faltered, "It is beautiful. Perhaps you could teach me, I would be so glad to learn to do something even half so fine," and was rewarded by a softened look from Anise.

A scream from the baby interrupted them, as he pulled a cup of tea over himself. Everyone reacted, scooping him up and lifting his little shirt away from his body, putting a cool wet cloth on his burned tummy. Sumera gave him her breast, and when things had settled down again, there was a feeling of warmth and harmony among the women.

Later, though, when Alev reached for the tea pot she dropped it, spilling tea all over. Reaching to catch it she scattered a plateful of little cakes across the wet cloth. Horrified, she burst suddenly into tears, and little Sakina promptly began to howl also. Not only her family but the visiting ladies as well gathered around her clucking words of comfort, and helped to quickly clean up the mess. In all, after their guests had gone into another room, the stiffness of strangers had left them.

Alev felt humiliated and furious with herself, but her mother and aunt agreed between themselves that things had gone well. "I think you can be happy in that household," Aysel told her seriously. "Not everything will always go smoothly, but be patient and willing, don't try to push yourself forward, and you should do very well. As a third wife, Mehmet will probably not be too demanding of you. If you are helpful to the other wives and submissive to them, you will get along. When you have your own children, you will come into some authority and honor of your own. Be patient."

Later in the evening, three of Mehmet's female relatives came to her and presented her with a beautiful ring set with a green stone, a gold arm bracelet, and clothing and shoes for the women.

They embraced her and welcomed her into their family. They seemed genuinely friendly and their kindness warmed Alev. Her mother smiled at her as if to say, "See, I told you it would be all right."

Tea was served again and further candy provided, and finally plates of fruit were offered to all the family members in the house. Outside a few people were still dancing. The big moon had turned silver as it rode high across the sky, and now it was well down in the west. Finally the musicians stopped playing, people began saying their farewells, and as the moon set the crowds melted away. Silence settled over the house. The family fell onto their beds in exhaustion, but satisfied that everything had been done properly.

Alev was too tired even to think as she went to bed that night, but in the morning as she lay warm and relaxed in her quilts, she realized that she was feeling a little bit excited about her wedding. A new life was always intimidating, but she could begin to imagine being happy.

THIRTEEN

A l e v ' s   W e d d i n g

The engagement established, the family began to prepare for an August wedding. This entailed a great deal of sewing and weaving for the women. Although a supply of beddings and linens had been being prepared for some years, their hasty move away from their home village had forced them to leave many things behind. Some of the newer, better items had been put into use, so replacements had to be made. Since there was a lot of work to do in the garden, and the boys were away working for others, each day was long and laborious. It was the season of the year when no rain fell, and under the hard blue bowl of the sky the soil baked hard as concrete. They toiled endlessly to bring enough water for the thirsty plants, while the weeds seemed to flourish with much greater vigor than their vegetables. After the late evening meal, they sewed or wove long into the night, falling exhausted into bed to rise early and begin again each new day.

As the day of her wedding drew close, Alev struggled to hide her panic from the family. There were so many things to be thankful for, she told herself. She would go to a settled home where they had accumulated many comforts, unlike her own sparsely furnished one where too many people struggled with too little to survive. The spring had been very hard for them, even with the generous help of the relatives who had taken them in. There had been little food and less fuel for warmth during the cold spring months

Once the spring thaw came, her father and older brothers worked long hours in the fields, hiring out to whatever farmer was rich enough to pay them. She and her sisters worked as hard, hauling water, tending the vegetable garden, repairing walls and animal shelters around the house, and doing the ordinary house work.

Although they had received a generous bride gift from Mehmet, the cost of the wedding celebrations fell heavily on the family. As the date approached, the responsibility of food preparations fell on the women in addition to their other work. The relatives from the town came again to help, but their lives were also filled with summer tasks.

All the family's winter food had to be preserved by bottling or drying, or by burying in the earth. They had already made the white cheese seasoned with garlic that was the specialty of the region, and it was buried in the earth to keep it through the winter. When the fruit trees bore, they preserved or dried the fruit. Some of it they mashed into thin sheets of paste which were sun dried. These were rolled up and stored away for the winter, when they could be softened again with boiling water.

They spent several long days peeling, dicing, and cooking the abundant crop of tomatoes from their garden to make the spicy tomato sauce that was so important in their diet. After it was cooked over fires outdoors in big iron pots, it was poured into jars that had been boiled to sterilize them. Olive oil was poured over the top before the lids were sealed down. Aysel's tomato sauce was famous for the special herbs she used, which were kept secret within the family. It was satisfying work, but sometimes Alev felt dizzy with exhaustion from it all.

The week before the wedding, there was a sudden change in the hot parching weather. By noon one day black clouds had gathered overhead. The air became still and heavy. There was an occasional rumble of thunder. It felt hotter than ever. The girls were working in the garden in mid afternoon when a sudden chilly wind blew across the hillside, carrying a blast of dust and small debris. Straightening her back, for a moment Alev welcomed the coolness on her sweat soaked body. Then she realized with alarm what it meant.

"Aliye, there will be hail. Come inside." She hurried the younger ones to the house, and even as they ran they heard the muted roar, like traffic on a busy highway. The first spurts of rain caught them as they reached the house, striking the dust with small explosions. Inside, catching their breath, they heard the sudden loud rattle of hail on the roof, and saw the grey sheets obscure the trees and garden outside the house. For many minutes the ice thundered around them, so loud they couldn't hear one another shout above it. Then it passed, leaving only the softer rain falling on the ruined garden and tattered trees. White piles of the sharp-edged ice balls covered the ground as far as they could see.

"Come," Aysel said. "Let's have some tea while the rain passes, and then we will go see what can be done." They tried to act normally as they spread the cloth and laid out their tea. Aysel took out a plate of sweet hard bread as a special treat.

The hail was a devastating blow, however. They had worked so hard, and needed the food from the garden to survive. They knew, without going outside, that it had all been destroyed.

When they walked through it later, the air was still chilly and great pools of runoff rain water lay among the melting piles of ice. Their hearts ached for the slushed and tattered plants beaten into the ground. The adjacent field of wheat, close to being ripe for harvest, lay in flattened rifts. Aliye couldn't stop the tears pouring down her face and sniffed into her sleeve, while little Sakina clutched a fold of her long skirt and sobbed in sympathy. Alev put an arm around her sister's shoulders and hugged her close.

"Never mind," she whispered. "There's time to plant some of it again. You won't starve this winter."

"But it was so beautiful," Aliye wailed. "We worked so hard." Every bit of the precious water had been brought laboriously by the women and children from the village standpipe. All day they had trudged back and forth with big plastic containers they carried in a harness, or dragged behind them on a little make-shift wagon.

Slowly, as vegetables ripened, things had gotten a little easier for the family. Now the hail had come and the situation looked bleak again.

They worked the rest of the afternoon carefully salvaging whatever sprouts and roots they thought might grow again. When the men got back from their work, Hassan promised that he and the other boys would dig all the soil again, turning it over to use the battered garden plants for fertilizer. Then they would bring new seeds, bulbs and seedlings and start another garden. "It will all be good as new again, you'll see," he promised. But thinking of the hard, hard work which lay behind them, the girls found his cheerfulness a small comfort.

That night as she lay in her bed, Alev worried about what would happen to her family. It made her fear the separation from them even more. Once she moved to her new home, she knew she would be allowed little freedom to see her own sisters and mother again. New brides were often kept confined in their new houses for long months at a time, even sometimes for years. They were not even allowed to use the telephone. She would be entirely at the mercy of the older wives, and even of their children. The farm to which she was going was on the far side of Cansu from her family's place. There would be no accidental meetings at the water pump or the food shops.

Sometimes a bride's family would be allowed by custom to come for one formal visit to see her in her new home. On the fifteenth day after the wedding, they would arrive laden with offerings of food and gifts for their daughter's new family. Timidly, Alev begged her mother to ask her father for this privilege. Aysel promised to speak with him. It was a frail hope, but it comforted Alev.

As the days sped by, in spite of her best efforts, Alev grew increasingly anxious. Although marriage was inevitable for a Kurdish girl, this leaving home and going to strangers was so painful to think about that she wished she could just go to sleep and never wake up.

Aysel had been working hard on the items for her daughter's dowry. When they could, Aunt Kader and the girls also stitched and wove to build up an acceptable stock of household items.

Such things were badly needed for their own home as they had lost so much when their village was bombed. All agreed without discussion, however, that the best work they could do should go with Alev to her new home, where it would help to give her status. By the time the wedding date arrived, there were quilts and braided rugs, knitted blankets, and embroidered table covers accumulated and stored in a big, carved wooden chest that Burhan had bought in town.

The last days before the wedding they worked almost without rest. Carefully planning for the best use of every penny, they prepared the spicy sauces and pickled vegetables that would accompany the wedding day feast. On the last day they stuffed endless piles of vegetables and vine leaves with the spicy filling of meat and rice to make dolma and stored them in the cool underground root cellar.

Mehmet had sent two of his farm hands with a dozen sheep, some of which would be eaten at the wedding feasts. It was an extremely generous gift. It warmed Alev's heart as she thought that she was marrying a kind and generous man, even if he was older than her father.

On Friday the women of Great Uncle Rakim's town family took the women of Alev's family to the hamam. There they all washed their hair, soaked and steamed, and were scrubbed and massaged by the bath attendants until they were pink and glowing. It felt wonderful to the hard-working farm women whose skins had been burned and dried by the sun and hot wind as they worked in their garden. At the end, fragrant lotion was rubbed into their skin. Then they sat in the adjoining salon and drank tea, relaxed and voluble. Friendly jokes mixed with sage advice helped to calm Alev's fears about what awaited her in her new home.

Alev's family went back to work at their house, but the younger town cousins took Alev to the beauty parlor where her beautiful long dark hair was curled and arranged in an elaborate pile pulled back from her face and up onto her head. Looking into a mirror, Alev saw that long curling locks had been artfully trailed to loosely frame her face, while the remaining wavy mass fell down her back, with ribbons and silk flowers braided into the dark mane.

As everyone cooed and exclaimed over her, she was reminded of the time when she was six and her hair had been cut short for the winter, as was the custom. She had been vain about it then, too, and had fought desperately to keep them from cutting it off. "I'm not a boy, I'm not a boy. I'll kill myself," she had screamed. She remembered still how she had stood with her back to a corner where she had taken refuge, breathless and sobbing with rage, beating the air with her fists and screaming at them all. They had promised her that it would grow back stronger and thicker than ever, they had given her a new scarf to wear for the winter, and the lady who had cut it had coaxed her back into the chair to have beautiful pink lipstick and fingernail polish applied, and in the end they had all laughed about it. It had, indeed, grown back more thick and lustrous than ever, she thought complacently. Things that seem bad don't always turn out to be so.

Her cousins went back with her to the farm house. There was a delicious supper prepared for them and then they worked together preparing the small, decorative packets of candy and nuts that would be handed out to the guests the next day. In a rare time of relaxed fellowship, they laughed and joked together. Alev thought sadly that there had been too little time during their busy lives for this kind of companionship between the two families.

Alev knew that at Mehmet's house his relatives had been gathering, some of them having come from long distances away. Because of his age and the fact that he had already had several weddings, it was not necessary that he celebrate this one with any particular ceremony. However, it pleased him to make it a festive affair to which he could invite all of his large clan. Now on this first day of the three day affair, there was feasting and dancing for them at his house.

The next morning those guests as well as many from Alev's far-branching family came to the bride's farm for the second day of the affair. Alev had been spirited away early to the large house in town, for she was not to be seen at this time. Mehmet too was strictly forbidden to appear until late in the day. He remained at home supervising the wrapping of the gift packages which would be distributed in the evening, as well as the important preparation of the henna for the henna ceremony which would climax that evening's festivities. Only at that event would the bride appear, and then only after she had been ransomed from her protective keepers by members of the groom's family. They would go to where she was hidden, and her relatives would pretend to refuse to release her until some ransom had been paid to them. Then she would return to her home for the beautiful and symbolic ceremony of the henna.

Several of the older women who had come to help sat on the breezy porch preparing the large piles of lamb and chicken parts that would be barbecued on coals back of the house. Pots of rice simmered on braziers in the kitchen. By evening mouthwatering odors drifted on the breeze, and everyone was filled with anticipation. .

Large numbers of people had appeared in their best finery, many of whom Alev's family had not yet met. The ladies' long skirted overdresses were of rich velvets ornamented with gold figures, or embroidered satins in deep, jewel like colors, complemented by white lacey blouses showing at throat and wrists. Some wore their best silk scarves, carefully color coordinated to match their outfits and draped in lovely folds about their necks and shoulders. Others covered their hair with the more traditional filmy white scarves edged in colorful crocheted designs.

Scattering around the farm, the men talked and drank tea. The women joined in food preparations, or sat gossiping in chairs placed beneath shade trees, and the children sat at their feet or clustered in little groups where they shyly got reacquainted with one another.

Out in the large field beside the garden, the younger guests danced most of the afternoon. Kadir had again been helping to provide the music. In a long, single line, men and women circled and circled to the repetitive chants of their traditional songs, following the familiar, intricate steps. Little fingers linked, or hands clasped either high or low as a particular folk dance required, they reaffirmed their identity as a nation. They danced the dances of their ancestors to the melodies that they had learned as small children at similar gatherings. As the long hours passed, each person's nature and identity was revealed, and young men and women came to know one another without ever exchanging a word. The older generations watched and gossiped, or rose to join for a short while in a happy reliving of their own youth and courting. Smaller children danced freely in the center of the circle, or joined the line. Linking hands with a favorite aunt or uncle, they fell naturally into step with the ritual patterns of each dance.

Late in the afternoon, sheets were spread on the ground under some trees, and the gifts brought to the bride's family were delivered and displayed. There were gifts of paper money offered to Burhan, while the gold and household goods became the property of the bride's mother. Aysel was very pleased by their abundance.

As evening approached, the groom arrived. Once again everyone sat down to long cloths spread with food about the house and porches. When the food and dishes had been cleared and tea with sweets served, they rose to dance again. From time to time throughout the evening, water, and small colorful packets of sweets and nuts were distributed among the guests. Dark came and lanterns illuminated the dancing circle, where glances exchanged between couples became bolder. In the flickering light, the traditional costumes became more beautiful and mysterious looking. Because of the government mandates against expressions of their culture, not many of the men wore the traditional Kurdish outfit of tunics worn over bloused pantaloons drawn tight at the ankles. The costume looked trim on fat and thin, young and old alike with its matching woven turban and cummerbund for the waist, but a law forbidding it was among the many laws designed to discourage the expression of ethnic differences.

However, most of the women wore the traditional long gowns open down the front over an underdress of contrasting color, cinched at the waist with elaborate buckles. Their full sleeves ended in long sashes that were loosely knotted low behind their backs. Full bloused white sleeves puffed out from under the dress sleeves, with wide edgings of lace coming down over their wrists to modestly cover their hands. The dances were modest as well, the long lines swaying forward and back in rhythm, although some people from the southern borders near Syria put more swing and sway into their hip and shoulder movement, in the Arabic style.

The moon was again full, although it rose later than the month before. It was still huge and orange above the mountains as the party bringing Alev and the henna arrived. Dressed in a red silk dress, she made her first appearance in public with dignity and modesty. As young girls dressed in their finest danced around her carrying small decorated bowls of the henna in which candles burned, a procession of the groom's family members came after her, bringing a beautifully decorated platter, resplendent with candles, filled with henna for the crowds. Some of it would be placed in the bride's palm, together with a gold coin, and her hand would be wrapped in a red silk scarf. Then the young attendants would pass among the crowd and all who wished could take some henna and put coins into the dishes. These belonged to the children who were serving.

The dancing began again, and went on far into the night as the golden harvest moon sailed across the heavens. Children climbed into grandparents' laps and fell asleep, as did too some of the grandparents, and still the music rose on the night air and the long lines of dancers moved forward and back, around and around.

Finally the musicians put away their instruments, the clarinet-like saz, the wooden flute, tambourines and drums. The last guests made their farewells. Alev with her sisters and mother hurried about settling the guests who were staying with them, so that dawn light was graying the sky when they were able to settle down together in the kitchen where they had set out their own pallets.

On Sunday morning, the third day of the wedding, all the guests of both families came to the bride's home to await the groom. Alev's father gave her the traditional gold coin tucked into a red band, to be tied around her waist, as well as a red scarf for her head. She had dressed herself this day of her wedding in the white wedding dress traditional to brides all over the world. She felt excited, beautiful, and stimulated by the unaccustomed attention she was receiving. A small crowd of little girls swarmed around her, eyes big with awe. When Mehmet arrived with a party of friends in an automobile to drive her away, although she had long dreaded the moment she hardly felt sad at all.

She hugged her mother and sisters, saluted her father with the filial pressing of his hand to her lips and forehead, and went away with her new relatives. Somewhat sadly, her family set their home and yard to rights. Their busy lives would resume as they had been, but Alev's absence would be keenly felt. Her calm, sensible nature had helped to carry them through many crises. Except for the one ritual visit, they might not see her again for a year or more; it was the way of their people. After loosing so much else so recently, it was hard to bear.

Aysel stifled a sob as she thought of her missing children, Aden and Mangat, Ruya and Songul, and now Alev. Kader took her into her arms with a sympathetic hug, and the two women stood in the kitchen listening to the empty silence which had replaced the noisy crowds. For several moments, each thought her own thoughts. Then Burhan called for Aysel, and they moved apart. Aysel hurried away, already distracted by the demands of her remaining family, but Kader stood a moment longer looking out of the doorway. "What is it all for?" she wondered, thinking of her dead husband, son and baby. As God wills, she hastily added piously, and went away to her own room, where her remaining children were fast asleep on their mats. Her mind emptied of thoughts as she too fell asleep.

When the customary time of adjustment had passed, Alev was allowed to entertain her family at her new home. She had not had any contact with them since the wedding, and she was missing her mother badly. Sumera and Anise generously helped prepare the special foods she wanted to serve, and everyone in the household worked with her to air and clean the house on the morning of the anticipated visit.

Aysel and Kader in their turn had prepared baskets of preserved fruits and vegetables, several jars of Aysel's special tomato sauce, and a beautiful crocheted table covering for Alev's new home. They brought colorful silk head scarves for Sumera and

Anise. Burhan came to see his daughter and brought a box of cig-
arettes and a beautifully carved Koran stand to Mehmet. Under
Anise's tutoring, Alev had embroidered a scarf for her mother
which she proudly presented, crediting her teacher's skill and
kindness as she did so.

Mehmet had invited the same female relatives who had
brought his personal gifts to Alev before the wedding, and they
greeted Alev kindly. She felt almost as if they were old friends.
They chatted about the wedding, remembering the good weather and praising the music and refreshments. Alev could even
laugh about her nervousness when she spilled the tea, and they
all remembered the excitement when the baby burned himself,
happily without any lasting harm.

To everyone's relief the visit went smoothly with good feelings
all round. The adults and older children sat in a circle around
the large central guest room, and Alev with Sumera and Anise
served plate after plate of carefully prepared foods, while the
older daughters of the household brought small glass after glass
of tea to the guests. Some of the younger children went outside
to play in the warm weather, and the babies tumbled around on
the floor near their mothers' feet.

When it was time to go, Aysel hugged Alev hard and kissed
her. "I'm so glad to see you can be happy here," she whispered.
"I thought you would be. It is the blessing of Heaven to you."

To Sumera and Anise she said, "You have a lovely home.
Thank you for making my daughter welcome here. You have
been like angels from heaven to her, and I can never thank you
enough, but if I may ever be of any service to you, please ask
me."

It was an unusual thing to say, but Alev could see that Sumera
and Anise were pleased and touched. Good relationships between the families of younger wives and her new married family
were not always the case. A calm, sensible person, Aleve would
have tried to make the best of any situation, but she felt she had
been very lucky in this marriage. The hardships of their move
to a new home, the sorrow of losing so many of her brothers and
sisters to the war, and her fears of a difficult time as a very junior
third wife were all behind her.

Alev said goodbye to her family with a much happier heart than when she had driven away from them to her new home. Then she had been excited, but also filled with apprehension. Now she felt reasonably confidant that she could manage her new role with some success. If she were blessed with a child from Mehmet, then she thought she would have a place to belong for the rest of her life. As she tidied up the room after the guests had all departed, she felt a pleasant sense of ownership in the fine furnishings and attractive ornaments. She hurried to the kitchen to help clean up there, and even Anise seemed satisfied, and spoke pleasantly to her.

The Wages of War

Ruya and Songul lay side by side, wrapped in one blanket. The night wasn't cold, and the rocky wall of the cave at their backs held some warmth from the fire that had burned against it earlier. Physically neither girl was hurt, but Ruya's mind felt bruised from the shocks of the battle they had just fled. Helicopter gunships had found them and poured bullets and rockets down upon them. They had been engaging about a hundred Turkish soldiers in a fire fight, and many had fallen on both sides when the world seemed to blow up around them. Then she saw the helicopters.

By some miracle neither she nor Songul were wounded, but when they made their way back to the sheltered ravine where their camp lay, very few others joined them.

Songul fell asleep as soon as they lay down, but Ruya's head ached violently as it had done in the mind-shattering racket of the battle. When she closed her eyes, scenes of bodies falling, smashed faces, blood spurting, limbs shot away filled her mind and she trembled with horror. It would have given her relief to cry, but all her tears had dried up long ago.

Finally she got up, carefully wrapping the blanket around Songul, and crept out of the cave through the sleeping figures that lay about on the floor. She touched the arm of the guard at the entrance, but didn't speak.

There was a tiny spring nearby and she drank, then washed her face. The night was soft with moonlight. God made the world so beautiful, she thought, but people make it so horrible. In a rush of revulsion she remembered the battle, and suddenly her stomach rebelled and she fell to her knees, retching until there was nothing left to come up. Still she vomited in dry heaves. Finally, in the depths of hopeless misery, she simply fell over on her side and lay there.

Someone was beside her. A man she didn't know lifted her to her feet and supported her with an arm around her waist. She sagged against him, not caring about proprieties. At last she could cry, and while she wept he held her against him.

When her storm of tears had passed, she knelt by the spring and again washed her mouth and face. Then she turned to her companion, seeing a handsome bearded stranger.

Startled, she looked over towards the cave where her comrades were resting. The stranger held out open hands to reassure her.

"I'm a friend. I belong to another group who happened along during your fight and joined in. Those gunships were bad. I'm sorry you lost so many fighters."

Ruya felt drained of emotion. She could think of nothing to say to him, but in a moment she forced out a thank you. Then she thought of how ridiculous this all was, sobbing in the arms of a stranger, and gave a watery smile. I'm sorry," she said. "That wasn't my first battle, but tonight something broke in me. You are very kind."

"It is always bad," he answered. "Sometimes I wish I could cry. My name is Anwar, and I come from the village of Kiziltas."

"Really? We come from Sicaksu, not far from there. My name is Ruya. My sister is with me, sleeping in the cave."

"Our group has only six men left in it. Our leader is Mahmoud Biter. He is a very great leader, " he added earnestly.

"Since both groups have had losses, perhaps they should join together. Do you want to meet our captain?" she asked.

"Let's wait until morning," he replied. "Everybody needs their sleep. Are you all right now?"

Surprised, she realized that she was relaxed and very tired. "Yes, thank you. I will go back now, and you tell your leader to come speak with our captain in the morning."

Suddenly shy, she stood irresolute for a moment, not knowing how to leave. Then she lifted her head and smiled at him, said a firm goodbye, and strode to her cave without looking back.

Anwar watched her, seeing the fall of long black curls down her straight back and her lithe, athletic walk. He remembered her softness against his body. An unfamiliar rush of warmth and longing, both joy and pain, made him feel weak. His throat filled with emotion; he felt both sad and incredibly happy. He seemed to be floating on air, not standing on a mountainside. After a moment during which he couldn't think at all, he decided he must have fallen in love.

In the morning the two groups joined forces, realizing that the soldiers were going to be sweeping the area looking for them. Their plan was to leave that place and work their way back to the original base from which Ruya and Songul's unit had been sent. For a week they moved about mostly at night, avoiding the searches of a large number of soldiers who were deployed in the area by the Turkish Army Once they attacked a small squad of soldiers that had become separated from their larger unit and killed every man. It was just at dusk, so their retreat was covered by darkness. They thought they had escaped cleanly, and then suddenly a bright beam of light swept across their line, and shots rang out. Beside Ruya, Songul gasped and stumbled.

From the guerrillas, answering shots smashed the searchlight, and in the darkness gunfire was random. Ruya reached for Songul and helped her with an arm around her waist. For five minutes they hurried along, then with a moan Songul collapsed to the ground. Someone Ruya didn't recognize stooped and lifted her in his arms, carrying her, so Ruya followed them helplessly.

After another quarter of an hour, they reached an area of broken rocks and caves, and stopped. There was no pursuit. The comrade who had carried Songul laid her down inside a cave, and Ruya dropped to her knees beside her. Blood soaked her vest, but her face was serene and peaceful. It was clear she was dead. For a time it didn't sink in, and Ruya sat there stroking her sister's hand. No tears came, for she was feeling no pain, just an overwhelming tiredness. Others came and sat beside her for a little, touching her hand or arm in sympathy. Someone brought her some tea, which she drank automatically.

Silence fell quickly, for everyone was exhausted, but Ruya didn't sleep. Through the night she sat holding Songul's hand. The dry, bitter smell of the crushed leaves on which her sister lay mixed with the salty smell of her blood. Forever afterwards that autumn smell of leaf mould brought back to her the memory of her sister's death. Now her mind was numb, and gradually a blackness fell across her soul.

They buried Songul and another comrade the next morning near the caves. For days they doubled through the mountains to avoid patrols. Ruya stopped caring where they were going and whether they did or didn't fight. She did whatever she was told, ate and slept when there was opportunity.

One early morning as they marched along, they were surprised by a helicopter that suddenly swept over a ridge and was upon them before they could take cover. It didn't attack them, but veered away back over the ridge, and they knew they were in trouble. It must have just lifted off when it spotted them, and that meant there were soldiers nearby behind that ridge.

Hastily they took cover, some in an area of broken rocks where they had a clear view of all approaches, and others up above on the hillside. Twenty minutes passed, then the helicopter returned. Behind it Ruya could see the blur of movement among the trees that meant camouflaged soldiers were moving in. As she had been trained to do, she waited until the figures of men were clear before opening fire. There were a lot of them, and she shot and shot until her gun was hot. At last she had no more ammunition.

It seemed to her they had been fighting for a long time. On the lower slopes of both sides of the narrow valley, many crumpled bodies lay. Lying nearby, half hidden by a rock, she recognized a special friend, Mehmet. She knew him by his distinctive big mustache and long curly black hair, but saw that his jaw, left arm and shoulder had been shot away and the ground below him was soaked in his blood. Dimly she thought that she should retrieve his gun because it might still have ammunition, but she couldn't move.

Finally she realized the firing had ended, there were no more soldiers on the opposite hillside. The helicopter had crashed and smoke still rose from its blackened ruins. On their side of the valley her comrades were beginning to move from cover. Numb and battered from the din of fighting, she stood up and joined the others. They followed their captain for an hour through the mountains and then took shelter in some caves high up on a rocky wall. Ruya lay down against the wall of a cave and sank into unconsciousness.

When she woke, she was cold, stiff and hungry. Carefully she stretched her muscles, trying not to disturb the others sleeping around her. The cave in which they sheltered was dark, but around the blanket stretched over its mouth she could see small gleams of light. It must be day. Above the snores and heavy breathing from the cave's sleeping occupants, she heard sounds from outside, voices and movement. Quietly she stood up and went out.

A fire was burning in a sheltered niche under the rocky cliff. Beside it she saw Anwar tending it and boiling a pot of tea. She clambered down the rocks toward him, careful not to dislodge any lose stones or make other noise. When she sat down on the ground near him, he offered her a tin cup.

"How is Ensar?" she asked fearfully. She had seen him fall and lie still during the battle.

Anwar moved his head to indicate the nearby cliff, beneath which she saw several bodies piled together on the ground.

"He's dead?" Shocked, she felt breathless. Impossible she thought. Not Ensar. During the time they had traveled together, she had come to admire and trust the rebel leader. Sitting by a fire in the evening, listening to Ensar, she could draw comfort from his wisdom and gentle strength. How could he be dead?

Anwar looked around to see if anyone was close enough to hear them. "Ruya," he said, speaking low. "I think we should leave. Can you go back to your home, do you think?"

Her mind seemed frozen. Songul dead. Ensar dead. Anwar wanting to leave. She remained silent, hunched over her tea.

"Ruya, we have to decide," Anwar insisted. "We have to leave this place and go somewhere, because the army has found us. They will come back soon. We have to leave, and probably our group will split up now without Ensar. I think we should go to your family."

Ruya knew that Anwar could never go back to his own family. His brothers had been taken away for questioning by the feared political police after he had left his village, never to be seen again. They had been tortured, killed and buried in hidden graves, so that the family couldn't even find their bodies. They blamed Anwar. He had received a message saying they had erased his name from their minds. He had told her this once, but they never spoke of it again.

Numbly she tried to consider. How could they leave? They were part of an army. They should find their way back to the training camp, perhaps, and get reassigned. But her heart sank at the thought. She was so tired.

She looked at the friends around her and saw how ragged and weary they looked. Anwar was right, they would probably drift off to their villages. How would her family react if she brought Anwar home to them? What would their village think?

She didn't even know anyone at her family's new village. People came and went between the guerrilla bands and the villages, so that she had heard about the new farm at Cansu, although she wasn't too sure exactly where it was. But there was less support for the rebellion in the north and she wasn't even sure of their welcome from her family.

"Wouldn't it be better if we went to a bigger place, Anwar, maybe to Van? Do you know anyone in Van?"

"I don't think so. Do you?"

She felt warmer now, and able to think. "If we go to my family, we must say we were married at your village. They will know it isn't so, but the villagers won't. They will take us in, and then we can plan what to do next.

"Wait here." Anwar left the fire, and returned in a few minutes with some bread and cheese which he gave to her. She ate hungrily.

"We have to bury the dead," Anwar said. "Afterwards, we will go."

The burial of their dead was done hastily. They feared the return of the soldiers. As Ruya tried to pray for her sister, she was interrupted by Anwar, who came up with his cousin Kerim. "Kerim wants to go with us," he told her. "Is it all right? Three of us will be safer, traveling."

They had to be very careful traveling. From a nearby village they caught a ride hidden under boxes of melons and canvas in the back of a truck. Before reaching the village where the farmer was headed, they climbed out and hid in the rocks until dark.

In careful stages, avoiding check points on the roads and all military bases, they caught rides or walked at night for three days and nights. Friendly villagers gave them food and sometimes hid them in a barn or out building. One man, out of kindness, drove them an extra hundred kilometers along their way.

At last they reached Cansu. Ruya and Anwar hid while Kerim asked the way to Burhan's farm. After dark, they went to the house and were hastily admitted. For any hint of their presence to reach the soldiers or police might be fatal for them all, and even lead to the destruction of their village. Ruya had not realized at first how dangerous it was for her family, and by the time she got to the farm she was wishing they had not come here.

She was not too sure of her welcome and greeted her father hesitantly with a filial salute, kissing his hand as she knelt before him and then lifting it to her forehead. Her mother pressed forward to embrace her, however, and then the others crowded around exclaiming and asking for news. She met Hatice, Hassan's new wife, already heavily pregnant, and learned for the first time of Alev's marriage and that her brother Mangat had also joined the guerrilla fighters. He had died during his first year, not yet seventeen years old.

When the sad news of Songul's death had been delivered, the three tired travelers ate hungrily and were soon put to bed. They slept around the clock. The family had wept to learn of Songul's death, but were overjoyed to have Ruya back unharmed. They all knew she couldn't stay long without being arrested, but they sat with her in the kitchen when she woke, urging more food on her and hanging on her every word. Sakina insisted on sitting on her lap, her soft arms wrapped around Ruya's neck as if she could hold her with them in that way.

Before the children, Anwar and Ruya kept up the pretense of a visit from their home in Anwar's village, but late at night they sat together with the elders and discussed future options.

"I want to go to America," Anwar said firmly. "I know it will take a long time, but we can go down into Irak to apply. I have a sister and an uncle in Texas. They will help us. I want Ruya to go with me as my wife."

"How will you live until you go?" asked Burhan. He knew this was not the usual wedding contract and there would be no money exchanged. But he was glad his daughter was still alive, and wanted her to find safety somewhere.

"I think we must go to Irak, where we can apply for visas to the US. Anywhere in Turkey we will soon be arrested," Anwar answered. "We will try to find work there, and live as a married couple."

Ruya thought about it. Anwar had not discussed this with her. Was it what she wanted? She said nothing, and kept her eyes lowered as the men spoke among themselves about the matter, freely giving opinions and suggestions.

America was so far. She knew no one there, had no family there. She would never see her sisters again. American women were so different, but perhaps Anwar's family were still following Kurdish customs. Could she fit in? Did she want to run away and leave her nation, to leave her comrades to go on fighting for its existence without her helping? Her head ached, and suddenly she felt overwhelmingly sleepy.

Without speaking, Ruya rose and left the room. She went to the women's room where her mat had been placed, and lay down on it. In a moment, without thinking anymore, she was asleep.

In the morning, she ate some bread in the kitchen where several of the women were drinking tea. Her sister Alev had been summoned, and had come along with her companion wives Sumera and Anise. They were full of questions, to which she found she had no answers. They also were free with their advice.

"How can you think of leaving?" sharply querried the second wife named Anise. "I thought you were so much on fire to free our nation?"

"Yes, what was the fighting like? Did you live in caves?" Aliye asked.

Relieved to speak about something she knew, Ruya turned to her. "Yes, we really did sometimes. But the fighting was very hard, and the marching through the mountains was hard, too. You should see how strong I am," she laughed.

But the talk quickly returned to the important decision at hand. "Do you really love him so much?" asked Alev gently. "What do you know about him and his family?"

"Can he take care of you?" asked Aunt Kader. "What can he do in America? Does he have work? Is his family rich?"

Little Sakina leaned against her and shyly reached for her hand. "Don't go away," she murmured.

Ruya felt her headache returning. "I'm going outside," she said. "I need to think about all this."

"I'll come with you," Aliye said. "I'll take you up to see the new calf."

Together the sisters climbed the steep hillside above the house, looking for the hollow where the cow had tried to hide her baby. When they found it, it's little white face peaked out from behind it's mother's bulk so appealingly they lost themselves in trying to pet it. As it ducked back and forth behind the cow, and she tried to keep herself between it and the girls, Ruya forgot her problems.

At last, breathless, she fell down on a patch of flowers and lay back, looking at the cloudless sky overhead. I wish I could just stay here, she thought. Why can't life be simple, like this?

Aliye sat beside her, plaiting a crown of blossoms. Shyly, she asked Ruya how she came to know Kerim. Ruya was surprised. She had never thought very much about Kerim. He was Anwar's cousin, and after their two groups joined she had come to know him as a comrade in arms. Now she understood that Aliye liked him. Aliye explained about the morning when they had left the area of their family village and come north to Cansu.

She had recognized Kerim immediately, as he had recognized her. There had been no chance for them to speak to one another, but she could tell that he had not forgotten her. Now with Ruya she spoke of marriage, wondering if Ruya thought that there was any chance for a guerrilla to come back to a normal life in a village.

Ruya thought about it carefully. She wanted to give Aliye hope and not crush her tender feelings, remembering how painful everything was for young love. But she knew there was really no hope for Kerim to escape the police for very long. Only if he surrendered and went to prison could he ever reenter his village, but the normal prison term was thirty years. He would be an old man when he came back. Not everyone who went to prison in this way came back alive. The war went on inside the prison walls.

Timidly, Aliye asked if she might run away to Irak with them and get married there as Ruya and Anwar planned to do. Aliye was still only fifteen. Ruya flatly rejected that idea. She and the others were trained to hard living. It would be hard and dangerous getting down to Irak, and hard after they were down there as well. The chances of getting to America at all were small, and Irak was a terribly dangerous place for Kurds. The Kurdish villages in the north had been bombed with napalm and poison gas, killing tens of thousands of people. Four thousand members of one important family had all been killed at one time by Sadam Hussein's government.

Aliye cried, saying she wanted to die if she couldn't be with Kerim. Ruya sighed, thinking that the world had come to such a place that there was little happiness for anyone, anymore. Without asking, the girls knew Burhan would never give his approval to such a match. Aliye was his darling, and might have been married off very profitably already if he hadn't wanted to keep her with him.

For a little longer the girls rested together, not speaking. Ruya knew her sister wanted to know more about the life she had led in the mountains. To her romantic soul, it all seemed dramatic and courageous. Ruya thought about how hard it really was, the cold and the hunger, and the fear.

Suddenly she knew she didn't want to go back. She would go to a new life in America. She did like Anwar, and they thought alike. They knew the same things. They were young and strong, they could make a new life. A new life in America.

F I F T E E N

R e f u g e   i n   I r a k

Although Ruya came under the strict rules of family life when she returned to her home, her long absence and unusual experiences gave her certain freedoms a home-bound daughter might not have had. Although she slept among the women at night, she was allowed to sit and talk with Anwar and Kerim. For fear of discovery by the police, they didn't dare go outside, and were prepared at any moment to hide themselves in the back bedrooms if anyone came to the house.

She had been touched when Anwar came to her in the kitchen where she was drinking tea with her mother and sisters. He asked her to come aside and speak with him, and led her into the front room. The younger children were there watching television, but with some authority Anwar walked over, switched off the set, and said firmly, "Please give your big sister and me some time alone in here." His manner was the same that had won her trust the night of the battle with the helicopter gunships, straightforward and direct, wasting no words, yet gentle.

When they were alone, Anwar took her hand and seated her on the bench which ran along the wall. Dropping down beside her, he said, " I'm sorry I spoke of going to Irak and America without talking to you first. I hadn't planned it, but at the moment I felt I needed to answer your father. I have been so busy thinking about what we could do, I forgot to ask you or…" Suddenly shy, he paused. She saw his face and ears were blushing red.

"Ruya, I fell in love with you in the first moments I met you. I want you to be my wife more than anything in the world. I want to take care of you and keep you safe. Please marry me. I know this is very strange, and not the way it should be done, but nothing is the same anymore. How can we, after what we have shared together, follow the old ways?"

To her own surprise, Ruya felt perfectly calm. She looked at his large brown hand enclosing hers, for he had never let it go. She saw perspiration on his forehead and knew this was a very difficult moment for him, and in that moment she knew she loved him too. It was no longer a matter of what she could and couldn't do. Instead she realized that she wanted to spend her life with Anwar, wherever they went and whatever they did.

She smiled, and took his hard brown paw in her other hand as well, leaning over to rub her cheek against his. "Anwar, I love you too. I do want to marry you and go to America with you. I want to be your wife forever."

Anwar held her hands very hard, smiling happily. "I think your father will agree. He didn't object the other night or tell me you couldn't go. I don't suppose he really knows what to do with us, since we have been away fighting together already."

After a moment he added, "I think we should go tonight. We are endangering your family by being here. Anyone might betray us. Are you ready?"

It felt to Ruya like her heart broke in half. The stab of pain made her gasp, and Anwar looked at her anxiously as all the color drained from her face. Ruya felt weak and suddenly cold and the room seemed to go dim. So soon. After being away so long, to leave them all so soon, and forever. She thought she might faint, and apparently Anwar did too, because he took hold of her arms above the elbows to steady her.

When she could breathe again, Ruya drew in several long, deep breaths while she thought. He was right. They had to go as soon as possible. Still held in his strengthening grasp, she stood up facing him.

"You are right, of course. I will go and tell Mother and the others. Will you please find Father, ask for his blessings, explain what we must do?" As an afterthought, she asked, "What about Kerim?"

Anwar looked unhappy, and let go of her. He turned away to the window without answering.

"Anwar, does he love Aliye?"

He nodded without answering, unwilling to give away his friend's secrets.

"Anwar, there isn't any way. Father would never let her marry him. He can't stay here anyhow, he would be arrested and go to prison, maybe even killed. Aliye thinks she loves him but she is young and doesn't know anything. Certainly she can't come with us. There is just no way," she repeated.

"I know," he mumbled.

"Well, tell him so," she said. "Tell him he must come with us so he won't be caught. If he can get to America with us, then perhaps Aliye can come to us when she is older."

Anwar brightened and turned back to her. "All right, I'll tell him that. He has already spoken to Burhan and been sent away with a flea in his ear. He is in the bedroom nursing his pain." It was clear to Ruya that Anwar felt little sympathy for his cousin's infatuation. It was certainly ill-timed.

The day seemed to both drag and fly. It was so strange. Ruya thought about it later when she had time, walking through the fields that night. They were circling the village outside the check points.

Her mother had wailed and clung to her, Alev had frozen in shock. Aliye, whose eyes and face were swollen from weeping, burst into tears again but Ruya knew it was more about Kerim than about losing her sister. The hours of waiting to leave had seemed to pass so slowly, when everything had been said. They moved in slow motion. Then, suddenly, the moment came and they walked out into the night.

Everyone wanted to press gifts on her, but they could only take what they could carry. Burhan had given them a little money, and Aysel had packed all the food they could carry. Now she tried to make herself understand that she was leaving her home and family, probably forever. But it wasn't her home, only a strange farm. And since Songul had died, the love she had felt kindle for Anwar that afternoon was the first happy emotion she had felt. She had already left her family long ago, she realized, and although she loved them all, her life had changed focus. Now, she realized, it had a new focus again, Anwar himself. He was now her life.

It was a warm evening. The air smelled of ripe fruit and late summer foliage, and faintly of smoke from burned off fields and ditches. Dry leaves and grasses rustled softly under their feet as they groped through the shadows. They knew the moon would soon rise and they wanted to be well away from the village before that happened. The area around Cansu was not as rocky and mountainous as the southern borders where they had been fighting. It would not be easy to stay hidden either by day or night. There was not so much sympathy for the war here, and it would be risky to take rides from passing cars.

Burhan had given them the name of a relative in the next village south who might help them. If they could get there before morning, they could hide with him and perhaps he might help them to go farther.

In fact, he did. He was an ardent separatist, but too old to fight. He fed and sheltered them while they slept. Then he hid them inside a cargo truck he rented, put a false load of vegetables in it to hide them, and drove them far south to the Iraki border. That night they went up into the mountains by horseback with a band of smugglers, and were left on the Iraki side well before sun-up.

It had all been easier than they could have hoped. They had sent a message back to Ruya's family that they were well on their way, so their hearts were quite high as they climbed through the jagged rocks of the northern Iraqi mountains, always going east and down toward the cities of the plain.

They were not quite safe from soldiers. The mercenaries and special forces of several nations fought over the ground where they were traveling with no regard for the arbitrary lines called borders by their distant governments. Their small group were well trained in scouting and hiding their tracks, and when daylight came they hid in caves. After several nights they came down out of the mountains to the city they planned to settle in. Suliemani was large enough for them to lose themselves among the large Kurdish population. While damaged, it was still unde-stroyed. Although none of them had any relatives here that they knew about, they found people friendly enough, or at least indif-ferent to them.

One day they met some old comrades who, like them, had left the fighting and were trying to rebuild their lives. Banding together gave all of them courage. Irak was safer than Eastern Turkey had become for them. After all, it had all been Kurdistan for centuries before the border lines had been drawn dividing it into Turkey, Syria, Iran and Irak. The Kurdish people were aware of that, however much their assorted governments forced them to hide the knowledge.

Anwar and Ruya had no trouble finding an imam to marry them in the Muslim manner. Afterwards, Kerim still lived with them. In the way of refugees everywhere, he had become their family. He never spoke of Aliye, and respecting his pain they didn't mention her either. They didn't speak of the past at all, but lived for the moment.

Together the friends worked, in construction when they could find work, or in road building or whatever labor came along. Ruya found a job as a waitress. She made little money but she was allowed to bring home food sometimes. Soon she was pregnant. When her condition began to show, she stopped working and stayed at home.

One day they ran into another old comrade from their guer-rilla days who had opened a fruit and vegetable stand. He took Anwar and Kerim in to work with him, and soon they expanded into other goods, maintaining a small market. Anwar was clever at figures and they were making enough money for all of them to live. One day their benefactor disappeared, no one knew where. Kerim and Anwar gave money to his wife, and then the market became theirs.

Their first days in Irak they had applied to the United Nations Refugee Commission, and after some months of delay a file was opened for Anwar and Ruya, although Kerim was never accepted. When Ruya's baby was born, Kerim moved to another room nearby which he shared with yet another guerrilla who had left off fighting.

The days passed easily enough for them all, although they felt unrooted, as if they were drifting in limbo between a former identity and one they hoped to attain in the future. Months stretched into years.

SIXTEEN

*K a d e r   M a r r i e s
a n d   A y s e l   G e t s
S i c k*

After Kerim left with Ruya and Anwar, Aliye pined through the rest of the fall. She went listlessly through her daily tasks, harvesting the late fruits of garden and orchard, bottling vegetables for the winter, drying apples and herbs, cleaning, cooking and always there was the never-ending job of carrying water. Each day was a repetition of the same numbing chores, and she blindly came and went as she was directed, her mind far away from it all.

Meanwhile, the others of the family were involved in a new excitement and therefore less mindful of Aliye's pain than they might otherwise have been. Ahmet, a brother of Burhan and Kadar's late husband, asked to marry Kader. He had lost his wife in childbirth. With very little debate, his offer was accepted. Although Kader and her children had become an important part of the family, it was better for her to have a husband of her own and she looked forward to mothering his five children. Along with her three it would be a respectable family to care for and she would feel she had regained her place in society.

Ahmet was a policeman in Van, and as such commanded a good income which supported a substantial home. Although his parents lived with him, he assured Kader that it would be her house to manage. It was a good marriage and the family rejoiced for her, even though her leaving would be a real loss to them.

They hurried to complete the celebration of the wedding before snow set in. Ahmet made generous provision for the feasts just as Mehmet had done for Alev. There were fewer people at Kader's wedding than Alev's. Kader's family lived farther away and her clan was neither so large nor so wealthy as Burhan and Mehmet's were.

She had grown somewhat apart from her family over the years, and they lived mostly in the south. She might have gone back to her own village for the wedding, but she felt much more a part of Burhan's family in Cansu now than of that past life. It suited both her and Ahmet to have the wedding in Cansu, which was not too far for his family and friends from Van to come. It was much safer and easier to travel in their area than it was in the south.

On the last day, when he and his friends "stole" his bride away from Burhan's house, they drove straightaway to Van and he took her to his home there. In no time, life resumed a busy pattern for both Kader and Ahmet as if they had been together for years. By great good fortune they liked each other, and Kader found Ahmet a warm father and an easy man to live with. She settled down with great contentment, feeling as if she belonged in a way that had never quite been true under Burhan's roof, even though everyone had made her welcome there.

In Cansu, with Kader gone, Aliye was forced from her dazed heartbreak by the realization that Aysel wasn't well. Sakina confronted her one day by the sheep pen where goats and sheep were milling aimlessly while Aliye ignored them, her mind a thousand miles away.

"Aliye, look what you're doing. The goats are in the garden and your head is in the clouds as usual. You have to help more."

To Aliye's bewilderment, Sakina began to cry. Quickly driving the goats back into the pen and latching it, she turned to her little sister. "What's the matter, Sakina? You aren't crying over a few run-away goats, are you?"

"There's too much to do," Sakina sobbed. "Mother isn't well and Aunt Kader and Alev are gone and you just sit around lost in your own world, and Hatice and I can't do it all." Sakina cried harder than ever, as if she couldn't stop.

Aliye sat down by her and put her arms around her. When Sakina's sobs had finally died down to an occasional hiccup and snuffle, she timidly ventured to ask. "I'm sorry, Sakina. I didn't realize, truly. What do you mean, Mother's not well?"

Sakina rounded on her, blazing. "She's sick. She's sick, sick, sick! How can you not see it. You're the most selfish thing I ever saw." She burst into tears again, and Aliye realized that she had truly been blind to the world around her.

Thinking, she remembered that her mother did spend a lot of time sitting. But she had thought it only proper that everyone spare Aysel, as the matron of the household, and let her sit while they worked. She had noticed that Aysel was pale and much quieter than usual, but had supposed it was the sorrow of losing so many children, and then Kader.

Suddenly panicked, Aliye stammered, "What, what is it, Sakina? What is wrong with Mother?" Fears flooded her mind. Not Mother, they couldn't lose Mother. All the others could go, but her world pivoted around her mother.

"We don't know," Sakina wailed. "She won't talk about it."

"Well, how do you know she's sick?" Aliye demanded.

"Can't you see? She throws up everything she eats, and blood comes out of her stomach. She's getting so thin, and has bad pains. She's weak, she can't work." Sakina buried her face in her hands and wailed louder.

Aliye felt bewildered and shamed, that all this had been going on around her and she hadn't noticed. She felt angry, too, and wondered if Sakina was letting her imagination run away with her, but then she caught herself. Now that her eyes were opened, she realized that her mother was weak, pale, and listless. She put her arm around Sakina's shoulders and waited for her to stop crying.

Trying to think what to do, feeling Sakina's small back shaking with her sobs, she felt deep pain for her little sister. She had been trying to carry the whole burden of the family on her little shoulders and she was still only a child. Aliye's shame burned within her and she resolved to forget about herself and give all her strength to her family.

She began to murmur endearments to Sakina, praising her for all she had done and promising to help her. She stroked the little girl's hair, mopped her wet face and wiped her nose as if she were a small child. When Sakina was quiet, Aliye lifted her to her feet and spoke cheeringly.

"Come up to the house, now. We'll take Mother some tea and talk to her about seeing a doctor. I'm sorry I haven't helped you, but I will from now on. You'll see, the doctor will make Mother well and I will help you and Hatice. I love you. I've been selfish, but I'll forget Kerim and serve our family from now on. I'll make it up to you, Sakina. I promise."

Sakina's downcast eyes told Aliye she wasn't yet quite forgiven, but the little girl went docilely back to the house with her sister. In the warm kitchen Aysel was sitting bolstered by pillows in a chair by the stove, while Hatice sat nearby on a stool preparing tomatoes to cook for the tomato paste they all loved.

Aliye went to her and said, "Hatice, I'm sorry I have been so selfish and blind. I will help you more. Sakina showed me what I've been like, all wrapped up in myself. I really want to do better and be more help."

Hatice looked at her, surprised. Aliye had always seemed distant, lost in dreams and books ever since she had known her. Although she did what she was told to do, she never saw what was going on around her and rarely acted on her own initiative. That she would suddenly change was hard for Hatice to believe. She saw Sakina's swollen, tear-stained face and thought that she had gotten through Aliye's guard, but in her heart she didn't really expect Aliye to change very much. People were what they were, in Hatice's experience.

Aliye went to her mother and knelt down beside her. "Mama, Mama, what is wrong with you? Sakina says you are sick."

Aysel smiled fondly at her pretty child. "Now, I'm not very sick. Don't you worry. It will go away," she said. But Aliye looked at the yellow color of her mother's face, her sunken eyes with heavy brown circles under them, and the thinness of neck and wrists where they peeped out from under the long sleeves and high neck of her dress, and felt a chill strike her blood. Her mother was really sick, she could see it.

"Mama, we are going to see a doctor. You don't have to feel so bad. I'm going to speak to Papa."

Aliye stood up resolutely, pulling away from her mother's restraining hand. She had used a confident tone of voice, not wanting to reveal how badly frightened she really was. She wondered how long her mother had been ill while she was nursing her broken heart over Kerim. Never mind, she told herself. She wouldn't let herself think about anything but what to do now, about how she could persuade her father to take her mother to the doctor, and how they could care for her until she got better.

Burhan was not in the house, nor were the boys. She supposed they had gone to the town, or perhaps were even working somewhere. She went back to the kitchen and began to help Hatice prepare the evening meal. When Hatice asked her to clean the front room before the men returned, Aliye was glad for an assignment. She set to work with energy and dusted, mopped and straightened with a will.

Burhan came in and finding her still working there, asked her to bring him some tea. As she hurried out to obey, he set about starting the fire in the big clay stove in the corner of the room. When Aliye returned with the tea, Burhan was sitting in his comfortable chair reading a newspaper.

She placed a small table beside him and put the tea and sugar on it. Then she drew a long breath for courage and stood before him in an attitude of respectful waiting. He looked up fondly, and seeing she wanted to speak with him, asked, "What is it, child?"

"Papa, don't you think Mama should see a doctor?" she asked. She kept her eyes modestly on the floor, her hands curled by her sides in the manner proper for a daughter in her father's presence.

"Oh, a doctor," he answered doubtfully. "I think she will get better soon, and doctors kill people as often as they cure them."

"Papa, she is very sick. She can't eat, and there is blood from her stomach when she loses her food."

Burhan peered at her doubtfully. No one had told him this. He thought for a few moments, while Aliye waited before him, holding very still.

"Has this been going on very long?" he asked at last.

"She is very thin, and her color is bad," Aliye answered. She was unwilling to admit that she too had failed to notice her mother's illness.

"Well, very well then. This is Thursday. If she isn't better by next Monday, we will go into the health clinic in Cansu," he said gravely.

"Thank you, Papa. We need to know what is wrong with her. Perhaps the doctor can give her some medicine to make her well," Aliye smiled, knowing her father loved to see her smile. He smiled fondly back and turned to his newspaper.

SEVENTEEN

Patterns of Life

The days set by Burhan to wait before going to the doctor convinced them all that Aysel was very ill. She was so weak that Aliye had to help her dress to go to town. The family did not own a car, but Burhan borrowed one from his uncle for the day.

They went first to a people's emergency clinic in Cansu, but the doctor there sent them to the bigger hospital at Van.

It was late when they reached Van and went to the State Hospital, which was busy and crowded. Kader met them there and sat with them while they waited in first one waiting room and then another. Finally they were directed to an area where Aysel could be examined by a doctor.

After a long wait, a nurse came to escort Aysel to the examining room, and Kader rose to go with them. The nurse led them away from the family down a long corridor. As they passed from view, Aliye felt panic rise and fill her throat. She gripped the arms of her chair, barely restraining herself from running after her mother. Burhan gave her a reproving glance.

They waited for another agonizing half hour. Then Aysel returned leaning on the nurse and Kader as if she scarcely had strength to stand. Kader was carrying a handful of papers. The nurse explained that they must go to a different hospital, and that one of the papers Kader held directed them to a specialist they must see. When Burhan asked what kind of a specialist, she didn't answer him directly, but just said reassuringly that Dr. Carikci was the best man in town for his wife's problems.

It was getting dark when they went outside into the chilly winter evening. They decided it was too late to go to the new hospital. Kader urged Burhan to stay the night at her home. They had not planned for it, but she felt Aysel was too tired to stand the long drive to Cansu, only to come back the next day. Reluctantly, he agreed.

Although they were frightened and distressed, the children were also excited by the crowds and by all the colored lights along the streets. There was nothing like that to be seen in Cansu. At Kader's house her family greeted them warmly. While Kader and her mother-in-law prepared the food, Aliye bathed her mother's face, hands and feet with warm water, undressed her, and helped her into a nightdress. Aysel was barely able to lift her arms or sit upright, and her face was almost colorless. She was not able to eat anything, but the rest of them ate and quickly settled down for the night, exhausted from the long day of waiting.

They went to the new hospital as early as possible the next morning, but once again they had to wait. They were very cold after sitting in the drafty hall for such a long time, but finally they were taken up to the third floor to the doctor's offices. There they waited again. It was warmer here, and this time a young man brought them tea. Aysel seemed so exhausted that she could hardly sit upright in a chair. Aliye put her arm around her mother and helped her to move to a divan, where she could sit next to her and support her.

Aysel leaned against her daughter with her head resting on her shoulder, and closed her eyes. After a while she sat up in distress, saying she was sick. Aliye led her to the restroom she had seen in the hall, and held her as she vomited into the toilet. Bright red blood as well as a black stringy material mixed with the stomach acid, but there was no food in her stomach. She dry heaved for a long time after the last material came up, and then sank onto the floor, unable to stand up.

Aliye ran for the nurse to help her lift her mother, and after one look at the girl's white face the kindly woman hurried back with her to the bathroom. She saw in the toilet what Aysel had been vomiting, and told Aliye not to flush it down the drain. Together they lifted Aysel, half fainting, and carried her between them back to the waiting room.

After returning to the bathroom with a container to collect a specimen from the material in the toilet, the nurse, with Kader and Aliye to help her, took Aysel to an examination room and lifted her up to an examining table. She covered her with a warm blanket, and told the women to stay with her. Then she left.

Somewhat later the nurse came back into the room followed by a grey haired man in a suit. He asked a lot of questions of Kader and Aliye, sometimes checking a point with Aysel. She was able to answer coherently if faintly. Then he examined her carefully, and took a blood specimen for laboratory tests. Telling Aliye to wait with her mother, he went out with Kader and the nurse following, and was gone for a long time.

Later Aliye learned that during that long wait while she sat with her mother, the doctor was meeting with Burhan and Kader in his office to explain his diagnosis of the case. Although they would do all the tests to confirm his suspicions, he felt quite sure that Aysel had a large tumor growing in her abdomen. He said they would have to take a specimen from it surgically to determine whether it was malignant, but that he feared it might be. He said in any event they would have to remove the tumor because it was interfering with her digestion and elimination, and was causing her to bleed internally as well. He told Burhan that Aysel must stay in the hospital while they did more tests, and asked him questions about how he would pay for his wife's care.

Burhan was bewildered. A few days ago he hadn't even known his wife was ill. Now the doctor was saying something big was growing inside her and had to be taken out in a hospital. When he thought about it, he realized the doctor was saying it might be cancer. Without being told, Burhan knew that if it was cancer, Aysel would die.

The doctor took Burhan's uncle's telephone number in Cansu. He promised to call as soon as the laboratory tests were finished. Burhan and Kader walked out into the waiting room, where Hassan and Sakina were sitting. He explained to them that their mother was very sick and had to stay at the hospital for a few days. Sakina began to cry, and Kader sat down and pulled her onto her lap, comforting her. She felt glad that the other children had not had to go through all this.

Hatice had been tired and unwell the morning the others left Cansu, so she had stayed at home with Ridvan, the twins and little Osman. Although they hadn't known they would be away so long, they would have left some of the family at home to stay with the animals in any event. The animals couldn't stay alone, and there was always other work to be done.

Burhan left with an attendant to make the official arrangements for Aysel's stay, and the nurse summoned two men with a stretcher to move Aysel to another room. Aliye stayed close beside her, and in the waiting area the family stood up to go with her too, but the nurse told them to wait for Burhan. By the time he came back, Aysel would be all settled in a room and they could visit her there to say goodbye.

Aliye asked if she could go with her mother, but was firmly told she could not. She turned to Kader, who took her hand and sat beside her. They waited for a long time, feeling miserable and confused. Sakina leaned on Aliye and cried again. Hassan got up and went out into the hall where he began to pace up and down. He looked angry.

When at last Burhan returned, he was silent and withdrawn, his face stiff. The nurse gave them a note with the room number on it, and the doctor's signature so they would be allowed into Aysel's room. When they got there, however, Aysel was asleep, looking a strange whitish-yellow against the white pillows. Aliye put her fist against her mouth. She thought her mother looked as if she were dead.

Aysel was in a room with three other women, all of whom stared at the family without saying anything. Burhan put out his hand and touched his wife's hair, then turned away and left the room, saying "Come, children."

Burhan drove to Kader's house, and left Aliye to stay there with her. She could visit her mother whenever she was allowed by the hospital to do so. Kader would also go when she could steal the time from her busy household schedule. The rest of the family returned to Cansu, filled with fear for their wife and mother.

The doctor felt Aysel was not strong enough to undergo surgery, and encouraged her to take a few sips of soup or food as often as possible. Aliye was allowed to stay with her mother most of the time in order to help her. When Aysel slept, Aliye would cheerfully do any tasks the nurses gave her, and soon she was a favorite with them. She began to dream of becoming a nurse when she grew up.

Resting in bed didn't seem to make Aysel feel any better, but at least when she had to throw up she didn't have to get out of bed and go outdoors. With the help of some medicine, she was able to eat the thin broths they gave her and even some bread, without immediately losing them by painful vomiting. Her color became a little better.

Back in Cansu, the family waited anxiously. They had no phone, so knew that even if the doctor called, it might be hours before the message reached them from Burhan's uncle's house. For many days they waited, but the doctor didn't call. Finally they arranged for Aliye to call every other day at a prearranged time so that one of the boys could be waiting for the message. After more than two weeks had passed, the family was awakened by one of the boys from the town house. Aliye had called in a panic in the early morning hours. Aysel had begun bleeding very badly internally during the night and they had taken her for emergency surgery.

The family hurriedly made arrangements to go to Van. The snowy roads made driving slow and difficult, but Aysel was still in surgery when they arrived. The doctor came out with blood on his surgical scrubs to tell them she was very weak. He feared she might not last through the surgery. They sat in stunned misery, unable to believe what was happening.

The minutes dragged. No one spoke. Hassan got up and began to pace up and down the room. Everyone else in the waiting room stayed well away from them. Finally Dr. Carikci came toward them again. His face looked grey and deeply lined and his manner was so full of pain that they knew without a word what he would tell them.

He had seemed extremely kind and sympathetic to them all from their first meeting, and instinctively they trusted him. Now they could see that he felt their loss very deeply as he told them how sorry he was that she had passed so quickly. He said he was sure the tumor was malignant, and that even if Aysel had survived the surgery, she could not have lived very much longer. In this way she had been spared much suffering, he said, and he hoped that in time they would be able to see it in that light.

The arrangements to claim Aysel's body were quickly made. In shock, the family drove back to Cansu. Kader went with them, taking her youngest children. The funeral would be in two days. Aysel's own home village had been bombed and her family scattered, so there was no thought of going there. They sent messages to those of her family they could find. The many military check-points made traveling difficult at best, and now the snow-covered roads and closed mountain passes prevented many from coming. In Cansu Kader took charge of the arrangements.

They went through the motions of the funeral like sleepwalkers. Burhan seemed to be in a shocked daze, speaking only in monosyllables, and his sons stood mutely around him. Aliye and Sakina cried intermittently. They would subside for a little while and then, when one began to sob, the eyes of the other would well over and they would again dissolve in tears together.

Friends and relatives sat with them during the day and some stayed the night. Shariye and Yagmur from the town family helped to care for them and feed all the guests. Alev, expecting her first baby, spent the day but then returned to her home for the night. Many guests stayed through the next day, but then everyone left. The family began to confront the task of living without Aysel at the center of their household.

It had not been possible to notify Ruya in time, although in the following week they reached her to break the news. They had not even told her Aysel was sick, it had all happened so fast. She began to cry hysterically, and Anwar had to take the phone away from her, learn the cause of her distress, and then hang up to tend to her.

Although she had not told them yet, Kader was newly pregnant. Because of that and because she presided over a large, busy household in Van, she could not stay long with them in Cansu. Although she hated to leave them while they were still so lost in grief, she returned to her own family in Van.

Birth and death are the pulse of Kurdish life. Kader thought about it as she rode the bus back to Van. It seemed they were always in the midst of both loss and new life. Aysel had been a dearly beloved friend, like a sister. Now she was gone, but Alev was pregnant, and within herself Kader already felt the stirring of the new little person who was coming. She and Ahmet were delighted about the baby, and the children of their two separate broods, having gotten through the initial bumps and rubs of settling in together, were also excited and happy to have a new little one on the way. More children were always welcome in a Kurdish home,

As their grief began to be less overwhelming, Alev's pregnancy and Kader's news when it came helped Burhan's family to feel a little better. They stayed busy and maintained the farm and household in good order. Alev's baby came in the late spring, and they were both glad and sad again as they thought of Aysel never seeing her first grandchild. Mehmet, however, was delighted with this fruit of his old age. Kader's baby was born in midsummer, and both babies and mothers stayed well, a cause for general rejoicing.

The medical expenses from Aysel's illness had placed the family under a crippling debt. Life had begun to be a little easier for them as the farm met most of their needs for living, and as the younger boys came to an age where they could occasionally earn a little extra money working for other farmers. Salih was mechanically inclined, and sometimes helped at the garage in town, working partly as an apprentice but partly for small wages.

Now, however, they were forced to sell everything from the house and farm they could spare, trying to sustain the schedule of payments that the hospital had requested. Burhan's shoulders became bent and he looked much older as he worried about what to do. It seemed impossible that they would ever have enough money to pay it off.

In mid-summer the solution to their problem came as if by magic. Burhan was approached by a relative, who asked for Aliye as a wife for his third son. This man was a powerful figure in Burhan's clan, and the richest man in the area. He was thought to be a drug smuggler, but his uncles and brothers were important leaders in their part of Turkey. He drove big cars and kept an expensive apartment in Van, but also maintained an elaborate country house in his family's home village not far from Cansu.

Burhan had been told about this family, who were known for their lavish homes and expensive cars, but he had never met any of them. He felt poor, unimportant, and tremendously flattered that such a man would want his son to marry Burhan's daughter.

He told Aliye as one sharing a wonderful surprise, certain she too would be proud and happy. Moreover, he told her gratefully, he was sure there would be a generous amount of money offered which would save the family from the hospital debt.

While she wasn't happy about marrying someone she had never seen, Aliye tried to be glad that she would be able to help her family in this way. She was seventeen now, high time to be marrying. It was only because she had always been her father's favorite that she had been allowed to stay at home this long. Aliye did not want to disappoint her father. She supposed it would be nice to be rich.

In a few days the important man, Mahmoud, came to their house with the Sherif of Cansu and another relative, who was a judge, to make the formal arrangements. While the money he offered wasn't as much as Burhan had hoped, it would clear their medical debts with something left over to restock the farm. He found himself so overwhelmed by the status of his guests that he couldn't bring himself to bargain at all, but kept bowing and saying, "Yes, Sir, thank you, Sir," until they got in their glittering automobile and drove away again.

Once Burhan agreed to Aliye's marriage, his powerful relative insisted on speeding the matter along with no delay. Mahmoud wanted the marriage completed by the end of the summer. The date of the engagement party was set for late July, just as Alev's had been, and the wedding was to follow in a month, just as before. Mahmoud had let it be known that Aliye would be coming to a home that had far more of everything than she would ever need, so that there was no reason for her to bring linens or furnishings of any kind. Instead she and Hatice set to work making some special fancy lingerie, and some pretty gifts for the women of her new family.

Alev had learned needlework from Anise, who really was very gifted with fine embroidery. Now she brought Anise to teach Aliye and Hatice, and sometimes Sakina would sit with them to learn, too. The women had a good time putting tiny flowers made of silken ribbon, colored chrystal beads, and gold thread embroidery on silk shifts and fine cotton nightgowns. It gave them a chance to play with Alev's baby as well, and during these weeks the two families grew quite close to one another.

Alev was happy in her new home. She especially liked the oldest wife, Sumera, who treated her as a daughter. Sumera delighting in buying Alev pretty clothes and brushing her long hair into fanciful styles. With Sumera's comfortable presence and advice, her pregnancy had gone easily and the new baby became everyone's toy. He was healthy and cheerful and gave his father great pride, and this in turn increased Alev's status in the family. Anise was sometimes sharp and temperamental, but she was not especially jealous of Alev. She had her own place in the family spectrum and three children of her own.

Alev had expected to assume the place of servant to the two senior wives and she set herself to please them, treating them with equal respect. Because she quickly became pregnant, and because Sumera liked her and showed her special favor, her life wasn't difficult. It was, in fact, much easier than when she had been helping her struggling family to establish their new home in Cansu.

Her elderly husband Mehmet owned a great deal of land to the west and north of Van, as well as around Cansu. Those fields were farmed by members of his extended family who paid him a percentage of their harvests, so that he was wealthier than anyone really knew. A canny man, he was careful about his income and invested it in more land and some businesses in both Cansu and Van. He was not ostentatious about his life style, but during Alev's pregnancy he began building a new large house beside the older traditional mud brick one they presently occupied. It had three stories, and when it was finished, each wife was to have one of the floors for her own home, as an apartment separate from the others. This made Alev very happy.

The night of Aliye's engagement party was fine and dry, and everything went very well. Her future father-in-law, Mahmoud, had delivered a quantity of food to Burhan's home the day before the party, saying that a large group of his relatives would be coming and he knew that Burhan had been hard pressed because of his wife's illness and death. It seemed a very generous thing to do.

Aliye had still not seen Omer, her prospective husband, and she was careful to remain hidden in a back room of her home during the engagement party. Several relatives of Mahmoud had delivered to Burhan the money agreed upon and some gift items of clothing, with a beautiful new rifle with silver chasing on the walnut stock. Mahmoud's sister and her daughter visited Aliye and gave her an elaborate red satin dress for the henna party, a wedding dress they had ordered made to her measurements, a gold necklace with matching earrings, and a sparkling diamond ring of impressive size and worth.

It was a really breathtaking array of gifts, and Aliye felt intimidated before their quality and the sophistication of her beautifully dressed future relatives. She tried to talk to them about the tastes and preferences of her bridegroom, so that she could please him, but they laughed and changed the subject, saying she was so beautiful that he was certain to be very pleased with her.

As the dancing progressed outdoors, the visiting guests became very loud and boisterous. There was damage to several of the fences and outbuildings of the farm and the sheep and goats ran away to wander about the neighboring fields. It became obvious to Burhan that someone had brought alcohol, and he called his oldest son Hassan over to talk about what they could do. They couldn't find out exactly who had brought it, or even who had drunk it. They were ashamed, and Burhan resolved to ask Mahmoud to please guard against it happening again at the wedding.

However, with Mahmoud's contribution to the food, they had nothing to be ashamed of in the hospitality they offered their guests. When it was all over, Burhan felt philosophical about the damage to his property. A few days would set things straight.

There was no question but that his Aliye was marrying into some pretty high society, where she would have nicer things than he had ever been able to give her. He felt he had done well for her. Nothing warned him of the grief he was bringing upon his family.

EIGHTEEN

A l i y e ' s
W e d d i n g

For Aliye, the time between her engagement and the days of her wedding flew all too quickly. She missed Aysel every hour of every day, and she had not really stopped grieving for Kerim, although she tried to keep from thinking about him. Her more practical sisters might have successfully put his memory aside as something that could never be, and therefore was a waste of time. She could not.

Aliye had always lived in a world of dreams and imagination; in a sense it was her reality more than the humdrum details of daily life. Now she went through the motions of performing the daily chores, but her mind rested in a kind of vacuum. It was as if all feeling had been suspended. The other women tried to rouse her excitement about her wedding, but she responded dully, dutifully smiling and repeating what they said, but without heart.

Alev tried to remonstrate with her. She had been afraid, she said, but it had all turned out better than she could ever have hoped. Aliye must try to be happy and please her husband. She made the mistake of pointing out that Aliye was very, very lucky to have been chosen by such a rich family, but this drew a flash of anger. It was the first real emotion Aliye had allowed, and broke the dam of her reserve. She screamed that she was not a sheep or a donkey to be sold for family income, that she had dreams and hopes of her own that were now ruined. She broke into violent weeping, and rushed to her bed where she turned her back and refused to respond to Alev's apologies and entreaties.

She couldn't stay turned to the wall forever, though. Eventually she came back into the kitchen with swollen eyes and a sullen mouth. By then Alev with her companion wives had returned to their home, and only Sakina with Hatice were there to bear the brunt of her silent anger. They were abashed by it, but didn't understand what was wrong with her. They took the course of resolutely ignoring her mood and went about the business of preparing the evening meal, talking around her as if she weren't there.

Aliye's anger lasted for many days, but the men didn't notice and the women chose to ignore it. She felt so helpless that she stopped eating, but as her eyes grew bigger and her cheekbones more pronounced, it only made her beauty more appealing.

One day when she was at the standpipe drawing water for the house, an expensive car drove slowly by. Four young men in it all stared at her. Startled at first by the unusual attention, she straightened her back and stared back. Then she suddenly realized that this might be her prospective husband, and hot color flooded her face as she turned away and ran home.

She had left her water containers on their trolley at the standpipe, but she refused to go back to get them. Sakina snapped at her and told her not to be so lazy when it was her turn. She, for one, was worn out with all her airs and graces. Aliye burst into tears and ran to her bed to bury her face in her pillow in another fit of wild weeping. She felt utterly alone in the world and misunderstood. She missed her mother with an aching pain that made her ill. She thought of killing herself, but she was too afraid.

In spite of her fears and prayers, the first day of her wedding celebration arrived. Kader, heavily pregnant, came to help with the preparations. The town women also came and the kitchen was crowded with women chattering and working together in happy companionship. Not so many of Burhan's relatives came as in the past, but many of Aysel's came. Those who had not been able to come for the funeral were now taking the occasion to visit the family and express their sorrow at her death, as well as to celebrate Aliye's wedding. Ruya sent a gift and a loving message expressing her sorrow that she couldn't be there. She would still be subject to arrest if she crossed the border back into Turkey, but her forced separation from her family caused her great pain.

Because of their grieving, the family was not expected to entertain as fully as they might otherwise have done, but nevertheless there were crowds of people to feed and in some cases to house that night. At Omer's home, they knew, the large powerful clan would also be gathering in strength and celebrating in a much more elaborate style than they could match. As a sign of sorrow for Aysel's death, her relatives brought generous gifts to the family, meant to show support for Burhan during this difficult time.

Aliye rallied and did her best to be gracious and appear normal for the sake of her mother's memory. She sat in a back room and talked with the women who came, while the ladies of the family served endless rounds of tea. She made a public appearance outside when the gifts were presented, exclaiming and praising them. When the cloths were spread for the evening meal, she returned to her seclusion indoors, but continued to entertain all who joined her. Sakina with Osman, together with the younger children of her great uncle's family ran to and fro, serving the guests. Late into the evening Aliye maintained a smiling face and did all that was expected from her, but all the time she felt that inside, invisibly, her heart was being torn apart.

The next day she went very early in the morning into Cansu to stay hidden at the home of relatives. Soon many of her out of town relatives arrived and some went with her to the hamam for the ritual bathing and massage. Then they went to the hair dresser, where for hours her hair was carefully curled and coifed into an elaborate style that would enhance her beauty and honor her groom. She was made up with eye and lip colors that dramatized her dark beauty, and because she was naturally so beautiful the beautician outdid herself with extra effort.

As the sunset flared in the western sky Aliye was brought to the wedding park, a large public area which the groom had rented to accommodate all the guests. She looked stunning in her red satin dress and elaborate gold jewelry. Her arrival caused a stir of admiration as many people saw her for the first time. She saw that the crowd of guests was so big that indeed, there would not have been room at her family's farm for them all. She wanted desperately to run away, but of course she was the center of attraction. She knew she needed to be present for the all important henna presentation. The groom had not yet arrived, but his family had crowded the area to overflowing, and they were being very wild and noisy. She wondered if again they had brought alcohol, or if rich people always acted that way.

There had been no dancing on the previous day in respect to Aysel's death, but this night a large and famous band was playing and two large rings of dancers were enthusiastically circling the open central field. Aliye was led to a podium beside the dancing ground and installed there. Her father, Omer's mother, and her Aunt Kader were there beside her. An empty chair waited for Omer. To Aliye, it seemed to sit there ominously. The thought of Aysel not being there brought tears welling into her eyes, but she resolutely held them back. Nothing should be allowed to spoil her makeup.

She felt exposed and naked. She was accustomed to wearing a modest scarf and concealing clothing, but tonight her head was bare. The red dress was low cut and tailored to make the best of her slim figure, but she felt almost naked. Her neck was stiff from the elaborate hair style full of ribbons and flowers that had been arranged on her head. The sun had set and darkness had fallen, and she knew her heavy gold necklace and earrings were gleaming in the bright lights which shown down on the field from tall light poles. People kept staring at her.

She should have felt beautiful and honored and happy. She should be happy. Tears burned behind her eyes again. She felt ashamed to be on display before so many strangers. The dancing was wild, the crowds noisy and excited. She saw that instead of family members, hired waiters were serving drinks to the crowd that filled the park. They worked out of a kiosk that was set up near the gate, and she saw that they were openly serving alcoholic drinks as well as mineral water and juice. Her family would be upset. Turning to look at him, she saw that her father didn't look upset. He was beaming with pride. He was honored by this grand affair. Bitterness flooded through her.

Omer was suddenly there, appearing from behind their podium to slip into the empty chair beside her. He didn't look at her, he was watching the progress of the group bringing the traditional lucky henna through the crowd. Six beautifully dressed girls carried the henna forward in a white satin basket trimmed with gold ribbons, placed on a silver tray. The basket was surrounded by brightly shining candles. This group was followed by half a dozen younger girls carrying white candles trimmed with red and gold ribbons and smaller dishes of the henna to distribute among the guests. Aliye stood to receive the henna in her palms as was the custom, and Omer stood beside her. He still didn't speak, or look at her. She felt more of an object than ever, a dummy playing a role for the crowds.

The henna was distributed through the crowds, and she saw that refreshments were being served by the waiters. The dancing had stopped, and the musicians were taking a break, standing around the drinks kiosk. Omer left the podium, and in a moment she saw him laughing with the musicians and drinking a bottle of beer.

The large grey-haired man she recognized as Mahmoud stepped up on the podium to speak to her. He called a waiter to bring her something to drink and asked what she would like. She faintly requested fruit juice, feeling too overcome to lift her eyes to his. He exuded satisfaction and made a joke to her father, holding his hand and shoulder in a hearty embrace. She noticed that he did not speak with his wife or even acknowledge her. However, when he had left, the woman leaned over and asked her how she was.

She seemed kind, and Aliye was glad to talk with someone. She replied that she felt quite overwhelmed because there were so many strangers. The woman smiled and agreed that it was a large crowd. "My husband has many friends as well as family," she said. "You will become accustomed to meeting many strangers who come and go. It is our duty to welcome and serve them when we are called to."

She seemed to want to soften her remark, recognizing that she had not comforted Aliye's fears. "We have a pleasant life," she added. "We are many women in the house and you will find us friendly and helpful to you while you get used to us."

Aliye was grateful, and smiled her first real smile of the evening. "I don't even know your name," she murmured. "Shahrazade," the woman rejoined, smiling. "I am Shahrazade, and my son's wives are Nur, Esra, and Elif. They carried in the henna, together with my daughters Gomer, Rojgul, and Talia. You will get to know us all."

"Thank you, Shahrazade Hanim," Aliye whispered. She took her new mother-in-law's hand and humbly kissed it, pressing it to her forehead in a gesture of homage. Without looking into her face, she knew the lady was pleased.

Omer returned to his seat after a while, and this time turned to her to compliment her on how well she looked. He asked if she wanted anything to eat or drink, but his manner was impersonal and perfunctory. He did not act as if he wanted to know her as a person at all. Aliye wondered if he had wanted to marry her, or if it was all his father's idea. What did he think about her? His eyes strayed over her body as if he were undressing her in his mind. Was that all that marriage meant to him? She felt nauseous, and cold with apprehension.

Aliye, lost in her own emotions, didn't realize that her body language was full of rejection and hostility. Omer, meeting this wife for the first time, felt her dislike and didn't know how to overcome it. He was used to girls smiling and modestly flirting with him. What was he to do with a wife who didn't smile or meet his eyes, who looked as if she had eaten something unpleasant. No matter how pretty she was, who wanted a girl who acted like she couldn't stand him? But what could he do? His father had chosen her. It wasn't like he had anything to say about it. Well, he would teach her to behave better. A wife had to like her husband and be good to him. It was a stupid girl who acted like this. She would be shown her place.

The emotions of the bride and groom were clear to everyone watching. The parents reacted anxiously. Mahmoud came up to speak to the young couple, making a hearty joke he hoped would melt their coldness, but it frightened Aliye and angered Omer. Burhan leaned over to Aliye and spoke anxiously to her, admonishing her to remember who she was and try to behave better. She kept her eyes in her lap and twisted her hands, but this didn't hide the stubborn set to her lips or the stiffness of her shoulders.

Omer stood up abruptly and went over to a group of his friends. Aliye saw he look back at her as he made some comment that made his friends laugh uproariously as they also looked at her. Color bloomed in her face and tears rose to her eyes, but they were tears of anger.

After a time Omer joined the dancing and his exaggerated and rather unsteady movements showed that he had been drinking heavily. Later he disappeared altogether and didn't return to sit beside his bride until much later in the evening. The strong odor of alcohol accompanied him and his speech was slurred. It was agony for Aliye to sit there, feeling alone and frightened, for the hours of the dancing. The rigid smile she froze onto her face deceived no one, her misery was on display for all to see but there was no escape until the early hours of the morning, when her town relatives took her to their home to "hide" her until the groom came for her in the morning.

The First Night

Aliye lay awake most of the night. She had been taken to the house of her relatives in Cansu after the wedding party had at last ended. She had thought it would never end, that lifetime she had sat on that platform, smiling, being stared at. It had seemed like forever. When at last her cousins had come for her and she could go to their house, she had gone straight to the toilet and vomited.

They were all concerned, giving her a cool cloth for her face and water to drink, and then putting her to bed in a room by herself. She was thankful to be by herself, but in the corner hung the long white wedding dress, and that was enough to make her think she might throw up again.

Instead she lay tossing and turning through the night until the sheets were in a knot and her head was aching. Only after the sun had risen did she finally sleep.

She had only two hours of sleep before her cousins came for her and made a great thing of doing her hair again, of dressing her in the white wedding dress, of making up her face. They had asked the beautician from the day before to come to the house to do that for her. By ten thirty in the morning, she sat drinking tea in one of their back rooms where they had "hidden" her as was the custom. When the bridegroom arrived with his friends, there would be a pretense that she was not there and then in the end, after bargaining over the price, the bridegroom would pay a ransom for her and carry her off to his home for the third day of the festivities.

She wondered if an imam would even come to this wedding to bless it. She knew her father would want that, but the way Mahmoud and his family had acted, drinking alcohol and even dancing in the western fashion two by two, man and woman together, she didn't know if they would want a religious ceremony. She wondered, if the imam didn't come, would she really be married? A foolish flame of hope flared in her heart. If they weren't really married, ….. but what? What could happen? She was trapped in this marriage and it would be for life. Inside her something died, as if that instant of hope had been the last spark of her soul.

They waited and waited. It was the custom for the groom to come in the morning, but the hours passed, and Omer didn't appear. Although she dreaded his coming, she was ashamed that he was so late. The Cansu family tried to keep up a cheerful conversation, but eventually one or two at a time stayed to sit with her while the rest of them left to deal with their own affairs. Sakina had come over to keep her company, and she sat with her the whole time, but her frequent comments about how late Omer was didn't help Aliye's nerves.

It was the middle of the afternoon when at last the doorbell rang and a large group of men came into the house. It was clear at once they had been drinking again. They were loud and not very polite; joking, but with a jeering tone to it.

There was no fun in the bargaining. In an arrogant voice, Omer threw down some bills and commanded, "Bring me my wife." Seeing that he had no intention of making the traditional game of it, Aliye's great aunt came to the room where she was waiting and said, "I think you'd better come now, Aliye."

When he saw her, Omer looked a little shocked and seemed to soften. Aliye did look white and strained, her eyes deepened by dark circles underneath. He took her hand and led her to the car with ceremony, helping her to arrange her skirts inside be-

142

fore closing the door. The other boys jumped in the back and in another car they had brought, and they drove away. Aliye knew it was the last she might see of her family for some time, but she was so tired that she felt numb. She focused her thoughts on keeping very still, her hands folded in her lap, her eyes resting on them. She was terrified that she might throw up again. The thought of it almost made her faint.

She continued to be very careful throughout the rest of the day and evening, while a notary came for them to sign their formal license, and the imam came to read the Koran over them. They remained at the home of the groom, a beautiful large country house with smooth lawns and flower beds lining the driveway. There were people everywhere, everyone laughing, drinking, and dancing on the large smooth field behind the house. She knew none of them. There was a lavish formal meal on cloths laid on the porches and lawn, and then more dancing that went on far into the night. When darkness had truly come, there was an elaborate and lengthy fireworks display that delighted all the guests. After the fireworks, the dancing resumed. Aliye loved to dance, but she felt so tired and ill that she was grateful Omer didn't ask her to dance this evening. She sat and smiled and tried not to look sleepy, or bored, or sad, but she knew she wasn't achieving that smiling radiance that a bride should show.

At last she saw that the guests were making their farewells and leaving. When most had gone, Omer's family, parents, sisters and brothers all came in a group to where she was waiting. She saw that they were going to escort her and Omer indoors. They were making a lot of noise, with a forced gaiety, but she was so frightened that she could only continue to show a wooden control, her eyes on the floor. When they reached a closed door in the back of the house, they stood aside smiling, and Omer opened the door and led her in. He closed the door behind himself and stood against it.

The room was large and very clean. The big bed was freshly made with the covers folded back. Vases of fresh flowers stood on the dresser by the window and on the table by the bed. She was touched by how pretty it was, and turned shyly to Omer, almost smiling.

He was staring at her belligerently, however. Scowling, he asked accusingly, "What's the matter with you? You shamed me in front of all my friends, acting like you were going to a funeral instead of a wedding. Do you think you're too good for me? You, a stupid village girl?"

She was so shocked she couldn't speak.

He approached her menacingly. "Don't look like you don't know what I'm talking about. You're damned lucky to get me. Do you know how rich my father is? You'd better start acting like a wife should. Get me some wine."

She looked around to see what he was talking about. On a table set against the wall was a bottle in an ice bucket on a tray with some glasses. She went to it, saw that the cork had been opened, and poured a glass, which she brought to him. He took it from her without thanks, drained it and handed it back.

As she started to turn away to place the glass back on the table, Omer took her arm and pulled her to him, pressing a kiss on her. He held her roughly against him and kissed her hard, forcing his tongue into her mouth. She was bent back over his arm with no escape, but she felt choked and smothered. Dropping the glass, she arched back and pushed against him, trying to shove him away.

With one arm he held her, with the other he hooked two fingers in the neck of her dress and ripped it open down the front. Again pressing his mouth against hers, his free hand tore away her slip and bra. He squeezed her breast, hurting her, and then dropped his mouth to the nipple, sucking on it. Held less tightly, Aliye got her hands up to his shoulders and gave a hard push. She broke loose and backed away, looking at him in horror. She gathered up the torn pieces of her dress and pulled them together over her breasts, standing at bay against the table.

When he moved as if to seize her again, she reached behind herself and grabbed the flower vase by the neck. She had panicked beyond thinking, reacting wildly to save herself. Omer was infuriated. Too fast for her to react, he caught the wrist of the hand holding the vase, and slapped her hard with his other hand. Then he twisted her wrist, and the vase smashed on the floor. Twisting her arm behind her, he tore off her dress and undergarments. He shoved her at the bed and as she fell backwards across it, he fell on her and raped her, only tearing open his fly without taking off any of his clothing. In his rage, he pounded relentlessly at her virginity, tearing the tender flesh. He reached his climax, excited by her struggling beneath him and her cries of pain.

Aliye was sobbing hysterically, gasping and choking in fear. Lifting himself above her, Omer slapped her again and then punched her face. "I'll show you, I'll teach you," he snarled. "Be quiet! Act like a wife, damn you." Silenced, Aliye lay barely conscious, blood running out of one corner of her mouth. Her skin was mottled red and white from the blows.

Omer stood up and took off his clothes, leaving them where they fell. He got into bed beside Aliye and reached for her, running his hands over her body, exploring all her most private areas, arousing himself again. After a little, he pushed her over and climbed on her again, entering her and pumping with no regard for her groans. In truth, he liked it when each thrust brought a moaning grunt, it made him feel powerful. When he had climaxed again, he rolled off and fell asleep.

Aliye lay still until his snores told her he was asleep, then she curled her body away from his on the very edge of the bed. She hurt all over in a way she had never hurt before, her face sore, her head aching, and her body burning and aching inside and out. All day she had been longing for sleep, but now she lay tense and strained, starting each time Omer moved. She trembled when she thought of his coming on her again. How many times did they do it in a night, she wondered. Would he sleep a little and then come back again? What could she do? Nothing, she realized. This is what it meant to be married, they could come into you as many times as they wanted and you had to let them.

Hot tears ran steadily down her cheeks and soon her nose was running too. She sniffed and wiped her face and nose with the sheet she had pulled up over herself. Eventually exhaustion won over her fear, and she fell asleep. When during the night Omer pulled her to him and once again rubbed his hands on her body and then mounted her, she only half knew it and didn't react at all.

She woke in the morning to find him moving around the room, dressing When he turned and saw her eyes open, he pointed a finger at her. "You stay there," he said. "You don't have to come out today. I'll have some food brought to you."

"I need to go to the toilet," she said.

"There's a jar here in the room," he said. And I'll have the maid bring you some water. Don't go out," he repeated. He left the room, closing the door behind him.

True to his promise, a woman brought a towel with a pitcher of water, and a tray with breakfast on it. Aliye lay in bed trying to hide her face until the maid left. Then she got up, found the jar, washed using the towel dipped in the pitcher, and ate the breakfast. To her surprise she was very hungry and ate a lot. She was also very thirsty, and drank the whole pot of tea that had been provided.

The maid had picked up her torn clothing and carried it away without comment, and Aliye wondered if she was going to be confined by nakedness. When she looked in the wardrobe, however, she found a number of outfits that looked like they would fit her, with several pairs of shoes lined up on the floor. In the drawers underwear was folded, and in one of them were the pretty night dresses that she had made with her sisters. The sight of them caused a wave of misery to rise into her throat. She put one of them on, and then went back to the bed and lay down. She must have slept, because the maid came in again with more food and a glass of cola.

This time Aliye rose from the bed and sat at a little table by the window while eating. The maid changed the stained and tangled sheets for new ones and left the bed fresh and folded back as it had been last night. After she ate, Aliye dressed and sat down in a chair by the window. She was waiting there when Omer came into the room. He began to take off his clothes without saying anything in the way of greeting, but then when he stood there naked, said peremptorily, "Come to bed."

Aliye was afraid to defy him. She took off her clothes, folding them neatly and laying them on the chair, and then went over to the bed. He signed for her to lie down with a motion of his hand, and then climbed on top of her again. He took his pleasure from her without saying anything, then rolled over and went to sleep.

She didn't sleep again, but lay there afraid to disturb him while he slept. When he woke up, he washed and dressed, then said, "Mother wants you to come to dinner with the family. Get dressed and come out to the sitting room." He left the room, and Aliye rose, washed and dressed again. There was a little dressing table with a mirror, stocked with the basic cosmetics. As best she could, she tried to cover the marks on her face. The bruises had turned dark red and purple, however, so she had to join the family with the signs of her shame clear for all to see. It made her silent and closed, and the family misinterpreted that as pride and anger. They left her alone and talked around her. She did feel pride enough that she didn't let her hurt show.

At the end of the meal, the family fell silent, looking at her. She didn't know what to do. Then Shahrazade rose and spoke to her. "Aliye, let's go out onto the balcony."

Aliye rose and followed her mother-in-law through the house to a large balcony overlooking the garden. Lamps stood about in the flower beds, making circles of colored light in the midst of the green darkness. The house rose above them as a lighted ship might ride on a dark sea.

She had no idea what to expect. Was there help to be found here? Surely the marks on her face were a clear sign that Omer had abused her. Surely Shahrazade, who had seemed kind at the Henna Ceremony, would know that was wrong and would stop Omer from doing it again.

There were candles in frosted glass globes on the balcony, treated with chemicals to keep away the night-flying insects. Jasmine bushes twined their vines around the railings, and the heady fragrance of the flowers drifted to them on the slight evening breeze. Large cushioned chairs were placed around a white wrought-iron table, and when her mother-in-law sat in one of them, Aliye sank into another. She was prepared for comforting words, and eager to tell how awful it had been, how much she had been hurt. But her mother-in-law's face was stern, and her first words warned Aliye that there was to be no sympathy or comfort for her.

"We are beginning to think we made a very big mistake in choosing you, Aliye." Shahrazade's voice was cold. "We have welcomed you into our family with all attention and honor, and you have insulted us both personally and before our friends."

She paused, but Aliye didn't know how to respond. How had she insulted them? She had done nothing but try to do what she was supposed to do. As Shahrazade waited for a reply, she managed a feeble excuse.

"I didn't mean to. I didn't feel well." It was almost inaudible, her chin pressed down as she hung her head, her hands clenched tightly in her lap. Shahrazade looked at her sharply. The mention of not feeling well made her suspicious. Surely the girl couldn't be pregnant? No, the maid had said there had been plenty of blood on the sheets when she changed the bed.

"My son said that when he kissed you, you tried to hit him with a vase."

Aliye gasped. What a lie! But not exactly a lie, that was what had happened.

"Surely you understand that a man has certain rights with the woman he marries," the cool voice went on. "Has no one told you about the ways of a man with a woman?"

Yes, of course she knew. It was how babies were made. Married women laughed about it sometimes when they didn't know the girls were listening. How could they laugh about such horror? It couldn't always be like that. "He hurt me," she said miserably.

"Yes, of course the first time for a virgin there is some pain. It is her gift to her husband, her proof that there has been no man with her before him. That goes away."

"He hit me," she said desperately. Angered, she had lifted her head at last and was looking defiantly into the other woman's face.

"Omer is a sweet boy. He loves his sisters and is always kind with them. If you had not made him angry, he would never have hit you. You have shamed us all, but especially him whom you have treated as if marrying him were some terrible punishment. We are all angry with you for his sake. We are very disappointed in you."

Aliye was horrified. "It was all so strange. I was....." She couldn't express what she had felt, but she had never thought of shaming or angering her new family. Did they think she was in-

148

sane? She knew her whole life from now on depended on them. How did this all go so wrong?

"I never meant to shame you," she pleaded, desperate to set things right. "I want to please you and Omer, of course."

"Well, you have chosen a very strange way to do that," Shahrazade said drily. "I think I should have had a talk with you before the wedding, but I thought your family ..." She paused, remembering. "Your mother died recently, didn't she?"

A bolt of pain stifled Aliye. She remained silent, choked with remembering, but tears began to spill down her face.

Shahrazade was silent, her face softening.

"Well, perhaps this has all been a misunderstanding. I must instruct you. A man has physical appetites that women do not share, but it can be pleasant for us, too. More important, this is the means by which we conceive children, and that is our real pleasure in life. If you please Omer, so that he likes to come to you and doesn't go elsewhere for his satisfaction, then you will soon have a baby on the way. When you have born him a son, he will value you as a person and take pride in you as his wife. You will have standing in the family and in the community. You must take pains to please him in every way so that he gives you many children. Do you understand?"

Aliye nodded, but she was filled with misgiving. Could it all be set right?

Her uncertainty must have showed, for Shahrazade went on, trying to encourage her. She reached out for Aliye's hand, disengaging it from the other where they were still tightly gripped in her lap.

"We women in this family have a very pleasant life. We don't have to work hard in house or field as most women do. Our tasks are to please our husbands, and raise our children. My husband has many visitors with whom he does business, and he often likes us to entertain their wives. Occasionally if they are western visitors, we sit or dine with the men as well. He often travels, and he likes one or more of his sons to go with him. He likes the wives to go along when he does this. He chose you because you are so beautiful and he thought well mannered. As a village girl, we thought you trainable. We thought you would fit into our family well. Do you think you can do so?"

Aliye felt a terrible fear. What if she couldn't do this, what would happen to her?

Suddenly desperate to grasp what security she could, she looked up pleadingly. "Oh, yes, I want to," she gasped. "Please, I want to. Tell me what to do."

Shahrazade felt exasperated with the child, but tried to give a comforting laugh. "You silly little chicken, you have only to be sweet and pretty and obedient. It won't be hard." She rose, the interview over. "Now go back to your room, make yourself beautiful for the night." She looked critically at her daughter-in-law. "You are very thin, and quite pale right now. Perhaps it has been a hard time for you," she conceded.

"I will have some wine and refreshments sent up to your room, and hot water. Wash yourself carefully, put on one of those pretty night dresses, brush out your hair and wait for Omer. When he comes, serve him and be sweet to him. It will go better tonight." Nature will take its course, she thought, observing Aliye's frail beauty.

Icy fear clenched inside Aliye's stomach, as she thought of another night with Omer. But there was nothing she could say, or do.

TWENTY

The First Year

After their talk Shahrazade escorted Aliye by back hallways to her room, so that she didn't see any of the rest of the family again that night. She did as her mother-in-law said, washing her whole body, applying some of the perfume furnished on the dressing table, and putting on the nicest of her night dresses. She was brushing her long hair when the door opened and Omer came in.

"Well, that's better," he said, looking at her. But his eyes were hard and greedy, she saw no softness or affection on his face. She blushed to the roots of her hair and her eyes fell, but she stiffened her courage and looked up again, trying to smile.

"Hello, Omer," she said softly. "Would you like some wine?"

"Yes, bring me some wine," he agreed. "You should drink some, too."

He had little experience with women outside his family. His father kept his boys under strict control, and while he was not a religious man, he had strong village principles about what was correct. A few times with his friends, Omer had been with country girls who were free in their ways and allowed the boys to hold their hands, fondle them and even kiss them. In Istanbul his older brothers had taken him to a brothel where he had learned how a man was to act, but the woman was friendly and skillful and kind, and his fumbling efforts had met with extravagant praise, although he knew it was feigned.

Nothing had prepared him for the overwhelming rush of ecstasy he had experienced last night as he mastered his struggling, sobbing bride and poured his manhood into her. He had felt like the master of the world, the strongest man in creation, like he could command the sun, moon and stars. It had surged up in even greater power the second time as she lay trembling and moaning as he thrust into her, the heat in him almost destroying him with pleasure.

During the night when she had scarcely seemed to rouse from sleep, and in the afternoon when she had lain passive and dominated beneath him, he had felt the tensions of unfulfilled need building to their release, but it had been nothing like the first times. More than anything he had ever wanted before, he wanted to experience again that explosion of power and delight that had given him the most wonderful feelings he had ever experienced.

When he had joined his father and brothers after his bridal night, they had accosted him with friendly, ribald jokes. He was sure they could see that he had been successful, although he had learned in painful ways not to boast in front of them. He was not completely aware of how much they could see, of the new confidence with which he carried his head and the bold way in which he walked. His oldest brother Rajiv had laughed and said, "Well, I think our Omer has become a real man," and the others had laughed, too. He felt quietly proud, and remembered how good he had felt the night before.

A small twinge of uncomfortable feeling made him remember Aliye's white face bent sideways on the pillow, the marks of his blows on her white skin, a red thread of blood coming from the corner of her mouth. Her shadowed eyes had closed as if something in her had died. Well, he reassured himself, if they saw the marks on her face where he had disciplined Aliye, they would just think he was setting things straight for their marriage. They could tell that everything had worked out all right by how happy he was.

Now he reached out to take the wine from his bride's hand, noticing that it trembled as she held the glass towards him. A spirit of devilment made him drop it as he touched it, so that it lay shattered on the floor, the red wine spreading in a dark stain around it. He reached out and slapped her hard, saying "You clumsy cow." Aliye dropped to her knees beside the broken glass, then cowered back from him as he stepped forward, standing menacingly over her. He grabbed her arm, pulling her up and throwing her toward the bed so that she was sent sprawling across it as she had been last night. He felt the surge of energy within him, the sudden stiffening heat in his organ.

Again he fell on her in his clothes, opening his fly and kicking his pants off as he covered her. He put his mouth down and thrust his tongue into her mouth, and felt her start to struggle under him. The excitement of her movements was a white-hot heat in him. He reached for her breast and dug his fingers into it and she tried to scream, although the sound was blocked by his mouth on hers. He was in her now, and the ecstacy was the greatest yet, like flying among the stars, until it burst in an explosion of mind-numbing power that paralyzed him. He collapsed on her, unable to move, gasping for breath.

After moments, Omer gathered his strength and slid sideways off Aliye's body, still holding her motionless with his arm and shoulder across her. He felt the sobs that silently shook her body, but was too exhausted still to do anything. Aliye lay stiff, too terrified to move, trying to stifle the sobs that convulsed her. What had she done? What could she do? Was this to be her life? She understood all the women who had killed themselves. Uncontrollable, her sobs burst forth and she rolled away from under his arm and clutched the sheet to her mouth, but could not silence them.

Omer sat up and leaned over her, puzzled and alarmed. What was the matter with the silly girl? It was over. He wasn't touching her now. "Shhh, be still. I'm not hurting you. Aliye, be quiet." He slid his arm under her head and pulled her against him, anxiously patting her.

"Aliye, I'm sorry I hurt you. I'm sorry. Be still. It's over now. It will get better, Mother says so. Be quiet."

Gradually her sobbing stopped. She rested in his arms, which were holding her now without hurting her. She was too confused to think. When she was quiet, they slipped down into the bed and lay together, his arms around her. They fell asleep, and when they woke they lay quietly in the early morning light. They had moved apart, but now he reached for her and held her in the crook of his arm again, her head against his shoulder. He stroked her and thought about how beautiful she was, and presently was aroused enough to enter her again, but this time slowly and quietly.

He felt her stiffen in fear at first, but then her body began to move in a different kind of way. As he continued to move within her for his own pleasure, she pushed against him and he saw that her face had flushed with color and heard her begin to breathe roughly and then, as she arched upwards under him she gasped and he was suddenly bathed within her in hot burning liquid that drove him suddenly to his own climax.

This time when they rolled apart, Aliye felt relaxed and peaceful. She didn't understand what had driven her to reach for Omer's body to pull him close to herself, to press herself hard and harder onto him, or what had exploded like the most intense feeling of both pain and pleasure, but now she was happy. Perhaps that was what he had felt as well, and it had driven him so hard that he had hurt her without even knowing it. He had been so rough because he was being driven to find that release that she had just felt. It made her want to be close to him, to stroke his body, and timidly she did so. She realized he was asleep again. She continued to lie quietly beside him so that he wouldn't be disturbed.

TWENTY-ONE

Aliye Decides to Escape

When Omer and Aliye joined the family late in the morning, their parents were relieved to see the young couple looking relaxed and in harmony with one another. Somehow they had come to an understanding, it appeared.

Mahmoud left the house almost immediately, taking Omer with him, and Shahrazade invited the women to an afternoon at the hamam. Soaking in the steamy hot water, being gently soaped and pummeled by the masseuse, then oiled and depilated, was wonderful. Aliye relaxed and let her mind drift away from her problems. The dark bruises left by Omer's rough treatment were plain on her face and body, but no one commented and she felt unembarrassed by them, since the other women seemed to make no judgement one way or the other.

As they were served tea and little savory snacks in the comfortable sitting room beside the baths, the young women were merry and friendly to her, and Shahrazade benign. Aliye became more open and ventured a few remarks of her own, even laughing about some of the guests at the wedding.

Afterwards they went to the family hair dresser, who with several adept assistants set and combed each woman's hair in attractive styles. Outside the family home they wore scarves and modest coats, but inside the house among family and servants, their heads were uncovered. Their clothes, although traditional, were beautifully tailored of fine materials. After their hair was done, they were expertly made up to enhance their natural good looks, and the other women were generous in their compliments to Aliye. It had taken the whole day, and was early evening when they returned home, driven in a big car by one of the several young men who seemed to be on hand for all services required by the family.

Mahmoud and his sons were not at home, so the women ate alone and separated to their various bedrooms immediately afterwards. A maid arrived with wine and a plate of sandwiches and cakes, so Aliye assumed that Omer would come soon afterwards. She changed to a night dress and settled to wait for him as she had done the night before, but the hours passed. At last she went to bed and fell asleep.

She woke up with Omer on top of her, only partly undressed. He had been drinking, she could smell the alcohol. In a few moments she realized that he was very drunk. He was clumsy and unsure in his movements, mumbling incoherently. He was trying to push himself into her but didn't seem able to do it. Becoming angry, he cuffed her, muttering, "Help me, bitch."

She tried, not really knowing what to do but moving her body to accommodate his, spreading her legs and finally putting her hand over his on his organ. It wasn't big and hard as it had been before. Knowing nothing about male anatomy, she was puzzled. She had assumed that men must carry an erection all the time.

Omer was making a strange, snorting, snuffling noise as he frantically rubbed himself against her. When his wet face fell against hers, she realized that he was crying. "Omer, Omer, what is it? What's wrong?" she asked, distressed. It was the wrong thing to ask. He pulled back, lifting himself on one arm braced painfully across her chest, and began to pummel her with the other, slapping and punching her.

"Nothin' shwrong wi' me," he slurred. "You, whash swrong wi' you, you ugly bish?" He swung his fist against her several more times, and then suddenly collapsed across her. When she realized that he was unconscious, she pushed him off her and scrambled out of bed.

156

He lay across the bed, sprawled on his stomach. At last, when she had collected her wits, she undressed him and pulled his heavy body into place on one side of the bed.

She washed his face, streaked with tears and saliva. She folded his clothes neatly and placed them on a chair. There was vomit on the floor where he had thrown up, and she used towels to clean it up. Then she washed her own hands and face, put on a clean night dress, and climbed back into bed. Eventually, she fell asleep.

She woke before he did, and was sitting dressed and groomed at the bedside table when he opened his eyes. He groaned, and pulled the covers over his eyes. "Close the curtains," he ordered. His words were muffled, and she didn't understand.

"What did you say, Omer?"

He emerged from the covers to growl, "Close the fucking curtains. The light hurts my eyes." She hastened to do so.

He collapsed on the pillows, and after a few minutes added, "Send for some coffee." Before it arrived he rose to use the chamber pot, then seized her wrist and pulled her back to the bed, where he fell across it and gestured blearily at her clothing. "Take it off," he ordered brusquely. She hesitated, stepping back. Anger flashed across his face, and he half rose threateningly. Hastily she unbuttoned her blouse and pulled it off, then stepped out of her skirt. He didn't wait for her to remove her underclothes, but reached out for her and pulled her down onto the bed.

She saw that unlike last night, he now had an erection. As before, he was rough with her, rolling onto her and pushing into her without waiting for her to become wet. She was still sore, and she shrank away and whimpered. Involuntarily she cried out, "Wait, wait."

She could see that her pain pleased him. He raised himself above her, smiling. "Wait, wait?" he mocked. "Wait for what, bitch?" He thrust himself into her, pounding cruelly. She could feel his excitement mounting to a frenzy. His hand groped for her breast, and he twisted her nipple hard. The pain arched her body against his, and he groaned, "Yes, yes!" He came explosively, grunting and shuddering before he fell down across her. She lay motionless beneath him, too filled with despair to move.

The maid knocked and then entered with a tray of coffee and rolls. Although he didn't open his eyes, Omer growled "Get out!" at her. She scurried out again, and he rolled over off Aliye. He pulled the sheet over himself, and after a few minutes he said, "Get me some coffee."

Aliye rose, quickly slipped on a night dress, and brought him a plate of rolls and a cup of coffee. He had pulled himself up against the pillows and took it from her without looking at her. After a sip of coffee, he pushed it back to her and said, "I like it sweeter, with more milk." She took it and returned with it after adding more milk and sugar.

"That's better," he remarked ungraciously, drinking it. "What a night," he added after a few moments. "My head feels like wedding drums in it."

"Perhaps I could rub it for you," Aliye offered. He looked surprised. After a moment, he said, "That might feel good." She leaned over and rubbed his temples as gently and soothingly as she could, letting her fingers slip into his hair and then down to rub the back of his neck. He sighed with pleasure and slipped down on the pillows. She took the cup from him and set it aside, also removing the plate of rolls from the bed. He hadn't touched them. His eyes closed as she continued to stroke his forehead and gently massage his temples. After a time she could tell from his breathing that he had fallen asleep.

Through the winter Aliye's marriage continued in the same patterns. The women of the family performed light tasks around the house, but there were servants for the heavy work. There were pleasant excursions for shopping, or to the cinema, or to the hamam, always escorted by one of the young men who worked for Mahmoud.

Once they all went to Ankara, the capital, and stayed at a relative's home. Twice she and Omer went with his father and another of his brothers to Istanbul and stayed in a hotel there. She maintained a calm and pleasant manner, visiting with all the people she met. She understood that Omer was proud of her good looks and wanted her to please the people they met. He bought her expensive clothes and shoes and sometimes a piece of jewelry. He liked to have her with him when he went to restaurants and the homes of friends, and visibly preened himself when people turned to look at her striking beauty. In public he treated her with courtesy, and spoke about her to others with pride and affection.

At night it was different. There were times when he was good natured in bed, even teasing or laughing with her. More often, he bullied her, enjoying her fear. It stimulated him sexually, and she learned to cry out and writhe with pain even before he hurt her very much, but sometimes that too backfired. If he thought she was acting, he abused her more to "teach her what really hurt." It was those times when he enjoyed the most intense sexual pleasure.

When she realized that she was pregnant, she hoped he would be more gentle, and told him in a way to flatter his pride. He looked hard at her swollen breasts and gently mounding stomach, and smiled cruelly. Her heart sank as she realized he saw only that she was more vulnerable, more easily hurt.

That night when he had rolled off her and fallen asleep, she thought hard. I cannot live like this, and he may hurt me so much I lose the baby. She very much wanted this baby to live, and not just for the status it might bring her in the family. She knew she had to find a way to escape but as she thought about it, she realized desperately that it was impossible. She had no where to go. If she ran away back home, her father might kill her.

She had tried again to talk to her mother-in-law about the problem. Whenever they went to the baths, the marks and bruises on her body were clear for all to see. She had begged, protesting that she did everything she could to please Omer and never refused him anything. Shahrazade had looked sad, to give her credit.

"I know, my dear, and I have asked my husband to speak to Omer. He says Omer protests that he loves you dearly and that you make too much of the normal enthusiasm of lusty love making. You have a very white skin that shows every small contact too clearly." Although Shahrazade spoke firmly, she didn't meet Aliye's eyes. There was something in her manner that told Aliye she knew very well what was happening, but was not prepared to do anything to stop it. There would be no help there.

If she ran away, she knew there was really no place she could go. Mahmoud was a rich and powerful man, honored and court-ed by other important people. He commanded a large number of young relatives whom he kept about him to do whatever er-rands and tasks he set them. They would hunt her down. Even if she did somehow manage to escape to some place where no one could find her, how would she live? She couldn't work, had no experience getting around in the world. She knew no one outside her family.

In the East, in their world, there was no place where any wife could escape her husband for long, no matter what he did. Her male relatives would feel their family was shamed and would in all likelihood kill her. If she were brought back to her husband, he would keep her a dishonored prisoner if he didn't kill her. She thought again of killing herself, but found she couldn't do it. Hope had died, but the will to live had not.

When the family learned that she was pregnant, they were very pleased for her. They had a special celebration, but a quiet one among themselves. First pregnancies were chancy and it was bad luck to make too much of it. When the baby arrived safely it would be a different matter. Omer appeared proud and happy enough about the baby before his family, but that night cruelly teased her by pushing and punching at her stomach, frighten-ing her. "Do you want to grow fat and ugly so soon?" he asked. "I am proud of your good looks and enjoy your body. I'm not ready to give you up to some small, naked scrap of flesh who will make you gross, your breasts sagging, your beauty gone. Time enough for that when I'm tired of you." She thought she would faint from fear. He exploited her fear for his own satisfaction, and for a time replaced some of the physical torture with that emotional one.

Before that had palled for him, she received a respite. Omer with the other young men of the family had gotten into some kind of fight with another clan from a nearby province. Two of their men had been killed when guns were fired off. Aliye was shocked and sorry, for one of the young men who died had been a favorite of the women. Only seventeen, he was often the one assigned to drive them about or stay with them when Mahmoud and his sons were gone. His name was Baran, and it seemed impossible to her that he would never again be with them, or enjoy the normal pleasures of life like marriage and a family.

She knew when their family organized a night raid and killed six of the other family, because Omer had been very excited about it. He had come home wild and somewhat drunken, boasting of his own exploits. Although she was horrified, she pretended to praise him and it was one of the rare nights when he made love to her without hurting her.

Mahmoud with senior family members met with the other family and arranged a financial settlement of $120,000 paid in gold to compensate the families of the men who had been killed. A truce was established, but even so it seemed wisest for Omer and Rajiv, the other son most involved in the raid, to go to Iran for a period of time while things cooled down. Aliye was left alone to spend the last months of her pregnancy in peace, and during that time she became close to Rajiv's abandoned wife, Nur.

Nur was slightly older and not so strikingly beautiful as the other wives. She had met Rajiv in university, and had been his own choice for a bride, although her influential family pleased Mahmoud well enough. Nur and Rajiv had a peaceful and pleasant marriage, and she missed him very much. They wrote and telephoned each other frequently. It was obvious to both of them that things were very different between Omer and Aliye.

Nur was educated and well read. She found in Aliye such a hungry mind that she took her under her wing and spent long hours teaching her. She loaned her books and guided her reading. Aliye idolized her.

In early July, Aliye delivered a strong baby boy. Mahmoud named him Zafer, Victory. Secretly she thought that, although he couldn't have known it, this birth was her victory over the suffering that he wouldn't admit. She loved the baby dearly, and the family embraced him among their numerous other young in the way that Kurdish families do, loving and indulging without stint or restraint.

When Zafer was four months old, it was judged safe for Omer and Rajiv to return. Aliye had hoped that a fine son might change or at least soften Omer, and she had worked hard to bring her body back into shape so that he might not feel his son had cheated him of any pleasure. Her hopes were vain.

In public Omer played the proud husband and doting father, but he had the baby moved out of their bedroom to the care of a nursemaid after its crying disturbed his sleep, or interrupted his sexual activities with Aliye. However, he liked her breasts swollen with milk and commanded her to keep on nursing the baby. He too liked to suck milk from her nipples, or press it out to run in streams over her breasts. The pain it caused her stimulated him.

For his own satisfactions, he was as cruel as ever to her. He devised new ways to cause her pain that would leave no visible signs as evidence. Aliye understood that it was an addiction for him, something he could no longer do without. She realized that her very life was in danger from Omer. His craving for the sexual stimulation that her pain gave him was pushing him farther and farther down the path of seriously injuring her.

Although Aliye knew better than to complain in any way to her friend, Nur sensed that her sister-in-law's life was troubled, and felt an intense sympathy. Nur had already borne three daughters, and perhaps this was the reason she took a special interest in Zafer when he was born. After their husbands' return, when Aliye had to spend so much time with Omer, Nur gave lavishly of her time to the baby, holding and comforting him when Aliye could not.

Sometimes after some particularly painful night with Omer, Aliye would appear limping, or would be unable to sit still for very long in one position. A few times she couldn't get up and would spend the day in bed. When Nur visited her, she could see that Aliye's condition was physical, not an illness. One day she spoke of it.

"He beats you, doesn't he?" she said out of the blue. It had just burst out unplanned. Aliye had long since shed all the tears she had, and merely nodded her head in tired assent. "Why does he do it?" Nur continued. "I know you. I know you never defy or disobey him."

"He takes pleasure from it," she said dully. "It gives him more satisfaction."

"That's terrible," Nur said indignantly. "I'm going to tell Rajiv."

Aliye sat up, panicked. "No, no, don't tell anyone. He might kill me if you did." Her terror, which had drained her face of all color, was so pitiful that Nur hastened to promise to say nothing, trying to calm her.

The next time that Aliye was unable to leave her bed, however, Nur waited until the men were gone from the house and came to Aliye. "Did he hurt you again?" she asked.

Aliye twisted weakly in bed, and said bitterly, "He always hurts me."

"You have to get away," Nur responded.

"How can I get away?" Aliye demanded. "He would kill me."

"You have to go," Nur repeated. "Would your family help you?"

"You know how powerful Mahmoud is," Aliye protested. "He would just kill them too."

"I think Mahmoud would protect Omer and let him get by with anything," Nur said, "but I don't think he himself would order anyone killed because of you."

Aliye was quiet, thinking about it. She couldn't think, her mind was too numb and confused. Anymore she hardly ever thought about anything, just how to propitiate Omer when he came to her to reduce the hurt as much as possible. At last she asked it. "How could I get away? We are always together. I would be missed at once."

"I have thought about it," Nur said quietly. "I thought of a plan, maybe not the best, but do you want to hear? We could work it out better together."

Aliye looked at her wonderingly. Nur was risking her own security and happiness for her. She nodded, afraid even to commit to listening to a plan, but also afraid not to.

"This weekend Mahmoud is taking Rajiv and me to Istanbul. I will ask Rajiv to ask his father to bring you and Omer, so that I will not be alone. They will be busy in meetings much of the day. I will bring all of my jewelry, as you also must do. I have a friend in Istanbul with whom I still exchange letters. We pledged our lives to each other when we were young, at that time of life when young girls love so passionately. She will hide you if I send a letter with you. She will help you to find a new life in Istanbul, and you can use our jewelry for money to live on."

Aliye thought very slowly, these days. She pondered what Nur had said almost as if it was someone else's life they were discussing. She wondered dimly if she wanted to make the effort. At last she thought of Zafer. "But, my baby. What about my baby? We never take the children on trips," she said.

"Zafer would be well loved and cared for here," Nur said firmly. "It would be no different for him than if you were dead."

Again Aliye stirred weakly in bed, turning her head fitfully on the pillow. How could she leave her baby? Nur reached down and took her cold hand in her own strong, warm one. "You must fight, Aliye. You must fight to live."

It stirred something within her. Yes, she wanted to live. Sometimes she thought she didn't, but if she could escape the terror and pain of her life with Omer, she did still want to live. Could this plan work? Could she do this? If she disappeared in Istanbul, surely Omer and Mahmoud couldn't blame her family, who would know nothing about her. Would it make trouble for Nur? No, how could she be blamed? Could she leave Zafer? It cut like a knife in her heart, but she knew that Omer would soon kill her anyhow, or cripple her so that she couldn't have a life with Zafer anymore.

"Yes." She turned her head to Nur and spoke more strongly. "Yes, I will do it. Ask Rajiv to ask his father to include Omer and me on the trip to Istanbul."

TWENTY-TWO

Aliye's Escape

The flight from Van to Istanbul was short, barely two hours. They were met at the huge international airport by a van driven by one of the familiar young men of the household. How that was arranged Aliye neither knew nor cared. The drive into the city along the sparkling waters of the Bosphorus had delighted her the first time she saw it. On the landward side of the freeway huge walls built by the Roman Christians still stood against invaders, but they had failed in the end to keep out the Turks. Now great domed mosques towered above the city on every hill, although she had seen some of the beautiful Byzantine churches that remained in the city as well. The road passed under a giant aquaduct, standing for seventeen hundred years but now surrounded by modern glass and steel office towers.

Today the hour long drive through dense traffic seemed endless to Aliye. She was exhausted by the time they maneuvered the tangled system of freeways and crossed the giant bridge over the Bosphorus. It was beautiful to see the ships crowding the blue water and the ornate palaces and mosques that lined its shores. She should have been entranced, but she was too ill and frightened to enjoy it.

Back on the Asian side of the city, they arrived at their hotel and checked in. It took all her strength of will to smile, to speak pleasantly to the strangers who joined them for dinner, and finally to endure one more night with Omer. The last time, she promised herself. The thought gave her courage to resist him when he began to torment her in preparation for their nightly sex.

"Stop it. Stop hurting me," she flared. "You are supposed to love me and care for me. I have always tried to please you. I gave you a son. "

Omer looked surprised. "Well,well," he sneered. "Where did that come from? Has the little worm turned?"

"Why do you do it?" She was genuinely curious.

Omer stood up and went over to the small refrigerator and took out a bottle of vodka. He poured a drink, and tossed it off. She saw that he seemed shaken.

When he turned, he stared at her for a long minute. "I don't know why I do it," he said finally. "It makes me feel so powerful, I have such wonderful sex when I do it. I tell myself I won't, but when I am with you it seems you give me reason. I get angry, and then the sexual release is so good, it feels so wonderful. I just need it," he finished lamely. "I can't live without it," he added more aggressively.

"But you are going to hurt me permanently, cripple me perhaps, even kill me," she protested. "I'm a human being too. You haven't the right to hurt me all the time just for your pleasure."

"You're my wife, I own you," he said flatly. "I have the right to do whatever I want."

She stared at him, and saw that for him that was the final word. However, he turned away and dressed again, and then went out shutting the door firmly behind himself.

She had been asleep for a long time when he came in, very drunk. Without undressing he fell on the bed and was immediately unconscious. She got up and undressed him, washed his face and hands, and folded the covers over him. Then she climbed back into her side of the bed. Her decision was made. Tomorrow she would leave forever.

In the morning the wake-up call came at eight o'clock. Familiar with Omer's hangovers, Aliye called room service for coffee and rolls. She brought him a glass of water with two Excedrin, and a warm damp washcloth. He accepted her service in silence, and got up to pour his own coffee when the room service tray arrived.

He looked terrible, yellow and bleary eyed, but he dressed and shaved carefully and went out. His father required prompt attendance at whatever meetings were scheduled.

Aliye drank a cup of coffee and nibbled at one of the rolls as she showered and dressed, but she was too excited to sit down to eat. She packed the small suitcase she had brought with the clothing she planned to take with her, and her jewels. Before she was finished, Nur was knocking at the door.

She came in filled with excitement. "Are you ready? Are you still going through with it?"

"We talked last night," Aliye said. "I asked him why he did it, and he said I was his wife and he had the right to do anything he wanted to. He said he owned me."

"Yes, in a way that is true. I like Rajiv to feel that way about me," Nur said complacently. "But he loves me, he would never hurt me. Why does Omer hurt you?"

"He says it makes sex so exciting for him. He says he means not to do it anymore, but then it feels so wonderful that he just can't stop."

Nur stared at her. "That is what he said?"

"Yes."

"Then you have to go," Nur said flatly. "You have to go."

"Yes. And I'm ready. How do I find your friend?"

"I've thought about it. Mahmoud has many powerful friends who could help him find you. We have to be very careful to leave no way he could trace you. We mustn't phone from the hotel, or use a taxi near here. You had better stay inside for several weeks once you get there, just so no one can find you. They might think to check my friends in Istanbul, although I will act as surprised as anyone when you are gone.

"I will say you felt sick and didn't want to go out this morning, so I went out shopping alone. When I came back, you didn't answer my knock, so I thought you were sleeping. You go out the service stair and the back door, and go along the side street to that big Benneton shop we like. Wait for me there. Don't go inside, because they might remember us. From there we'll phone my friend Magrit, and walk a little farther away and take a taxi. Or better yet, the Metro, where no one can trace us."

Aliye looked at her with admiration. "You have been thinking. I'm going to have to learn to do that," she said.

Nur went over to the suitcase and dumped her purse into it. "Here is all my jewelry," she said. "I got up in the night and took a hundred lire out of Rajiv's billfold. He will know I did it, and probably he will know why, when you disappear. But he won't give me away. Maybe I can show him something new he hasn't seen yet and tell him I used the money to buy it."

Aliye couldn't wait to get away. She put on her coat and tied a scarf over her hair.

She fastened her suitcase and put it on the floor. Turning to Nur, she put her arms around her and kissed her. "Thank you. Thank you for saving my life. Be careful for yourself."

"I'll go back to my room to call Shehrazade. I'll tell her you are sick and I'm going out shopping for a little while. Lucky she always stays in bed all morning when we travel. Then I'll meet you at the Benneton store."

On their previous trips to Istanbul, they had always stayed at the same hotel and shopped at the same stores, so Aliye had no trouble finding the Benneton. Waiting there, Aliye felt her blood pounding in her head, and then running like ice water through her veins. She pressed back against the building, suddenly afraid that somehow Omer would find her. The policemen passing in pairs with their automatic rifles over their shoulders frightened her, as if they might snatch her up and return her to her captivity. The crowds of people passing on the sidewalk were self-absorbed and indifferent. It seemed like hours before Nur appeared, but when she looked at her watch she saw that only forty minutes had passed.

"Sorry it took so long," Nur chirped as if it was all a lark. "That big oaf Bektas thought he should come with me, and I had to go in a department store and act like I was trying on clothes before I could get away from him. I've got a phone card," she added. "There's a telephone kiosk down at the corner." They hurried down the block. Aliye couldn't escape the panic that stopped her breath and prickled her skin. She could almost feel someone following her. Her knees felt weak, and the greasy smells of the Istanbul street, where breakfast borek was being sold in every other doorway, made her nauseous.

At the telephone, Nur entered the booth and dialed a number. Aliye saw her talking earnestly, and taking some notes on a small writing pad. After a few minutes, she popped out and picked up the suitcase, which Aliye had set down.

"Right, let's go. We catch the Metro just a few blocks from here."

Aliye had never ridden the Metro. She felt weak with thankfulness that Nur was with her to help her. She hurried along, and in a moment took the suitcase back from her friend. She was on her own now, and would carry her own burdens.

After the Metro, they took a taxi cab to a neighborhood far out in a distant suburb. They got off at a small supermarket, and Nur told the cab to wait for her. Then she hurried with Aliye around the corner and down a street of tall apartment houses. They stopped before one she recognized by consulting a note in her hand. She rang the bell, and when the door was buzzed opened she pulled Aliye inside. As they approached the elevator, the door opened and a blond woman came out.

"Magrit" caroled Nur, and the blond woman grabbed Nur and hugged her exuberantly. "Magrit, this is Aliye. Thank you so much for helping her. Look, Magrit, I didn't realize how much time this was going to take. I have to get back. I'm so sorry there isn't time to visit after so long. Maybe next time I come we can get together. But I really have to get back now."

Aliye realized they had been gone for so long that Nur was in danger of being suspected. She hugged her friend and kissed her cheeks. "Thank you so much. Thank you. Be careful of yourself. I'll let you know somehow when I get settled in a new life. I love you. Goodbye."

The tall, blond Magrit was watching this with a quizzical look on her face. She could tell from the intensity of the two women's manner that this was no small problem. Well, no doubt she would hear all about it from this white faced, anxious girl her friend had brought to her. She and Aliye watched as Nur hurried out the door and back down the street to her waiting taxi cab.

Magrit turned and opened the elevator door, inviting Aliye to enter with her suitcase. Upstairs she ushered her into an attractive upscale apartment, and showed her to the guest room.

"Here's the toilet next door if you need it," she said, "I'll go make us a cup of tea and you can tell me all about this adventure."

Aliye hardly knew what to tell this stranger. She was not sure what Nur had written, to secure this refuge for her. She was not sure how long she would be permitted to stay, or what she was going to do afterwards. She took off her coat and scarf and hung them in the wardrobe, fluffed her hair and used the toilet to give herself a little time to think. When she joined Magrit, she had made up her mind.

"I don't know what Nur told you," she began. "We are married to brothers, and while Nur's husband is good to her, my husband was very brutal and was on the way to killing me. I had to escape him. In our world out in the east, a woman may not leave her husband. He will kill her. Nur took a big risk to help me, but we believe her husband will protect her. I need a place to hide for perhaps a month, because my father-in-law is very powerful and will be able to search everywhere for me. When the search has died down, I must go somewhere and start a new life."

"Nur told me you were in danger of your life," Magrit agreed. "You are welcome to stay here for as long as you need to. My husband Uur is a lawyer and may be able to do something. He has agreed with me that we want to help you."

Aliye looked at this savior and the tears spilled over. Suddenly she felt the release of what she had done. She had escaped. The ordeal was over. As Magrit stood up and came around the table to her, she stood up too and came into her arms. The flood gates of her tears opened, and she sobbed out her fear and pain in her new friend's embrace.

The next month passed quickly for Aliye. Magrit and Uur had a well stocked library, and it was heaven to her to pass her days reading or watching television. They all agreed that it was best if she didn't go outside until the search was over, but after a month Uur found her a job in a library, where she could work among her beloved books and where she felt as securely hidden as she had in their apartment.

After two months, Nur felt it was safe to write a letter to her old friend Magrit as had been her custom since college. By this time Aliye was starving for news and she felt weak with relief that her friend was safe. Nur tried to write positively, but most of her news wasn't good. She began with news of little Zafer, knowing how much Aliye must miss him. He was well and happy, too small to really miss his mother, she thought. She went on to write that Omer had been furious, as they knew he would be. With his father, he had gone to Burhan, sure that her family had somehow played a part in Aliye's escape. They had seen that they were entirely innocent, and indeed knew nothing about why Aliye would want to leave. In fact, Hassan accused Omer of foul play, and promised to get Kader's husband in Van to look into it.

Omer knew he had nothing to fear from the law, which would never offend his powerful father, but Burhan and Hassan were so angry and frightened at his news that he recognized they had not themselves helped her to escape.

Since Aliye's family had not helped her, he turned back upon Nur and accused her. She protested innocence, but it was not only Omer who suspected her. Shahrazade, and worse, Mahmoud's man Bektas, knew how long she had been away from the hotel that morning. Shahrazade also knew that Nur was no longer in possession of most of her jewelry. Rajiv, of course, knew she must have had something to do with Aliye's disappearance but he never asked, and when his father asked him what he knew, he could truthfully say he knew nothing about it.

Faced with his family's lack of cooperation, Omer turned his own bitter enmity against Nur. He threatened her, and in the end his parents would stand behind him whatever he did, she thought. He frightened her, she wrote.

Worst of all, she was sorry to have to write, was that Aliye's young brother Kadir who played the saz with the musicians in Cansu, had somehow been killed in a nasty accident. Walking across the fields at night, coming home from town, he had fallen into the canal and his neck had been broken. It would have been sudden and he had not suffered, but it was sad that one so young and talented should die. The letter ended with Nur's assurances of her fondest love to both Aliye and Magrit.

Aliye was heartbroken about her brother. So many had been lost from her family. Now Kadir, who was always laughing and clowning. His twin Salih was as serious as Kadir was playful, and now she knew he would feel like less than half a person. It was far too late to go to the funeral, and she didn't dare even to write or telephone her family for fear Mahmoud would be told of it. She had known she had to disappear entirely when she slipped away from Omer, but it was so hard.

After several more months passed, she made a friend of one of the women who came to do research at the library where she worked. Elif was plump and pretty, with laughing eyes. She was outgoing and had struck up conversations whenever Aliye was working the check-out desk. One day she invited Aliye to go out for coffee after her work day ended. Elif was a student at Istanbul's famous university, studying law. There had been a chair of law there for seventeen hundred years, she told Aliye. Her father was a judge, and had raised her with great freedom. Her bubbling personality was contagious and cheered Aliye up. She felt more alive when she was with Elif.

Elif had sparkling dark eyes and wore her long hair loose about her shoulders. Her prettiness and her vivacious personality attracted many young men, and their respectful attendance on her began to reassure Aliye somewhat about the company of men. At first painfully shy, she gradually learned to talk and laugh over coffee with the students who clustered around Elif. She was unaware that her face was softening, and her eyes regaining a spark of laughter in their depths.

After several weeks, the two young women decided to take a small apartment together. Elif was tired of living in university housing, where there was never any quiet or privacy. Aliye saw it as a chance to take one more step out on her own. She thought that her move could only be welcome to Magrit and Uur, generous as they had been in taking her in.

One evening after she and Elif had been living together for about four months, they received a visit from Magrit and Uur. They brought with them a stranger, whom Uur introduced as Ison, a lawyer who was practicing in Van. They had met at a conference that day, and Uur had prevailed on him to come home for supper. Afterwards, he had brought him to Aliye, thinking that he could safely transport a letter from her back to Kader in Van, who could carry it to her family in Cansu. Ison had agreed that he would do so with complete discretion. No one would be able to connect him with Aliye, or find her from her letters to Kader if she was careful in what she wrote.

Aliye and Elif's tiny sitting room was so crowded by three guests that Elif took them and went to a nearby café to pass the time while Aliye composed her letter. When she joined her friends after three quarters of an hour, she saw right away that Ison and Elif had formed a strong attachment to each other. Ison took her letter, and promised to continue to act as a go-between, taking letters from Kader and mailing them to Elif. It was clear to all that there would be some personal correspondence between Elif and Ison as well, following the same pathway.

When the first letter came back from Kader, Aliye learned that Alev had given birth to a fine strong son the previous March. She now had two sons of Mehmet's old age, and very proud he was of it, too. Hassan and Hatice now had four, having had twin girls the last time. The babies were small, but growing well. She herself and Ahmet had a second child, and Sakina had come to stay with her to help her with the babies. It was good for the girl, because in Van she could get better schooling than at the village.

Burhan, bless him, had married a widow lady in Cansu, a distant relative whose husband had never come back from fighting in Irak. Two women in the house might make some problems for Hatice, but such things could be worked out. Ridvan and Salih were old enough to go out to work, so another woman to help around the house might be a blessing.

She was sorry to report that one of Aliye's sisters-in-law had died. The one named Nur, a nice lady as Kader remembered her, had fallen down some stairs and broken her neck. It was a shame, but went to show that riches didn't protect you from bad luck.

Bile rose into Aliye's throat and she thought she was going to throw up, but she couldn't move. She was sure that Nur's fall had been no accident, and the knowledge that she had been the cause of her friend's death turned her blood to ice. She sat frozen in place, so that Elif asked with alarm, "What is it, Aliye? You're white as a sheet."

Aliye sat paralyzed, unable to speak. Elif came over and took the letter from her hand, glancing at her staring face for permission but taking the letter anyhow when Aliye made no response.

When she read through to the news of Nur's death, she gasped, "Oh, no. Aliye, did they kill her? Surely not."

Aliye nodded. She still couldn't speak. Twisting her hands together, she bowed her head and a strange, groaning noise came out of her throat. Then in a choked, grating voice she said, "I killed her, Elif. I killed Nur. It's my fault." She groaned again, rocking back and forth in her chair.

Elif knelt beside her, wrapping her arms around her friend. "No, no, you didn't. It wasn't your fault. You just escaped for your life, and you had a right to do that. What kind of people are those, who would have let Omer kill you and who killed Nur?"

Aliye was inconsolable. She moaned over and over, "It's my fault. She died because of me. I should have stayed. It's my fault."

At last Elif got her to rise and go to her bedroom, where she undressed her and put her into bed. She had used some sleeping tablets when she lived in the university dorm where noise roared day and night. She found one of these and made Aliye take it.

After some thought, Elif waited until she was sure Aliye was sound asleep, and then went to Magrit and Uur's apartment, where she told them what had been in the letter.

Uur groaned.

"What is it, Uur?" Magrit asked him. "Surely we can somehow expose this wicked family. They would have killed Aliye, and they have killed Nur. We have to do something." She was seething with grief and rage.

Magrit had lived most of her life in Turkey, where her Swedish father managed a large insurance company. She had gotten some of her university education in America and worked as a well-paid executive in an advertising firm. She was insulated from the life of the average Turkish worker, and nearly ignorant of the customs still practiced in the east of the country.

Uur was folded over in his chair, his head in his hands. "Magrit, I'm sorry. Really, we can't."

"Why not?"she raged. "What do you mean, we can't? We must hire detectives, I'll go out there and tell what I know to the police. It's clear that Nur was murdered."

"No, Magrit. You can be sure it won't be clear. It will be very carefully arranged to look like an accident." Uur pursued his angry wife across the room until he caught up to her and took her into his arms. Holding her and speaking very slowly and forcefully to her, he said, "Mahmoud is a powerful and wealthy man, and he is a dangerous one. No one would dare to investigate his family, no official would risk offending him. If you were somehow able to bring any threat to him, you might have an accident too. And no one would investigate that, either."

Magrit stared at him in shock, his intensity holding her still before him.

"Now listen to me, Magrit," he went on, still holding her in front of him and speaking very earnestly as he locked his eyes to hers, "you must promise me you won't talk to anyone about this. First of all, you would endanger Aliye. Have you thought of that? And you would endanger yourself, and perhaps me. And Elif as well. Now promise me," he demanded.

Magrit collapsed against him, burying her face against his chest. After a few moments she began to sob. He led her to a couch and sat down with her, where he stroked her hair while she continued to cry.

Elif signed to him that she was leaving and went unattended out the door. What Uur had said had sobered her, as well. Better than before she realized how much risk Aliye and Nur had taken, getting Aliye away from her marriage. She wondered if

Ison fully realized how important the secrecy of their arrangement was. Would he give away any details of Aliye's location to anyone? Surely if he worked out there in the east, he would realize. She thought she would caution him in her next letter, however.

In the morning Aliye woke, heavy eyed and lethargic from the sleeping pill, but seemingly in her right mind. Elif made coffee and they sat together at the table, making plans. There was more news in the letter after the terrible paragraph relating

Nur's death. Elif had read the letter again after coming back from Uur and Magrit's, and now she urged Aliye to read on.

Kader had passed on the news that they heard very rarely from Ruya in Irak, but that she and Anwar were doing well there and were still hoping to be sent by the United Nations to America. She didn't know whether to mention it, Kader went on, but did Aliye know that Kerim was still with Ruya and Anwar? They partnered together in a produce store, and apparently Kerim had not married. She enclosed Ruya's address, for there was nothing to keep Aliye from corresponding with her directly.

The letter closed by assuring Aliye that there seemed to be no more unpleasantness with Omer and his family. Apparently they had given up on finding her, but she should still be very careful. She shouldn't try to get in touch with her father. The plan using Ison as a go-between was a good way to exchange news and she looked forward to another letter from Aliye. Kader would continue to be careful, too.

Aliye thought about the letter for days. Should she go to Irak? She was still married to Omer. Could she use her Turkish identification card to cross the border, or would she need a passport? Would she have to go to Van to get the proper papers? Even if she didn't have to go to Van, could she be traced by some informant so that Mahmoud could find her? She was terribly afraid that if she used her identity card to cross the border, she might alert Omer to where she was. He might have thought of her doing so, and probably had contacts that would inform him. Would she be safe in Irak once she got there, or would Omer hunt her down? And could he claim his legal rights and take her back? She wondered if Kerim would still want her when she was married to another man?

Some of these questions, Uur would be able to answer for her. She decided to talk with him first and get his advice. Then, if it seemed possible for her to go to Irak, she would write Ruya and ask her advice on the matter.

The next day after she left the library, she went to Uur and Magrit's apartment. They welcomed her and over tea she explained her situation. They urged her to go to Irak as soon as possible, arguing that as long as she was in Turkey, she was not safe from Omer and his powerful father. Uur assured her that she could use her identity card to cross the border. No other paper work was necessary, and it would be nearly impossible for Mahmoud to find out that she had done so.

Aliye returned to her apartment facing the extreme effort of leaving everything familiar to her for an uncertain future with a man she really didn't know at all. She spent most of the night tossing and turning, unable to reach a decision. Aliye was a dreamer, never one to make firm decisions and then act. Days slid by while she agonized over the matter. When she shared her dilemma with Elif, the practical Elif sided emphatically with Uur and Magrit. Aliye would never be safe in Turkey, and going to Irak was the best hope she had. Still, Aliye wavered, and could not bring herself to a decision.

Finally, still uncertain, she wrote to Ruya explaining her situation and asking her advice. Before Ruya's reply reached her, violence in her homeland changed her life again.

TWENTY-THREE

Patterns of
Death

While Aliye struggled to make up her mind about going to join Ruya in Irak, violence erupted once more in Cansu. It would change her life and, in the end, bring it to a tragic close.

In Cansu one dark winter afternoon in December, Ridvan was riding his bicycle home from his job in town. It had started to snow, and big wet flakes were piling up fast on the road. He had no warning when a heavy vehicle struck him from behind. The driver sped on, leaving the boy sprawled on the pavement. He was taken to the hospital in Van, where he lay close to death for many days.

Kader's husband Ahmet questioned Ridvan for the police, but he couldn't remember anything, not even where it had happened or what he had been doing there. It seemed at first there was no way to find the person who had done it. However, there had been witnesses of the accident, and they were relatives of Burhan's family. They were afraid to speak to the police, but privately they told Hassan that they had recognized the vehicle as Omer's, and that he was driving it.

Burhan and Hassan now knew from Kader about Omer's cruelty to Aliye, and how that had driven her to flee her marriage. They knew Omer's father would protect him from any legal action even if the police could be persuaded to investigate, and they knew that the witnesses would be afraid to testify formally about what they had seen. The accident to Ridvan cast suspicion on the "accident" that had killed Kadir, and they knew about Nur's death as well. They felt their own lives were possibly in danger, and certainly Aliye would die if Omer could find her. Soberly, they prepared to kill Omer.

In Mahmoud's family, other tensions surrounded Omer. In the summer, one of the young women who worked in the house had fallen down, or jumped, from the roof terrace and been killed. Although such things were kept from the ears of Mahmoud and certainly from Shehrazade, it was generally known within the household that Omer had been very familiar with the girl who fell off the roof terrace. Another girl had been with her, working to prepare some vegetables, but she wouldn't speak about what had happened and was so distraught by the accident that she was sent home to her village to recover herself. A few short weeks later, she disappeared. No sign of her was ever found, but her family suspected that she had been killed because she knew too much.

Brothers of both girls were among the young men who served Mahmoud and his family. Eventually it came to Mahmoud's ears that one of them had threatened to kill Omer. Mahmoud was disturbed that there was so much disorder in his house, and knew well enough what its source was. He sent Omer a hundred kilometers away to oversee one of his large farms on the north shore of Lake Van.

It was not safety enough, as it transpired. Omer had only been at his new post a few weeks when he went missing together with two of his young men. Weeks later, after much fruitless searching, his body was found under water near the shore of the lake. He had been shot and thrown into the water, tied by ropes to a large stone. Nothing was ever discovered to show what had happened to his two attendants.

Five days after Omer's body was pulled from the lake, Burhan and Hassan were found dead from bullet wounds in front of their farm house. The police report stated that an unidentified car with unknown assailants had driven up in the night, honked until the men came outside, and then shot them dead. The women of the family with their children had not seen it happen, only heard the gunshots. The case was held under investigation for several weeks, and then laid aside, unsolved.

At about the same time as the other murders, the bodies of two young men were found in a ditch outside of Van. They were identified as servants of Mahmoud, but no one had seen the shooting and none had any idea who might have done it. That one of them was the brother of the young woman who had fallen from the balcony the previous year was not mentioned by anyone to the police, nor did they ever discover that the other was the brother of a girl who had disappeared from her village several months earlier.

When she received the momentous letter telling her of the death of her father and oldest living brother, Aliye once more broke down. Even the news that Omer was dead and she was free from him failed to stem her tears. She cried hysterically all night and into the next day, unresponsive to any effort to comfort her. Her grief was so uncontrolled that Elif was afraid Aliye might kill herself. To prevent that, Uur and Magrit helped her sit beside their weeping friend all the next day and night, until finally she regained some semblance of rationality.

However, she didn't really recover from her prostration even after she got up and dressed. All day she sat, white and huddled as if nursing a pain in her stomach, by the window of the apartment. That she was unable to attend her father and brother's funerals seemed to be more than she could bear. Again and again she would break into sobbing, wringing her hands and wailing that she would be better dead. She was inconsolable. She was still in this state when, late in the afternoon, Elif brought her Ruya's letter from Irak.

Aliye seemed not to understand or care, at first. The slanting sunshine falling through the window should have warmed her, but she sat wrapping her arms about herself as if bitterly cold. When Elif put the letter in her hand, she let it fall without noticing, so Elif picked it up again and opened it. She knelt beside her friend, her arm around the thin shoulders, and held the letter coaxingly in front of her.

Ruya had written the letter before the fearful news of Omer's death and her father and Hassan's murders had reached her. Its calm, conversational tone comforted Aliye and seemed to draw her back into life as she read it. Making ends meet in Irak was difficult, Ruya wrote, but they were doing well enough. There had been more than one panic during their years there, when it seemed the army might kill them all in Sadam Hussein's mad attempt to repopulate the north of the country with Arabs whom he could control. In a second major gas attack like the one that killed all the people of Halabja, almost the whole Kurdish population of northern Irak had fled into the mountains, but after a time people came back again.

Ruya praised Kerim, who had been a faithful friend and supporter. She wrote that he had never shown the least interest in any other girl in all the time they had lived in Irak. She was sure he still loved Aliye.

She and Anwar had made no progress in their efforts to go to Anwar's family in the United States, but they were still hopeful. Not yet knowing of Omer's death, Ruya wrote that Aliye might be able to divorce Omer from Irak, without going back to Van. If Aliye and Kerim were married, then although he had no relatives in either the US or Canada, they might be able to follow because she and Ruya were sisters. Even if they couldn't go to America, they made a good living from the market in which they shared ownership, and so Aliye could count on that.

Ruya advised against Aliye's getting in touch with Kerim unless she was sure she wanted to come to Irak to marry him. Nothing would stop him from going straight to Istanbul to claim her if he knew she was there, Ruya said. She wrote that she thought Aliye would surely be safe from Mahmoud. His power could not reach that far into Irak. She closed with loving words of welcome and longing to see her sister again.

Aliye sat holding the letter against her breast. After a little, she got up and washed, and then ate some soup. She still felt desperately guilty and unhappy about being separated from her family during such a terrible time. However, Ruya's letter had given her some hope again.

Ruya's brisk and breezy tone sounded like she was happy enough. Just having her sister know where she was came as comfort to Aliye in her terrible loneliness. In Cansu, no one knew where she was. She was not yet ready to make a decision about going to Irak, but she told Elif that she thought she could probably be happy there, as long as Ruya was there. After a week at home, Aliye started back to work at the library, and her friends waited patiently for her to decide what she was going to do.

In Van, Sakina continued to live with Kader in order to attend the better schools there. Kader tried to comfort the young girl and help her recover from so much tragedy. Although she and Ahmet had a large and thriving family, she lavished special care and attention on Sakina. She felt it was her debt to Burhan and Aysel for saving herself and the children of her first marriage. Ridvan, Salih, and young Osman, the last of the brothers, remained in Cansu to assist Hassan and Burhan's widows in their daily struggle on the farm. In Van, Kader poured her love out to Sakina as if trying to make up to her for all the losses.

Sakina loved school and was always the first student in her class. When she got a scholarship to one of the special private secondary schools in the city, Kader prevailed upon Ahmet to allow the girl to accept it and continue her education. He was dubious, but decided to indulge his wife, to whom he was truly grateful. She was a good wife and marrying her had turned out very well for him. He understood her sense of debt to his brother Burhan, and allowed her pampering of Sakina in order to keep harmony in his home.

A month after Omer was buried, Mahmoud, with his characteristic confidant use of power, had Ahmet brought to his home and made him a proposition. They had liked Aliye, he said. She was the mother of one of his grandsons, a likely little fellow, he added indulgently. They had assumed the responsibility for her welfare and were willing to resume that commitment. There would have to be a period of mourning for Omer to keep up appearances, but she could spend that in their home. He understood that life with Omer had been difficult for her, but if she were willing to return to be the wife of his younger son Ferhat, the family would receive her with no hard feelings. Of course there would be no further money changing hands, but Aliye would have a safe and comfortable home if she chose to return.

It seemed to Ahmet an honorable and satisfactory outcome to what had been a bad situation. He agreed straightaway to try to bring Aliye back as soon as he could get in touch with her. Kader was not so sure Mahmoud could be trusted, but she had heard nothing more from Aliye to suggest she was thinking of going to Irak. Perhaps Aliye would welcome the chance to return to her son and the people who had been her family. Mahmoud was known as a generous man, and he had chosen Aliye before. She was of his clan, and had given him a grandson. Perhaps it would be all right.

Kader and the lawyer Ison had faithfully kept Aliye's secrets, and no one else knew how to get in touch with her, not even Ahmet. Kader agreed to write to Aliye and tell her Mahmoud's proposal. If she wanted to return to Van, someone from the family should go to Istanbul to travel back with her, they thought.

At this time Ahmet was in charge of an important case, and his boss was unwilling to give him time away. Ridvan was still handicapped by his injuries from the accident, and as the oldest remaining male, was needed at the farm. Ahmet and Kader decided the matter was important enough to justify sending Aliyie's brother Salih to Istanbul to bring her back. Kader was reluctant to reveal Aliye's hiding place even now, but agreed to write to her to set up a meeting place where she could speak with Salih.

When Kader's letter reached Aliye, asking her to meet Salih, she sat down and burst into tears again. She wasn't even sure why she was crying. Of course she wanted to meet her brother. The offer from Mahmoud was so unexpected she could hardly take it in.

Kader had not only relayed Mahmoud's offer, but also wrote that Ahmet strongly endorsed it, feeling it was much the best chance that Aliye had. She expressed her own belief that Aliye should take some time to decide whether she could ever be happy again in that family before she answered.

Kader added that the family farm in Cansu was now occupied by Hassan's and Burhan's widows, with their children and the three remaining brothers, Ridvan, Salih and Osman. The property rights to it had reverted to Burhan's male relatives, which was only right as they had owned it before he moved onto it. They would look after the women and children. Perhaps Aliye might want to return there, if she didn't want to go back to Omer's family.

When she could finally emerge from her shock enough to think about the offers in Kader's letter, Aliye was in a quandary about what to do. The relief of knowing that Omer was dead somehow helped her to accept her guilt for all the deaths that had followed her flight. What preoccupied her now was how to choose what to live for. She was not unhappy in her present life working at the library. She was a widow and could go to Irak to marry Kerim if he still wanted her. But she also had now been given the opportunity to return to her son and help raise him. She knew she would never want to go back to the farm in Cansu, but to be close to her family again appealed to her.

Aliye understood that Mahmoud, having acquired her by marriage contract, considered her his property as well as his responsibility. He was free to decide however he might want to dispose of her. He had always appeared quite fond of her, and it had been he who had selected her for Omer. Apparently he still liked her and was willing to give her to another son. This was not a thing to discard lightly.

It didn't take her very long to decide. She sent a note to Kader through the lawyer Ison. She agreed to Mahmoud's offer, and would meet Salih at the bus station if he came to Istanbul for her. He would have trouble finding his way around Istanbul, she thought, so she would meet him when he arrived. She would like to show him the sights of the city before they came back to Van together. She asked Ahmet to represent her to Mahmoud and agree to his disposition of her affairs. She said she was willing to marry Ferhat, if that was what the family wanted. She would observe whatever period of mourning they wanted her to keep.

She wrote to Ruya to tell of her decision, asking her to keep Kerim from ever knowing that she had at one time had a choice. It was too far away, she wrote. It wasn't the thought of their hardships but of going from there to America that seemed too difficult. She could never live that far from the rest of her family and from their beloved mountains. She knew if Ruya were ever free to make the choice, returning to her own family would be her wish, too. She closed with love, wishing her sister all the best that life could bring. However she thought as she sealed the letter that life was a very chancy business.

She filled her days with packing and with saying goodbye to all the friends she had made during her year in Istanbul. She would miss these friends of her loneliness, she thought, who had comforted her when there was no family left of her own. But then she realized proudly that she had somehow made a life of her own that wasn't just a part of a bigger family. In a Kurdish family, everyone is closely enfolded into the family unit. No one did anything by himself. She felt happy inside thinking about how she had found new friends and done a job and lived in a big city all by herself. Some good comes from everything, she thought.

When she went to meet Salih's bus, her mind was full of the things she wanted to show him. She hoped he would want to stay a few days with her so that he could see Istanbul before they went back to Van. She didn't really know him at all. It had now been three years since she had spoken with him. He would be eighteen, she thought. No, maybe still just seventeen. The age she was when she married. She wondered if he was still so serious and purposeful. It was his twin, Kadir, who had been full of wonder and excitement about the world. Poor Kadir. She knew he would have loved Istanbul.

It was a long ride on the city bus to the terminal where she would meet her brother. Through the dirty window, she watched the seagulls circling the domes and minarets of the elegant mosques that stood everywhere on Istanbul's hills. Late summer sunshine sparkled on the ornamental flower beds that filled the traffic circles. Tall buildings of colored glass and metal made fantastic shapes against the almost cloudless sky. The sea that wrapped the edges of the city shone blue with white ruffles on the wavelets. When they passed the massive city walls built almost two thousand years ago, she thought about the history she had read in the books at Uur and Magrit's house. She didn't suppose she would ever get to come back again, but it had been nice living here for a while.

She reached the big bus terminal with plenty of time to find where Salih's bus would park, and sat down to wait for him on a bench beside the numbered quay. His bus was late, and she bought a tea from the vendor who circulated among the crowds carrying a silver tray of small, steaming glasses, each covered with its own little saucer on which were balanced two sugar lumps and a spoon. She marveled at the hundreds of people all coming and going on their own private journeys. She had gotten used to crowds, living in Istanbul. Cansu might seem rather dull, she thought.

The big painted bus wheeled into the parking spot before her, the sign in its front window clearly marked Van. She stood up eagerly, wanting to be sure that Salih saw her. People were coming out both the front and back doors. Anxiety gripped her stomach. Would they recognize each other? Then she saw him, and of course she knew him. He saw her too. He was climbing down by the back door, and she started toward him. She didn't see the gun, or understand when something slammed into her chest, knocking her down. She realized she was lying on the pavement, and she could hear people screaming around her. Feet scuffled about her head. She died without understanding that her brother had killed her.

TWENTY-FOUR

A New Life in America

The news that Salih had killed Aliye reached Ahmet quickly through his police channels. He left work to go home and break the news to Kader and Sakina. They were devastated by the shock, and Ahmet stayed with them the rest of the day. He telephoned the news to Cansu, but left it to the town branch of the family to carry the terrible news to the widows, Ridvan, and Osman. He shook his head sadly as he thought of the terrible fate that had left only a few of their family alive.

Ridvan and Osman would be grown men with families of their own by the time Salih came out of prison. Ruya with Anwar could not return from Irak. Hassan's widow Hatice would in all likelihood remarry and his children would grow up in some other man's home. As a policeman, Ahmet was familiar with tragedy, but he thought that some fearful curse must have been spoken over Burhan's family, that so many had died or been taken away, in such a short time. He began to attend the mosque more piously, feeling that by doing so he was somehow protecting his own family from these disasters.

After some months Salih was tried in Istanbul and sentenced to fourteen years in prison. Ahmet tried, but was not able to arrange for Salih to be brought back to Van. The judges in the eastern part of Turkey recognized such murders as "honor killings," and were traditionally lenient about them, but in the Europeanized west, they adopted a tougher stance.

Mehmet appealed to Mahmoud to use his influence to get Salih a reduced sentence, but Mahmoud was unwilling to intervene. He said that if he had been willing to take Aliye back into his family, Salih should have respected that and not acted on his own.

Ahmet was satisfied that Salih had indeed acted on his own, in grief for his murdered father and brothers. Kader, however, thought that Mahmoud had deceived them, luring Aliye out of hiding so that Salih could kill her. Such things happened. She thought that Mahmoud couldn't help, because if he intervened to help Salih, it would throw suspicion on him as the instigator. Prudently, she kept her doubts to herself.

Sakina grieved for her sister unreservedly, but Kader felt that there was a certain measure of justice in her death. Three men of her family and perhaps her sister-in-law had died because she ran away. Her husband had been killed as well, and Ridvan almost killed. Kader's grief was for the warm, vital family which had embraced her such a few short years ago. Almost all of them were gone, now. She grieved most of all for Sakina, who had suffered the loss of so many of her family.

Privately, Ahmet thought Kader seemed more grieved by all the losses than Sakina did, but perhaps it was only that the girl was so young. She seemed to insulate herself from everything around her and live in her own mind, and in her books. All her energy was directed toward her schoolwork. It didn't seem natural to Ahmet for a girl to like books, or to be so stubborn and hard headed, for that matter. He worried about where it would take her.

In the spring of the following year, Kader received a letter from Ruya informing her that they had finally been accepted by the United Nations to go to America. They were going to a place called Texas, where Anwar's father and sister were already living among a large community of Kurds. Perhaps she would be able to help her family once they were in Texas, as everyone there was very rich, she had heard. Ruya said nothing about Kerim, and Kader assumed that he was not going to go with them.

Kedar replied, telling what family news she could and wishing them well. She had written at the time of Aliye's death, a heavy letter carrying the sad news of all the family losses in Van and Cansu as well as in Istanbul. Ruya had not replied at that time. This letter was the first time Kader had heard from her since that long ago, fateful letter sent while Aliye was still alive in Istanbul and choosing her own fate.

Ruya had not written because she had fallen into a heavy depression. Aliye's decision to return to Van instead of joining her in Irak had been a blow, following quickly upon the terrible news of the deaths of her father and brother, and the tragedy of Aliye's murder. Salih's imprisonment was a foregone conclusion. So many of her family gone in such a short sequence of years, and she trapped in Irak, unable to return to them. That she could not go back to her home and grieve with those who remained of her family was a burning acid in her soul that never stopped hurting. Almost worse was that there was no place to return to, no place that she could think of as home. Cansu had never been her home. Her home lay mouldering under a shroud of new vegetation that had overgrown the ruins of their old village, Sicaksu.

She kept busy, of course. There was always work to be done with three babies and the little store downstairs under their apartment. Suliemani was a busy thriving place in spite of the opposition of the government under Hussein. It was beginning to look as if the Americans were going to come over and do something about Hussein. They had been protecting the Kurds in the north from aerial attacks ever since the Kuwait war. Still, there was a constant fear of further attacks on the ground, and fear of what would happen to them all if America did invade Irak.

Anwar was sorry for Ruya, but impatient with her too. The past was behind them. They were safe for the time being. He was much more optimistic than she about their future. They had done well enough with the produce market and then the grocery. He was sure they could manage just as well when they got to the US. He never doubted that they would prosper.

After their initial acceptance by the UNHCR, nearly a year dragged by with no further activity on their case. They burned with impatience. Ruya had another baby. Finally they were called for another interview, and then after three months they were told a date for their departure to Texas in four more months.

When the assignment came from the U.N., with characteristic energy Anwar set to work putting everything into order. Kerim had given him what money he could to buy out the grocery. It was their plan that when they were settled in America, they would sponsor Kerim. He would sell the grocery and bring the profits with him to invest in whatever new business Anwar had started. Their lives were entwined as closely as if they were brothers. He had been as disappointed as Ruya when Aliye decided not to join them in Irak to marry Kerim. He had been angry when the outcome of it all was only more death. But, being by nature optimistic, he had put it all behind him as Ruya had been unable to do. Now he was fully focused on their new life in Texas.

Anwar bought as many things as he could to transport to America to provide for his family when he got there. The woman at the UN had told him not to take anything beyond their immediate needs for a few days. In Texas the U.N. would provide for them for the first three months, and by then they would have work and be able to buy what they needed. Anwar didn't really believe her. It was his experience that no one gave you anything for free. He knew his sister's husband would help them, but the less you had to take from relatives, the better. There were always strings to that, too.

He bought new outfits for all the children, and a warm shawl for Ruya. They would take pots and dishes, and the best of the rugs and blankets she had made for their home. He himself had a suit in the western style, although he wore Kurdish clothing for everyday. The journey would take a day and a night, so they would pack bread and cheese and olives just like any journey. Of course he understood that they would be flying through the air over the Atlantic Ocean, but who knew what food there would be on the airplane? Not good Kurdish food, he was sure. When the time to go finally came, Ruya went mechanically through her daily tasks and all the sorting and packing for the

192

journey, feeling like an automaton. She had experienced too
much loss, and this was the final and greatest loss of all, the loss
of her family ties and her homeland. She was sure she would never again see a familiar face, or the place of her birth and happy
early life. Sometimes she was not sure who was living inside her
body; it seemed it was someone she didn't know.

Between them Anwar and Kerim made all the decisions and
most of the preparations. When the family went to the airport,
only Kerim went with them and stood at the window afterwards
to watch the big silver plane taxi away and rise into the sky. He
felt bereft. They were the only family he had left. Anwar had
been certain they would continue their partnership in America,
but in his heart Kerim wondered if he would ever see them again.

He had never spoken to anyone about Aliye's death, but at
the time something inside him had died as well. More than he
had realized, he had been waiting for her somehow to come to
him. He knew from Ruya that Aliye had run away from her marriage before Salih shot her, and he imagined that she was trying
to get to him. In his heart, he had always been waiting for her.
Now, he thought, he must try to find someone else to marry. He
left the airport with new energy, as if Anwar left his energy behind when he flew away.

The long journey with two stopovers in the strange, sterile
airports passed like a dream for Ruya. The children clung to
their parents, big-eyed at all the amazing things they were seeing. They were together on a chartered United Nations plane
with a lot of other refugees and a guide, so that there was someone to tell them where to go at each stage of the trip. Anwar
knew some of the others in the group, and when they were off
the planes, the men would gather together to smoke and talk. It
helped them to feel they were more than parcels being shipped
to some unknown destination. On the planes, they had to sit
in their seats with the safety belts fastened over their laps. They
felt like prisoners. The plastic containers of uneatable food
came periodically to each of them, but it neither looked nor
tasted like anything they had seen before, and it was returned
mostly untouched. Anwar was glad he had provided some good
food, but under the stress of so many new things, they weren't

really hungry even for the familiar tomatoes, olives, bread and cheese.

At last they reached their destination in Houston, Texas. Everyone clapped that they had arrived safely by the marvels of air transportation, and some of them kissed the carpet of the terminal when they at last came off the airplane. Anwar was too busy scanning the crowd looking for his sister, and Ruya was too numb, for them to show any emotion about reaching their new home.

Suddenly they were surrounded by a crowd of foreign people in the kind of clothes they had seen on the television, and everyone was kissing and patting them and speaking a broken mixture of Kurdish and a foreign tongue. Ruya shrank into herself, not understanding what was happening, and the children clung to her, burying their faces in her skirts. Only Semih, their five year old son, whose hand had been firmly clasped in Anwar's as they walked through the corridor leaving the plane, would look at these people. But Anwar belatedly recognized his father and then his sister. Instantly he was all exuberant hugs and cries of delight, and drew Ruya and the other children into their midst.

Ruya continued to feel dazed as they passed through the huge crowded halls of the airport and out to a parking lot filled with more cars than she had ever imagined. With all their bags, they were bundled into a large van, and together with two other vehicles full of the people who had met them, they drove out onto streets filled with vehicles.

The city went on forever, and the highways full of fast-moving traffic were terrifying to her. She closed her eyes, trying to calm herself. She held little Kader, her baby daughter, on her lap and the small, warm body with its familiar smell comforted her. Somehow they would survive, she told herself. They had been through so much already. They would make a new life.

At last they left the busy highways crowded with racing automobiles, and drove through quieter streets lined with big houses built far back across green fields. Each house was surrounded by more level land than they had had for their wheat in their old village, Ruya thought. Like the children, she became interested in what she was seeing and for a time she forgot to be afraid.

Their surroundings changed again. The houses were smaller and set closer together, with little fences around most of them. The smooth green fields as perfect as carpets were gone, and the ground around these small houses was often brown or full of wild uneven growth. Most of the people she saw were black-skinned Africans. At times they passed large buildings that she recognized as apartment buildings, but they were built of some material she had not seen before. Something small, like stones, but not the stone or mud nor yet concrete blocks nor marble. She thought it was as if the people here used paving stones to build their houses.

The van turned into a small road built very close to a small wooden house, and stopped right in the middle of it. She saw that it didn't go any further, but that they had stopped under a kind of roof, a roof for the car. How strange, she thought. The other cars stopped in the street, and all the people who had been at the airport came up to the house. They all went inside, and Ruya let herself be ushered in among them. Anwar's sister took Ruya to a room where their bags were stacked against the wall, and invited her to make herself comfortable there. She had showed her the door to the toilet as they passed it, calling it a "warsh room."

Ruya set about helping the children who had crowded close around her, taking off their coats and leading them to the "warsh room." She did what she could to make all of them as clean and presentable as possible, and then sat down on the floor among them to await what would come. Anwar came in and surveyed them with approval.

"This will be our room where we can stay until we find an apartment," he said. It is my sister's home, and they have this house to themselves, they do not share it with another family. We may have to live with others for a while until we can afford better, but I know I can work here and make us comfortable." He seemed excited and happy, and for his sake Ruya tried to look happy too.

With the help of the American officials who were assigned to them, they soon moved into their own apartment. To help with expenses, they took in three young single men who shared one bedroom. It was not any more crowded than the homes to which they were accustomed, although these were not their family. They were newly arrived from Irak, however, and had much the same experiences as themselves. They all got on together well enough. The men soon found work, Ruya cooked and cleaned for them all, and there was always plenty of food, in part supplied by the Immigration officials. Semih began to attend a nearby school, and there was a small park nearby where the other children played outdoors.

English classes were offered at night in a room of the same school where Semih went during the day. The children were allowed to play in a neighboring room, and Ruya attended regularly. Anwar's brother-in-law had presented them with an old black and white television. It ran most of the day and night, and from it Ruya soon learned more English than she was learning at the school. Several months passed.

One day she saw a sign in the window of a neighborhood laundromat, asking for someone to work there. On an impulse, she went in and spoke to the manager. They needed a person to work at night. That evening she spoke to Anwar about it. If they saved their extra income, they could perhaps start another small market of their own sooner than they had expected. If she worked nights, he and the other young men in their apartment could see to the children well enough.

Anwar at first refused to think about it. He left the house angrily and didn't come back until very late, by which time she was asleep. In the morning she persisted. It was no shame, she urged. In America a lot of women worked, and they did it so they could have a better life. If they had their own business, Anwar would make it successful just as he had in Irak. He was a good businessman.

Anwar's brother-in-law worked in construction. He was a good worker and always got jobs eventually, but he was dependent on contractors hiring him and very often was between work, never sure what would come next. He had found work for Anwar, sometimes doing the most menial things like cleaning buildings or loading trucks. It put bread on the table, but Anwar didn't like what he was doing. He was trying very hard to save money for a business of his own, and in spite of himself, he was tempted by Ruya's offer to work.

Finally he conceded, stipulating that it was just for a while, until they could buy into a business of their own. Ruya confessed her fears of being somewhere by herself at night; the thought of it had made her very nervous. Anwar agreed to walk with her to and from the Laundromat, and the young men who were their housemates offered to take turns checking on her from time to time. She thanked them, and went to make her arrangements.

When she started the job, she found that there were always people using the laundromat and she was never alone. She talked with anyone who was willing to put up with her broken English, and very soon she became comfortable in the new language. There were many Kurds in the neighborhood, and she could speak with them as well in Kurdish. She enjoyed keeping up on the matters which concerned the Kurdish people in particular. In fact, she came to love her work and the opportunity it gave her to be out of her home, in touch with new people and events.

In about a year's time, they had the opportunity to buy into a neighborhood corner grocery store. Anwar had made friends with the owner and had made suggestions for improvements that had won the man's trust. After school, little Salih would go in to help his father however he could, and Ruya left the laundromat and worked in the grocery some of the time as well.

Their partner branched out and opened another store in another neighborhood, leaving Anwar in charge of the first store. Then Ruya worked longer hours, bringing their two younger children to play in the stock room while the older children were in school. They continued to live frugally. They were building up a sum of money in order to expand their business, or buy into another.

They didn't forget about Kerim, and stayed in touch through the Internet. He bought another grocery store when the opportunity came, and wrote that he had a fund set aside for coming to America if the chance ever arose. The UNHCR had not yet accepted him as an applicant. Anwar worked hard to get him a visitor's visa to come see them in Texas. Unexpectedly, this was granted.

Hastily, Anwar wrote Kerim telling him the news. Sell your stores, he said. Bring your money to the US. When you get here, we will work out something more. You can stay with us, work with us. You will have to buy a round-trip ticket, but you won't have to go back. There are a lot of illegal immigrants living here, it isn't a problem. This is our chance.

Kerim believed him. He didn't want to live in Irak forever. Although the north where the Kurds governed was much more stable than the south after the Americans invaded, the future didn't look very promising. Northern Irak was booming with the money poured in by the Americans and by rich, returning Kurds, but Kerim wanted to be secure more than he wanted to be rich. Even if he didn't have the legal right to stay in America, the important thing was to get there, and then to stay there.

In northern Irak it was a time of expansion and growth and he had no trouble getting a good price for both his shops. Inside of three months, Kerim was on an airliner headed for the same airport where Anwar and Ruya had disembarked almost two years earlier. His new life had begun. He did not have a wife, but he felt sure he could find one in America. There he would have enough money to take care of a family, and they would be safe. Kerim sat looking out the airliner's window at stars in a clear sky, and for the first time he could remember, felt an unfamiliar happiness stir within him.

Sakina Goes to University

Sakina sat on the flat roof of the house, preparing tomatoes for the paste that was such a staple of their diet. Although the late summer sun shone hot overhead, there was always a little breeze on the roof. A small mountain of tomatoes beside her awaited her attention. Two of Ahmet's daughters worked alongside her, diligently peeling and chopping as they talked, but their attention was mostly on the behavior of their aunt Miryam, who had gone off in a fit at their cousin's wedding two nights before. She had fallen, thrashing and babbling, on the field where everyone was dancing. It had caused a great deal of anxiety as to what kind of bad luck it would bring to the young couple.

Sakina wasn't listening to what the girls were saying. She had been very interested in her aunt's condition at the time and had tried to restrain and comfort her, without really knowing what to do anymore than anyone else did. Sakina wanted to be a doctor, and she knew enough already to understand that Aunt Miryam had experienced a brain seizure of some kind. It had been her Aunt Kader who had dealt firmly with the afflicted woman, putting a stick in her mouth so she wouldn't bite her tongue and turning her on her side and then wrapping her in a cloth she

whipped off one of the tables so the woman didn't hurt herself
more.

Sakina was determined to continue her schooling, whatever
she had to do to make that happen. However, it helped a lot
that she had Aunt Kader's full cooperation. Through the years,
her aunt had argued and cajoled her husband Ahmet into allowing Sakina to continue in school. He had agreed for the sake of
peace in his household, but Sakina knew he thought it was a bad
thing for a girl to get too much education. She took great pains
to keep her grades the highest in her classes, even when she had
to study all night under her blankets, using a flashlight to read
her books.

Twice someone had offered to marry her, and Aunt Kader
had argued hard with Ahmet to refuse them. It was good of him,
Sakina thought gratefully, to let her go on studying. He had
borne the expense of keeping her for a long time, ever since her
father had been killed. Her father and Hassan, and Aliye too had
died at almost the same time. Almost no one in Sakina's family
was left at their farm in Cansu, which wasn't really their home,
anyhow.

She didn't remember their first home very well, but the others had always talked of it as if it was the most beautiful place in
the world. Kader remembered it, but not like the others did.
She had only lived there for a short time after her husband and
two sons were killed in the fighting, and she didn't really have the
same happy memories.

No one had happy memories of Cansu, Sakina thought. Her
memories were of too little food, and terribly hard work, and
Mother dying, and Alev, Ruya and Aliye going away, and Kadir
being found dead and then Ridvan being hurt so badly. Then
Father and Hassan were murdered Lastly Salih, whom she loved
especially because he read stories to her and talked to her about
interesting things, Salih had killed Aliye and was going to be in
prison for years and years. She sometimes wondered if he ever
got to read any books in prison. No one knew what his life was
like, there were never any messages or phone calls.

She knew why he had done it, but whether or not he was
right she didn't know. Without telling anyone what he meant to

do, he had just gone to Istanbul and shot Aliye because she had run away from her husband. Sakina knew that Salih believed the deaths of his father and brothers were Aliye's fault because she had left her husband. She wished she could have talked to him again, just once.

The late summer sun was very hot on her head and neck. There was a nice breeze this afternoon, and they had put a cloth on two poles over their heads as a sunshade, but the sun had moved down in the sky until it shone under the cloth, and it was still very hot. The girls beside her giggled and chatted as their busy fingers steadily reduced the pile of tomatoes, but Sakina hardly heard them.

In June, the national examinations for university admission had been held. Everything depended on them. If Sakina did well, if she scored highly enough, then she would be eligible to go to one of the better universities where medicine was taught. Even if she didn't do well enough to go to another city, there was a very good department of medicine for urology at the Hundred Years University near Van. She thought she would get a good score, she always had. Still, the waiting for the results was agonizing. Moreover, even if she made a high score, there remained the big question of money.

Every year since she moved to Van, in late summer a sum of money to pay for her school fees, uniforms and books had come in an unmarked envelope to Ahmet and Kader's house. It was always delivered by a messenger service. They didn't know from whom the money came, but it had been a big factor in Ahmet's willingness to allow her to continue in school. Every year a neat, politely worded note had been enclosed in the envelope directing the use of the money for Sakina's schooling. There was nothing to indicate who had sent it.

Now the question was, would there be enough money for university? First, of course, she had to score well enough to be eligible. But after that, she knew the only way she could go anywhere would be if her anonymous benefactor sent the money to pay for her education. Who could it be? She didn't know anyone who was wealthy.

She wished she could thank this person. Already she had learned enough to know she would never settle down in Van or a nearby village as someone's wife, condemned to a lifetime of housework and child bearing. But if the money didn't come for medical training, she wasn't sure what she could do. She would have to run away to some city in the western end of the country, and…. Well, somehow she couldn't think beyond that. She would just hope that the money would come. She was going to be a doctor.

The examinations had been very hard. Sakina had prepared as best she could, using the books sold in book stores with examples of the kinds of questions they asked. She was unnerved by the crowds of young people who thronged the city at the time the examinations were held. They came from everywhere, and there were hundreds of them. She wondered where they stayed at night, there were so many. So many applicants, and so few places at the universities. She knew that very few students from the eastern part of Turkey got scores high enough to be accepted.

The examinations were held in different places. She was assigned to her own high school, which helped her nervousness. The familiar face of one of her teachers, giving instructions and watching over the students as they wrote, was reassuring. The exam lasted for three hours of intense effort. Three hours seemed a terribly short time, when your hopes for the rest of your life depended on the results. Some people did take the examinations more than once. You were allowed to, but Sakina was sure that if she didn't do well this time, she would never get another chance. Ahmet would decide it was time for her to marry, and she would have no choice except to run away.

Afraid to even think of failure, Sakina wrote until the last possible moment, pouring words onto the paper as fast as she could. She was limp and exhausted afterwards, once the state of high tension wore off. For the rest of the summer, she waited for the results. Her nerves frayed, she was alternately absent-minded and irritable, snapping at the others in the family or bursting into tears when someone crossed her. She remembered Aliye when she had acted in this way, and how she had scolded her at the time. She was sorry, especially because she could never make it up to her. Aliye was dead.

At last August came and the hot days and nights seemed to drag even more slowly than before. She knew the results were to be announced any day now. It seemed as if she couldn't think about anything else. Whether she was working with the others, as she did now on the rooftop peeling tomatoes, or whether they were gathered at some festive wedding, nothing but the hope of going away to university engaged her thoughts.

At last the examination results were posted and Sakina learned that she had passed with high honors. She had almost no time to worry about whether the money would come. The evening of the day the results were posted, a messenger came to the house with the familiar brown envelope. When Ahmet opened it, he found two large packets of money. The note enclosed was as anonymous as the others had been, but stated that the money was to help Sakina attend the university of her choice, and that there would be an equal sum paid for her living expenses at the beginning of the new year. Her benefactor guaranteed her on-going expenses for the length of time she remained in university, provided she did well at her studies. It ended by wishing her well.

Ahmet sat fingering the bills, marveling. "Who can want to help you in this way?" he asked her. Sakina didn't know. She only knew that it was a gift of life to her, and she hardly knew whether to laugh or cry. She had chosen in her heart the university she wanted to attend, although it had seemed only a miracle could take her there. But here was her miracle in Ahmet's hands, and she needed only to find the courage to act on it.

"Do you know what you want to do?" came Kader's gentle question.

Sakina did know. "Yes, I want to go to the University of Izmir, to study medicine. It is the best of its kind, and this is enough money to live on the campus in a dormitory there." She spoke as if there was no question about it, as if her mind had always been made up. The others looked at her in wonder, as if seeing her for the first time.

Then Ahmet stood up and handed her the money. "We are proud of you," he said. "You are a very special person. For a long time I was not sure about letting a girl go to school, but no one could have brought this family more honor than you have done.

I will buy you all the clothes you need for your new life, and your aunt and I will drive you to your new home ourselves."

Kader gazed at him with her mouth open in mixed astonishment and delight. He smiled at his wife. "It is time we took a vacation," he said. We will take the young children with us, and before we leave Sakina at the university we will all take a holiday at the seaside. I have always heard that Eski Foca is a lovely place to visit, or perhaps we will go down to Kusadasi."

The family erupted into hysteria, overwhelmed by such an unprecedented treat. The children flung their arms around Sakina, jumping up and down. It took some time for the uproar to die down. Kader looked flustered, thinking of all the arrangements that would have to be made, but Sakina stood beaming, feeling that this was the happiest moment of her life.

TWENTY-SIX

No Longer Alone

Sakina sat in her cubicle at the library, but she wasn't trying to study. A book lay open before her, but she sat deaf and blind to everything outside her small, blank sphere of misery. She felt confused, destroyed by pain. She couldn't even remember how she had gotten here to the library.

After a time she rallied and gathered her strength, forcing herself calm down. Pressing her fingers against her eyes, she listened gratefully to the silence of the empty room. Mentally she stroked her frayed nerves smooth, calmed her emotions, slowed and deepened her breathing until she felt settled again. Until she was in control again.

In nice weather she could do this best outdoors, somewhere in a garden or near water. Today a February snowstorm beat against the windows of the library, the wind whining through the cracks of their loose fittings. When she had crossed the campus earlier today, hastening to her appointment with her advisor, she had been exhilarated by the biting wind, the blinding curtain of white pouring down from its inexhaustible source in the clouds. She had been full of confidence, full of joy. Everything was hard, but she loved her classes. She loved learning.

Phrase by phrase, her advisor had stripped her of all that. Every sentence peeled her belief in herself away, leaving her feeling naked and worthless. She was ignorant, he had said. She was stubborn and unteachable, he had said. His voice still droned in her ears. She was wasting her money and the valuable time of the university staff, he had accused her. She should go back to where she came from, and take the place assigned to women in her culture. She would never be a doctor, she couldn't learn to be a doctor, and women were not needed as doctors in any case. It was not fitting in her culture.

Nothing in Sakina's experience had prepared her to face personal criticisms like these. Secretly she had felt her willfulness, determination and her critical mind were her strengths, without which she could not have come so far. Her teachers had always encouraged and praised her. Her family had learned to be proud of her academic successes. They had supported her in her dreams of becoming a doctor, although there was no precedent for it among the people they knew. She was very proud of being different, of following such a different path from anyone else in the family. Now, this man whose support she needed was telling her that because she was a Kurd, a stubborn Kurdish woman, she could not stay at the university.

Sakina had not done well in her beginning courses. She had always done well in her classes in high school, but the university materials were taught in a different way. Instead of being told what they were supposed to know, and then tested to see if they had learned it, now she was given problems and expected to solve them. She was given books to read, and then tested over a vast amount of detail buried in them. There were many questions about details she had not known how to identify as important. In the examinations, she sat bewildered, unable to organize the information she had read in order to answer the questions that were asked. In the laboratory she was clumsy and confused among the tools and supplies the other students seemed to be familiar with. Where had they learned how to do all the things they were doing, and why wouldn't someone teach her how to do them too?

In spite of the overwhelming strangeness of it all, Sakina had never doubted herself. She had tried eagerly to learn, watching the others in the laboratory, but asking no questions. Questions were never allowed, in her experience. She had read all the materials over and over, and done the best she could on the examinations. There were few other women in her classes, and they had not been friendly. She didn't know how to talk with them. She had been brought up never to speak to men.

In the women's dormitories she didn't mix with the other students. Although she wouldn't have admitted it, they frightened her. She sometimes missed the familiarity of her former life in Van, but she hadn't really felt a part of the life there either. Her life was in her books. Her family had not played an important role in the life she had chosen for herself. Her family was mostly dead or gone away, and Aunt Kader's family was just a kind of living arrangement. Sakina was used to thinking of herself as different from the people around her.

Perhaps it had been all the loss and change in her life that had made her that way. Their family had been forced from their village, and on the new farm nothing was ever settled for long. The other members of her family had seemed to have little control over what happened to them, whether they had conformed to the patterns of their culture or had broken away.

In Sakina's eyes, they were all victims of forces outside themselves. From an early age, she had determined not to be a victim too. She had set herself to shape her own life according to her own plan. Focused on what she could control, she had learned to treat others as either aides or obstacles to her own purposes. She had successfully followed a path different from her family and cultural patterns, and she paid little attention to anything but her own plans.

Now she was being forced to realize that her own will, by itself, was not enough. Had she really been wasting her efforts all this time? Had it always been impossible? Sakina had loved her family and she would never intentionally hurt anyone. She simply didn't trust anyone but herself, and saw no model she wanted to follow except her own plan. She was far from unteachable, being eager to absorb any information or knowledge that she came across. The learning she desired, however, was scientific information. She had no interest in human relationships or the learning that came, not from books, but from interacting with other people.

Sitting hunched in misery in her quiet cubicle, her mind began to work again. How had she come to this place of failure? Ever since she entered the university, she had felt out of place, unable to connect to any of it. She had struggled as hard as she could to compete in a game, the rules of which she didn't understand. Now the person whose place it was to help and guide her had abandoned her, condemned her, and told her to give up and go home.

She had no home. She would not go back to Van to marry into slavery, if anyone would have a girl who had reached so far above herself and failed. As she faced the hopelessness of her situation, despair rose up and overwhelmed her. Sinking her head onto her arms, she shook with sobs that she tried to choke back.

She was aware that someone had moved a chair and sat beside her. Through tear blurred eyes she saw a brown hand cover hers. Gasping, she jerked back and tried to pull away, but two hands grasped hers firmly and held her. A man she didn't know was looking at her sympathetically, holding her hands. Soft brown eyes in a smooth brown face showed compassion and kindness.

"Now, now," he said. "I'm a friend, I won't hurt you. What in the world is so terrible, that you should cry like that?" He proffered a large white handkerchief, clean and neatly folded. "Wipe your face," he said prosaically, releasing her hands.

Stiffly defiant, Sakina did so, a last sob hiccupping through the folds of cloth. His chair and body blocked her way out of the cubicle, or she would have run away.

"I'm Ibrahim Coban, a law student here. Tell me what is wrong, maybe I can help you." His manner was so calm and earnest that her fear and anger faded, but to speak with a strange man about something so personal was impossible. Her throat filled again with tears, but that was impossible too. She refused to cry again.

Something in the kind brown eyes regarding her so calmly drew her to speak. In desperation, she blurted out her story, that she wanted to be a doctor, to help people in the East, but her advisor had told her she was worthless and had to go back.

"I can't go back," she wailed. "I won't live like that, a slave, bearing children until I die. I can learn. I have always made the best grades in my classes until I came here. I just don't know how to do things the way they do them here."

"What is it that you haven't been able to do?" Ibrahim's soft voice was matter of fact.

"The questions don't ask what the book says, and there is so much material to read. They ask you what you would do in a new situation, and they haven't told you the right answer. In the laboratory you have problems to solve and I don't know what to do. I don't know how to use the things there, how to cut or melt or burn things like everyone else seems to know how to do."

"You are from the East?" Ibrahim asked. "Tell me about your schools there."

"Well, there are a lot of people in the classes, like here. In the upper schools that wasn't so, but most of the girls weren't interested in science, and the teachers didn't know much. Our books were old. I mostly learned literature and history, and read whatever I could find to read about science for myself."

"Did you learn how to read background material about a problem and then work out the solution for yourself?"

"No," she said. She hung her head as if she were a naughty child.

"I think that is your problem," he said. "You haven't enough practice in solving problems and thinking for yourself."

Sakina was silent. It was right, but what could she do about it? She slumped in her chair, for the moment defeated again.

Ibrahim watched her, and in a moment spoke cheerfully. "So you need practice, right? Would you like some help, practicing?"

She lifted her head warily, once more alarmed. What did he mean?

Ibrahim smiled at her. "Look, I won't hurt you and I don't want anything from you. You know we do things differently here than in the East. You can come for a pizza with me now, and we can talk about how you can learn to solve problems. No harm will come to you, and no one will think anything bad. I just want to help you," he added persuasively.

She studied him, struggling within herself. Never could such a thing happen in the East, but she knew it was true here at this university. Boys and girls met freely for food and drink, walked and talked together in public places. She knew from the girls' talk in the dormitories that no harm came from it, and sometimes real friendship would grow between students of the opposite sex. In fact, the boys they met seemed to be almost the only thing the girls talked about.

Ibrahim had a round, cheerful face. Even though he was being sympathetic, his warm brown eyes seemed to sparkle with laughter as if he knew a secret joke. Heavy black eyebrows nearly met over his nose, his eyes were set in a thick fringe of long black lashes. His expensive looking overcoat hung open over a red cashmere sweater. Without thinking about it, she registered that he must be wealthy. She saw that although his lips didn't smile, he was laughing at her.

"Well, will I eat you up?" he asked.

She had to smile. "No, I guess not," she confessed.

"Come on, then. Let's go have a pizza at the Roma Café, and talk about problem solving. I'm studying law, and I don't know much about laboratories, but I do know about gathering and organizing materials." He stood up and replaced the chair he had moved in order to sit beside her. He waited while Sakina pulled on a coat and wrapped a muffler several turns around her face, then led the way out of the library.

Outside, the blizzard still filled the air with gusting curtains of white. Ibrahim took Sakina's arm and pulled her along through the streets and into a warm, crowded café. Emerging from her own wrappings, she saw that snow was piled on his crisply curling black hair, and on the shoulders of his thick overcoat. They stood, dripping and panting, inside the door. The hot air and loud laughter washed over them, and Sakina felt excited and scared. She didn't know that it made her cheeks scarlet and her big black eyes sparkle, or that as she brushed the snow off her head she pushed back her headscarf so that a few raven tendrils curled around her forehead.

Ibrahim reached over and brushed the snow off her back and shoulders, while she wiped the trickles from her face with her knitted muffler. Greatly daring, she reached up and drew it across his head, wiping the snow from his hair. When he smiled at her, her eyes dropped modestly, but the flash of shy appreciation in them enchanted him.

A waiter led them to the second floor and found them a table in a corner alcove. As they sipped cokes and ate their pizza, they got acquainted. She was surprised to learn that Ibrahim was from the Kurdish northeast, a member of a prominent Kurdish family. He had lived and studied in Europe, however, and was frank to say that he felt there were many things in their Kurdish culture that should change.

"I believe that men and women should have equal opportunities, and equal protection under the law," he said. Her face showed her surprise. "We will be much richer and stronger when we free our women," he went on. "Our nation will be much stronger when there are human rights for all people."

"Life is so short and uncertain in the East," she lamented. "My mother and father, three of my brothers and two of my sisters are dead, and another sister lives in Irak, waiting to go to America."

"I know. Quite a few of my family have died in the war as well."

"Why are you studying the law?" she asked.

"Well, most of the men in our family are in the military," he replied. "But I don't believe that war is the best way to solve our problems and build our nation. I believe that if there is a fair system of laws, administered fairly by the courts, people will be free to prosper and there will be less fighting. I want to be a judge. I hope to become a judge for a family court that will help to eliminate the feuds and honor killings that rob us of our life's blood, our young people."

"I want to bring medicine back to our land in the East, especially to help women," she confessed eagerly.

"I'm sure you can do it," he said warmly. "We need that. Now, let's talk about how you study in order to organize materials for the kind of examinations they will be giving."

When Sakina was back in her dormitory late that afternoon, she lay down on her bed and curled up around a pillow. Ignoring the noisy revelry of the other students that surged around her, she marveled at how much her world had changed in one short day. From self confidence she had been thrown into an abyss of despair, ready to kill herself. From that black pit, she had been lifted to a kind of joyous excitement new to her, that had nothing to do with her renewed determination to become a doctor. Ibrahim had been able to restore her sense of pride, her belief in her own ability.

More than that, she had found a friend. They shared a vision of helping their own people, the Kurds. She could imagine them returning to the east together, working together to make their world a more modern place. She sighed happily.

TWENTY-SEVEN

At Cross Purposes

Proudly Sakina stood on the stage among the graduating seniors of the medical school. Far from the first ranks of her class, she was content to have overcome the handicaps with which she had entered the university. Being from the eastern part of Turkey, her preparation for university life had been very poor, but with determination and help from sympathetic friends and teachers, she had succeeded. She was now about to become a doctor. There was still a lot of hard work ahead as she did her practical training in a hospital in Van, but she was graduating.

Seated below the stage in the large auditorium, her Aunt Kader and Uncle Ahmet smiled at her, or so it seemed. She didn't really know if they could see her from so far away. It didn't matter, they knew she was there and they were proud of her. They didn't know that she had nearly been forced to give up and leave in the first year. They didn't even know her friend Ibrahim, who had saved her from giving up halfway through her first year and helped her so much ever since.

She wondered if anyone else in the audience had a personal interest in her. Someone had continued to send large packets of money twice a year to pay her way through the university. Always the money came to Ahmet's home by courier in a plain brown envelope. There was always a short, anonymous note directing that the money be used for her education. Sometimes there was a line of approval or encouragement. Nothing more. Over all the years, no one had been able to guess who took such a personal interest in her achievement. Would the mysterious benefactor have wanted to attend her graduation? Might he or she reveal an identity now that she had finished?

When the graduation ceremony was over, Sakina joined her aunt and uncle at the reception given by the university for all graduating seniors. She was eager for them to meet Ibrahim. His cheerful trust in her had kept her head above water when she hadn't known if she could go on. His practical advice and sharp mind had helped her overcome every obstacle. He, himself, had graduated today with both a law degree and the requisite credentials to be the judge he wanted to be.

Ibrahim found them as they stood, sipping the fruit punch and receiving the congratulations of other friends and faculty. Sakina proudly introduced him to her aunt and uncle. He had heard a great deal about them, of course, and they of him and it was almost like friends meeting one another. Then Ibrahim pulled Sakina away to meet his parents, and calling an apology, she followed him.

She was a little shy about meeting them, for she knew them to be an important and wealthy family in Agri. They had long been aware, however, that Ibrahim's interest in Sakina was more than casual, so they met her politely. Their pleasant manner didn't conceal the serious scrutiny they were giving her, as parents still had a lot to do with choosing marriage partners for their children in the East. Their son deserved the very best. They had taken pains to check Sakina's background, and it was not distinguished. Village people, with several children dead in the rebellion and one brother in prison. Not auspicious, however commendable his crime of killing a sister who had shamed her family.

Her parents were dead, and the relative who had sent her to university was only a policeman. One wondered where the money for medical school had come from. They were not very happy about letting Ibrahim marry this person, if that was on his mind.

After a few minutes of talking, it was quite apparent to them that Ibrahim was very much in love with this girl. Sakina was very pretty, and today she was radiant with happiness at having graduated. She had the nice manners of a village girl, modest and respectful of her elders, but also a quiet dignity. She seemed to be a person of strength and character.

When they talked about it later, Ibrahim's father said, "Ah, well, if he has set his heart on her, let him have her. She seems a good girl, and the day of fathers making alliances to benefit their families has passed. Anyhow, she has no father and he wasn't of much account when he was alive. We don't have any other girl in mind. Let him have his way."

"Yes, but is an educated girl who wants a career the right thing for him?" asked his mother. "I would rather see him settle down with a girl who will stay home, cook for him and give us babies. Anyhow, there is a girl I've always had in mind for him, my niece Cidan. She would be a perfect wife."

"He has known Cidan all his life and never showed any interest in her. I don't think Ibrahim will marry whomever we choose for him, my dear. He has followed his own plan for his life for some time now, and I think he means to continue to do so."

Ibrahim's mother sighed. What her husband said was too true to be disputed. She also felt quite sure Ibrahim would marry whom he pleased, and in the end, this girl did seem to have nice manners. She looked to be modest and well brought up. But a doctor? Would she want to work after they were married? What kind of a home would that be for Ibrahim? She sighed again. She knew her own parents were going to be very critical.

The two families had dinner together that night at a restaurant. Before they went to meet Sakina's aunt and uncle, Ibrahim came to his parents in their hotel room and asked their permission to propose to Sakina.

"We can follow the proper way of doing things, Papa," he said earnestly. I want you to go to Ahmet and ask him to give Sakina to me, and if he feels he is due some kind of settlement, I will agree to pay him anything reasonable. And I will pay it from my salary, you don't have to. But I want to be sure Sakina will agree to marry me before you speak to Ahmet. I know she loves me, but I am not sure she wants to marry before she has practiced as a doctor. She has very high ideals of helping our people in the East, and we have never talked about whether she can manage that and a marriage as well. I need to ask her."

"Ibrahim," his mother implored. "Wouldn't you be better off to marry a traditional girl who would stay home to take care of you and have babies?"

"I love Sakina, Mother," Ibrahim said patiently. "I don't want any other wife. She will make me very happy, and we will have babies. Neither one of us wants fourteen children in the old way. That was always foolish. People did it because so many children died. Sakina and I both want to help our people to live in the new way, where there is less fighting and killing, and better medicine, so that every child who is born can live and grow up to be a useful citizen. We both want to work for this purpose, each in our own way. We will be a perfect couple. We will be perfectly happy."

His mother looked sad and unconvinced. She could not imagine the world had changed that much. His father look resigned. He saw there would be no dissuading his son. "Very well, Ibrahim. When you tell me, I will speak with Ahmet and see what his feelings are about all this. I see your mind is made up."

During the elegant dinner at a fine hotel, conversation was stilted. It was difficult for Sakina's aunt and uncle to fine any common ground with Ibrahim's parents, or with the young graduates. As soon as he could do so politely, Ibrahim asked Sakina to walk outside with him, and she was glad to escape. Behind the restaurant, the hotel swimming pool was bordered by a rose garden. A soft warm breeze blew just enough to stir the flowering branches over their heads, and the evening perfume of the early summer roses filled the air.

Ibrahim was wearing a dinner jacket and looked darkly handsome. Sakina had put on a peach colored chiffon dinner dress that drifted about her in soft folds and molded against her curves provocatively. The half-length sleeves were cut like the petals of a flower and fell open revealingly as she moved her arms, then fell closed again. Pearl drops in her ears gleamed within her dark curls, and a simple strand of pearls lay against the modest neckline. She had become accustomed to wearing her hair loose and uncovered, as head scarves were forbidden at the university. A few loose tendrils curled about her face, but a mother of pearl clip shaped like a flower restrained the rest of the dark shining mass that tumbled down her back.

Sakina paid little attention to her appearance most of the time. She had very little extra money to spend for dresses in any case, but Kader had ordered this dress made for her and brought it as a graduation present, expecting there to be some kind of festivity after a graduation. She had hustled her niece out to a coiffure in the hours before dinner as well, knowing better than she that appearances were important to people like Ibrahim's parents. Kader had a pretty good idea that Ibrahim would propose marriage, even if Sakina did not.

Sakina's thoughts were all on returning to Van and starting her work in the hospital. She couldn't wait. Her whole life had been spent in struggle, it seemed to her. All of it was to attain what she now possessed, a medical degree. Her mind was full of plans, and she hadn't given a thought even to where she would live in Van. Vaguely assuming that she could stay with Ahmet and Kader, she was thinking about what kind of specialized training she wanted to pursue, and with which doctor. She had an appointment the next morning with her advisor to discuss this. Although he had done his best to discourage her at first, he had come entirely around to championing her as she had proved to him that she could do the work, and was eager to follow his advice.

She chattered eagerly about her plans to Ibrahim as they walked, the soft lights beside the pool fading into semi-darkness as they turned into a walk that entered the rose garden. When he turned to her and took her hands, she broke off to smile a question at him, but without a suspicion of what he meant to do. He pulled her toward him and kissed her. It was their first kiss, but at first she lifted her face trustingly. She felt a fountain of happiness bubbling up inside of her, overflowing, and her kiss was the natural expression of this joy which she assumed he shared. They had both realized big dreams today.

Ibrahims arms tightened, he drew her hard against him and kissed her hungrily, thrusting his tongue into her mouth. Sakina was startled. She tried to pull back, but for a moment he held her fast. Then, reluctantly he lifted his mouth from hers. Her name was almost a groan on his lips.

"Sakina."

He saw her eyes wide with fright, her mouth still open in dismay. He held her tight, afraid she might run away if he let her go. "Sakina, I love you. Marry me. Marry me and we will both work in the east as we planned, but together. I need you."

"No. No, Ibrahim. I can't marry, I have work to do. I don't ever want to get married. You know that."

Sakina was white with shock. His proposal felt like a betrayal. Surely everything he knew about her should have made him know she wouldn't marry anyone. Marriage was entrapment, slavery, a loss of everything she had worked for. How could he, who she thought of as a helper and friend, how could he now want her to throw it all away. What kind of friend was that?

When his arms loosened around her, she tore herself away and ran blindly back toward the dining room. Snatching up her purse and light jacket from the table, she said without preamble to her aunt, "Come on. We're leaving." The four at the dinner table stared at her, disheveled and obviously very upset. Sakina didn't wait for questions. She turned and walked quickly out of the restaurant, signaling for a taxi. She was already inside it when her aunt and uncle came hurrying out after her, and although very bewildered, they climbed in too. She offered no explanation when she had the taxi driver drop them at their hotel, merely saying she would see them tomorrow.

Ibrahim had rejoined his parents in the restaurant, but only long enough to tell them what had happened, and why he thought it had turned out as it did. He understood enough to realize why Sakina had reacted as she had. He was kicking himself mentally for not preparing her better. He believed they could marry and both follow their careers, but he hadn't understood just how deeply Sakina believed that she could not do both. To her marriage meant the kind of bondage she had seen among the women of the villages. She had no concept of anything different.

He tried to explain to his parents what had happened. His mother gave an exasperated sigh, feeling bitterly that young people might have changed the world but they still had a lot to learn. She knew her son was not ready to hear anything she might have to say right now, however, and wisely kept her silence.

"She may have graduated medical school," his father said angrily, "but she hasn't learned anything about life. You're way above her and she would be lucky to get you. Our family doesn't have to go begging to village orphans to find wives."

"I don't want any other woman," he said earnestly. "She is the only one for me, and I will wait as long as I have to." He rose, wanting to go off by himself and think it through. He still believed he could find a way to persuade her. Excusing himself, he left his parents and began to walk the streets. Eventually he found himself back at the campus, and for a while he stood outside Sakina's dormitory, wondering if he could explain himself to her. Finally he saw the building go mostly dark, and gave up, returning to his own apartment.

In the morning, Sakina didn't answer her phone. When he went to her dormitory, he found she had checked out. She was going home, leaving the university, the desk clerk told him. He didn't know which hotel her aunt and uncle had stayed in, so he couldn't think of any way to find her. He decided he would have to return home with his parents for now, but he resolved to go to Van to try to talk with her very soon.

They flew back to his home city, but for the next several days both his father and mother attempted to argue with him, trying to talk him out of his fixation on this one unsuitable girl. To escape them, he drove to Van. He had heard of a possible new court being established there, a family court. It was exactly what he wanted to do, and he very quickly made the connections with family members and friends that were necessary to help him get the appointment.

After some thought, once he had taken care of all the business he could do on the court appointment, he sat down and wrote a letter to Sakina. In it he apologized for his behavior the night of their graduation. He said as honestly as he could that he was in complete sympathy with her ambitions, and wanted her to pursue her career as a doctor. He promised never to interfere or make demands that would take her away from her work. But he told her again that he loved her, never wanted to marry anyone but her, and believed they could both marry and follow their own careers. Marriage didn't have to be like the ones in the village, he reminded her. She knew that. At the university they had known women professors who both worked and had a family. He begged her to meet him and talk with him about it. He added the phone number and his extension at the hotel where he was staying.

Ibrahim bought a large, beautiful bouquet of flowers and tipped the florist to deliver it. He slipped the envelope with his note into the bouquet. Then he went back to his hotel room to wait anxiously for her reply.

Several hours later his phone rang. Sakina spoke hesitantly, her voice soft. "Ibrahim, I'm sorry I ran away. I can talk to you now. But I don't want to get married. You know how I feel about being a doctor. I don't think I will ever want to get married. You are my best friend, but that is all I want you to be. Can we go on the way we were?"

"Sakina, I shouldn't have asked you so soon. I didn't realize how strongly you felt about this. I don't want to just be your friend, though. I want you to marry me. I don't know how we can go on if you won't."

"Ibrahim, I think we can't agree on this. I'm sorry. Maybe you'd better not call me again."

He didn't know what else he could say. He said good bye, and hung up. Then he lay down on his bed, trying to think how to go on with his life without the wife he had counted on.

When Sakina hung up, she stood biting her lip. She refused the emotions that were welling up inside of her. She would not throw away her whole life, she told herself for the hundredth time. She was a doctor. She had already begun her training at the hospital, and had come home for a few hours of sleep before returning for night duty. Finding Ibrahim's flowers and note, she called him impulsively. But she told herself there had been nothing to think about. There never had. Marriage was unthinkable. She lay down, but although she was very tired, she couldn't stop her thoughts from churning around and around.

When she had to go back to the hospital it was very hard to get up. Once on the ward, however, she lost herself entirely in her work. In the late morning when she returned home, she saw the flowers and waved at them irritable. "Get rid of those," she said to Kader. She went to her room and fell onto her mat, asleep almost before her head dropped onto the pillow.

For two months she worked without time to think about Ibrahim. He began his new work setting up the family court, and it engrossed him, but Sakina was always at the back of his mind. Although Van is not a large city, their paths never crossed.

Working with little sleep, rarely stopping to eat, Sakina grew thinner and paler. Kader watched her with anxiety. One morning when she came into the house, Kader saw the unmistakable signs that she was genuinely ill. Bright spots of color on her cheeks stood out against her white skin, and sweat glistened on her forehead. She drooped at the door, too tired to take off her shoes and jacket, or seemingly to move any farther.

Her aunt hustled her to bed, and called a doctor. He diagnosed fever and exhaustion, and prescribed bedrest. He promised to make her excuses at the hospital. Sakina fell at once into a restless sleep, but soon woke calling out and flailing her arms. Kader soothed her back to sleep, but soon she was tossing back and forth and crying again. Only late in the day did she settle into quiet sleep. That night she was worse, however. She woke delirious, and Ahmet had to help Kader hold her in bed. At last they got her settled, and Kader got into bed with her to keep her quiet when she woke. In the morning the doctor came and gave her an injection to help her relax. When she woke, she didn't know where she was, was very restless and seemed to be in pain. For two more days she continued in the same way. Afterwards she had no memory of these days, remembering only her wakening on the fourth morning, when she opened her eyes to see Ibrahim sitting beside her bed. She was startled. For two months she hadn't seen Ibrahim, and she felt a burst of anger at her aunt who would let him in to see her like this. She rolled away from him, pulling the light cover almost over her head.

"Go away." After a moment of silence, she added, "I don't want you to see me like this."

"Dearest, I don't want to see you like this either. You are very sick. Kader was so worried she called me. Sakina, I love you. Let me help you through these hard times."

"It's just the training," she protested. "I'm tired. It has to be like this, while I'm learning. I'll be all right."

Ibrahim reached for her hand, and held it. "Sakina, I know you have to work hard.

I won't do anything to distract you or make things harder for you, but I've missed you.

I don't want to live without ever seeing you."

They had been so close at the university, seeing one another almost daily. Suddenly Sakina realized how much she missed Ibrahim, too. His warm hand holding hers felt wonderful. She didn't want him to ever let go.

She rolled back to look at him. There were tears in his eyes.

"Ibrahim, I'm sorry. I'm sorry. Could we, would you…," She paused, thinking about it. Why had it seemed so impossible to her? She knew Ibrahim. He wouldn't expect her to be like the village women.

"Ibrahim, do you really think we could get married and I could still work at the hospital? I don't have any time to cook or clean."

"You silly duck, of course you don't. Of course we could. I kept telling you we could both work, and we'll get someone in to clean and cook. You know I'm proud you're a doctor, and I know it will take all your time to be a good one."

She lay back, gazing at him. He now held both of her hands in both of his, smiling at her through his tears. Suddenly she smiled back. "Then all right. Let's get married."

He lifted her hands, pressing his lips to them.

TWENTY-EIGHT

Family Life in Texas

Ruya paused at the foot of the driveway and honked to warn the twins to clear the way for her. They pulled their small bicycles to the side, and she pressed the garage door button. As it swung open, Semih came across the front lawn to lean in her window.

"Mom, can I go over to Shane's house?"

"Have you finished your homework?"

"Yeah, all done. And I swept the garage out," he pointed proudly.

She smiled fondly at her oldest son. "Be back by six," she answered. He pushed away from the car and ran across the street to his best friend's house.

Ruya drove into the garage, then unloaded two bags of groceries from the back seat of her small Toyota. She went into the house through the door which led directly into the kitchen, pushing the button to close the garage door with her chin.

Leaving the groceries on the counter, she went on to her bedroom to change her work clothes for more casual ones. Dropping the neat navy suit jacket on the bed, she pulled off her white silk blouse and stepped out her short heeled navy pumps and the straight skirt which matched the jacket. Gratefully she peeled off her hot panty-hose, tossing them into a hamper in the closet, and pulled the pearl earrings out of her ears, rubbing the lobes.

Standing in bra and panties in front of the dressing table mirror, she surveyed herself as she enjoyed the coolness of the air conditioned bedroom. The sweat drying on her body sent a little frisson of chill across her skin. She still looked pretty good, she thought. Firm breasts, tight tummy. Her hair was still black and glossy. She left it long, although it was hot that way, because Anwar liked it. One evening a week she attended a ladies exercise class at the local community center.

Pulling on some jeans and a cotton T-shirt, she went back to the kitchen to prepare supper. Her daughter Kader, named for Ruya's Aunt Kader, came into the kitchen and opened the refrigerator.

"Mom, may I have some chocolate milk?"

"No, wait for supper. You can have some then if you want." Ruya was putting away groceries. "Kader, have you finished your homework?"

"Didn't have any today. I know all my spelling words."

"Will you shell these peas for me?" Ruya poured the plastic bag of peapods into a strainer in the sink to rinse them, then put the strainer and another bowl on a towel on the table. She knew Kader liked the raw peas and enjoyed opening the green pods and popping out the little green balls.

Kader settled happily at the table, and Ruya continued to work at the stove and sink. They chatted about Kader's school, and the problems of her best friend Susan, who had a crush on one of the boys in class. Ruya thought about how different her own school had been from the large, well-equipped brick and glass building her children attended. She said nothing of that, however, just encouraging the little girl to chatter on. She felt closest to Kader, her youngest. She and Anwar had agreed that in America, their four were a large enough family.

She had been too busy, anyhow, to have more. She had taken an active part in building up their three small supermarkets. She managed one of their stores now, and also took responsibility for most of the non-grocery purchasing for all three. It was a lot to do along with the children and the house, but a Mexican girl, Elena, came in three times a week to clean for her.

Kerim still lived with them. He was in charge of hiring and firing their help at the super markets; he was very good with people. It was Kerim who had somehow found Elena to come and help her. Elena was wonderful, sweet and hard working and always willing. If any of the children were sick and had to stay home from school, Elena came to sit with them.

When their dinner was simmering on the stove, Ruya went to the front of the house to check the mail. As she had hoped, there was a letter from Aunt Kader in Van. She went out onto the front porch and sat in the swing to read it. It was filled with family news, and Ruya devoured it eagerly.

In September she was going to return to Van for Sakina's wedding. With her new American passport, there would be no trouble left over from her days of fighting for the guerrillas. She was going alone, except for twelve year old Semih to escort her. Neither Anwar nor Kerim wanted to go back and they pled the demands of the stores as their excuse. However, they all wanted Semih to see the homeland of his parents. None of their other close relatives had come to Texas, so Anwar's father and his sister and her family, who had lived in Texas much longer than they had, were the only family members their children knew. It was another of the differences from Kurdish life as she had known it in Turkey.

Kurdish families were so close. She had never quite, in all these years, gotten used to the loneliness of living with just Anwar and her children. She missed her sisters so much. She was grateful that Aunt Kader wrote regularly, keeping her in touch with those still living in Turkey.

Kader had never been allowed to go to school. Her father had thought that it was a great shame to the family for a girl to have any education. She had taught herself to read and write after she had lost her husband and two sons in the fighting, when she came to live with Ruya's family. Ruya knew Aliye had helped her, working at night in the kitchen of their house in Sicaksu, the village Ruya still thought of as home. Although Ruya had left home to become a guerrilla at almost the same time Kader came, it had been Kader who had written her during the years she and Anwar lived in Irak, and it was still Kader who kept in touch with her now they lived in America. Kader, who was not much older than herself, really, but who had three living children by her first husband, and three by Ahmet, her present husband. He himself had five by his first wife when he married Kader. A respectable sized family by Kurdish standards. In addition, Kader had raised Sakina, Ruya's youngest sister. Sakina was now a doctor, about to marry a judge in Van. They had met at university. Ruya paused to marvel at how fast the world changed.

She leaned her head back, closing her eyes and remembering. Some things had changed, but many hadn't, she decided. Alev still lived in a very traditional way, as a widow who had stayed on with two companion wives and their many children when their husband died. They lived in a big house in the same village where she had married. Kader wrote that she seemed to be happy. Aliye was dead. Things hadn't changed fast enough for her.

Songul had seen none of the changes. She had died very young, shot while fighting for Kurdish independence. That struggle still existed as a cloud over the daily life of her people in eastern Turkey, Ruya knew. Some had not given up the struggle, and the Kurds were suspect to the rest of the nation of Turkey.

What would it be like when she went back, she wondered. Her life in America was so different from the way it had been before that it was like two different worlds. Was she a completely different person? Yes, she thought she was. Would these people she was going to visit think she was the same Ruya they remembered? Had they changed? Had the Kurds still living in Turkey changed from the way they used to be when she lived there? Suddenly she was afraid.

It wasn't Ruya's way to shrink back from a problem. To realize she felt uneasy about something was to jump up and get busy. Going back into the house, she tossed the open letter on the pile of mail for Anwar and Kerim to read. She went back to the kitchen where Kader was just finishing the peas, and took the bowl from her.

"All right, Pumpkin. That's good. Thank you. What do you say we make a cake for dinner? We can make a chocolate one, Papa's favorite."

Made in the USA
Monee, IL
08 March 2021

62273115R00134